The Grotto

by

Fredrick Cooper

The Grotto

Cover Art by *Kim Mendoza*

The Wild Rose Press, Inc.
PO Box 708
Adams Basin, NY 14410-0708
Visit us at www.thewildrosepress.com

Publishing History
First Edition, 2022
Trade Paperback ISBN 978-1-5092-3771-5
Digital ISBN 978-1-5092-3772-2

Published in the United States of America

As they pulled away from the boat harbor, a lone raven and the resident seagulls lined up on the outer pier like friends and family waving to their loved ones on a departing cruise ship. She glanced at the spot where the Sherry J had been. She wondered if they would find the boat. Would her mother be aboard it, or would they find her already at the Grotto? Brooklyn thought about what Old Frank told them about the place. That it was dangerous and she shouldn't go there. But here she was—headed for the Grotto with her new friends. She shivered and pulled up the collar on her army jacket in response to a sudden chill on the back of her neck.

Praise for Fredrick Cooper

"Set against the backdrop of the Alaskan wilderness, Fredrick Cooper's latest novel is at its heart a coming-of-age story. The Grotto showcases the importance of friends and family in times of need, who, even in the most desperate of circumstances never leave your side. The narrative is well-paced, and the plot is filled with thrilling moments of suspense and intrigue. Brooklyn's relationship with the inhabitants of the tiny Alaskan town of Chatham, and the way they develop throughout the story make for a thoroughly engaging reading experience. The characters are lively, with distinct personalities that make them all the more compelling."

~ Pikasho Deka for Readers' Favorite

Dedication

This novel is dedicated to my little sister, Karen.

PROLOGUE

Southeast Alaska, Winter, 1916

The captain of the *Clara* tooted the ship's steam-operated horn announcing arrival at one of the coastal freighter's frequent stops along Southeast Alaska's Inside Passage. The long, deep-throated sound echoed off the rocky shore and the cloud-shrouded mountains. With a shift of a lever on the brass telegraph, the captain signaled the engine room to reduce to half-speed. The ship turned to starboard and anchored in a small bay off of Chatham Strait. At ninety-eight feet in length and with a shallow draft of six feet, the *Clara* was well suited for delivering supplies to the small, remote mining camps and communities in places with uncharted waters. Her rusted steel hull bore the scars of many years of service and harsh winters. Her decks and yawning cargo holds held everything from barrels of liquor to thousands of cases of canned salmon. But delivering food supplies and household essentials to native villages, fish canneries, and mining camps, the backbone of the young territory of Alaska, were her mainstay cargo.

The weather had been brutal. On this particular wintry trip, the pilothouse and wood deck of the *Clara* sparkled with frost, turning her into a ghost ship. The ice-covered rigging on her masts hung like a pale spider's web, ready to snare an unsuspecting victim. Below her icy deck, the engine rumbled in her belly like a hungry sea monster, ceasing its roar as if in respect to the silence of the inlet.

The captain surveyed the shore of the small bay. There were no broad beaches or docks lined with men anxious to receive his cargo—only a lonely, rocky shoreline and stands of dense timber. Yet, just beyond the edge of the snow-blanketed forest was a mining camp and hungry miners waiting to be resupplied. A door below the pilothouse opened, and four men emerged. They moved cautiously forward on the slippery deck in response to the captain's orders to lower a shore boat. Minutes later, two grumbling and swearing deckhands swung a heavy box of provisions over the rail. They lowered it in a sling to the small launch now tied alongside the ship. The other two men waited impatiently in the launch.

Isaac Johansson, the first mate, stood ready to receive the box. He was a tall, slender man and wore a long, heavy parka, gloves, and a wool cap to protect him from the bitter Taku Glacier wind blowing in from the strait. His immediate job was to deliver winter supplies to a dock serving a small gold mining camp that lay less than a quarter of a mile inland. The mining camp was fifty miles south of Juneau on Baranof Island.

Johansson placed the box next to several others already stowed in the bow. The fourth man, Ollie, sat waiting at the oars of the launch. He resembled a trained circus bear with his short, stocky body bundled in a furry coat and his head fully wrapped in a wooly skull cap. His dark beard and mustache sparkled from bits of ice.

"That's the last box," said one of the shivering men on the deck. He stuck his hands under his armpits to warm them. Johansson nodded and pulled a canvas tarp over the boxes.

"You ready for me to untie the lines?" The man said.

"Yup, let'm go." Johansson took a seat on the covered boxes. "I'll be real happy to hand over these supplies to those Chinks and get back on board. That is if I don't freeze to death while the Swede takes his sweet time admiring the scenery instead of just getting us to the dock."

"Ya ain't to blame my rowin' for slowin' us down, by gosh," said Ollie. "You get those crates ashore right quick, or by ya mother's cold grave, I'll leave ya with those Chinamen to dig for gold nuggets in this frozen earth until ya skinny fingers fall off."

The two deckhands laughed and then hurried back inside for hot coffee and the heat of the cookstove in the ship's galley. Only the captain from his lonely watch at the wheel saw Ollie row the boat over to the mouth of a stream half-hidden in ice-covered rocks. Then it disappeared into the dark opening of the Grotto.

The Grotto was one of many unique geological features of the karst or limestone formations of the region. The unusual formation had been laid down during the Middle Jurassic to Late Cretaceous time, over 65 million years before. There were limestone outcroppings, caves, sinkholes, and caverns throughout several of the larger islands, of which Baranof Island was one. Water had created these features, and Southeast Alaska received lots and lots of rain—on average 220 days and 150 inches per year.

The stream that had carved the Grotto flowed from a lake maybe a mile to the west. In late summer, the color of its streambed turned red from the thousands of migrating salmon lying side by side so thick that the gravel bottom became obscured. Where the stream reached tidewater, it carved its way through a formation of white marble, now worn smooth and polished from thousands of years of erosion.

****

As Ollie rowed the launch into the Grotto, Johansson admired their surroundings. It formed a graceful arch high over the stream, reminding him of pictures he had seen of Venetian chapels with their marbled walls and vaulted ceilings. The walls and the bedrock of the stream glistened in the dim light that penetrated the sanctuary. Dripping water formed long icicles along one side, looking very much like a massive, soundless pipe organ.

Despite the cold, Ollie was sweating in his heavy coat as he powered through the outflowing current, trying to reach a small wooden dock just beyond the upstream end of the cavern. Logs and overhanging tree branches made it difficult to maneuver the small boat. Johansson called out directions as they moved upstream. When he turned to look back at the oarsman, he caught a glimpse of something large and dark that surfaced, and moments later, disappeared in the icy water behind their boat. Whatever it was didn't resurface. He took it for a harbor seal on its way back out through the cavern to the bay.

Johansson turned his attention to the small landing ahead of them. On the shore near the end of the dock, he saw a man sitting under the low branches of a cedar tree. A broad-brimmed hat obscured his face. Johansson waved and hollered a greeting.

"Hello ashore."

He received no response. The boat was now within a few yards of the dock.

"The dock's just ahead," warned Johansson, keeping his eyes on the man. "Looks like someone's waiting for us, but he must be asleep."

A moment later, the boat touched the dock and slid along its edge. Johansson stepped off the boat, tied the bowline to a post, and then hurried over to the still figure. When he stooped to shake the man's shoulder and peer at his face, he staggered back in horror. The ashen face was raked with deep red scratches and bites. The man's mouth and eyes were frozen open in a silent scream. On the dead man's jaw, hung icicles of pink froth.

"One of the Chinamen?" Ollie asked, catching up with Johansson, who was kneeling and examining the body.

"Yeah. There's something wrong here. Looks like the man suffered a nasty death. I'm going up to the mine. You better stay with the boat."

"Ya leavin' me with that dead Chinaman? What about the supplies?"

"Yeah, and be ready to leave in a hurry, but not before I get back, you hear? And leave the supplies in the boat."

Johansson stepped around the body and headed up the trail, slipping and sliding on the frozen ground. The light rain had stopped, but now a fresh, thin layer of ice coated everything. It fell like shattered glass from the branches and brush that he grabbed to stay upright.

His destination was a cluster of buildings the miners used. It was a small operation—nothing like the big Treadwell mining camp near Juneau that employed hundreds of miners. The miners he was looking for were all Chinese exiled from the Treadwell mine after conflicts between the whites, Indians, and imported Chinese laborers. Hard rock miners were a tough breed, and fights were common. But the Chinese had lost and been evicted by the mine managers at Treadwell.

It took Johansson a while to reach the small cluster of cedar clapboard shacks nestled at the base of a tall granite slope. The upper part of the slope, stripped of trees cut for firewood, was obscured by a low-hanging mist. Snow and freezing rain covered everything. Ice-encrusted tree stumps cast weird shapes on the barren ground. Entering the main area of the camp, the entrance to the mine was easy to spot. A pair of narrow gauge iron rails used to pull out the ore carts extended from the opening like the fangs of a serpent. Yet, the whole scene was still and ominous. Johansson shivered as he looked for anyone in the camp. The image of the frozen miner coupled with the dead quiet of the camp reinforced a chill that crept up his back.

"Hello? Is anyone here?"

He scanned the shacks as he hollered. The stillness clung to the camp like the ice that coated everything around him.

Johansson frowned. No smoke rose from any of the chimneys, and none of the miners came out to greet him. He picked his way across the clearing towards the largest of the shacks. It served as a bunkhouse and kitchen. Its door hung open. On the floor just inside the doorway, he could see another body. Just as Johansson started towards it, two dark shapes leaped over the corpse, one after the other, and charged out the doorway. They scampered over the icy ground and up an incline to the entrance to the mine. Startled, Johansson slipped and fell. He scrambled to his feet and looked after the shapes. They were river otters and they stopped just outside the mine, turned, and faced him, standing on their hind legs. They had sleek brown bodies and dog-like heads. Their bared, sharp teeth and black, beady eyes gave them a menacing look.

On the ground near them lay the body of a third miner. The animals stood over it staring at Johansson, unafraid of his presence. They began bobbing their heads and making threatening yowls and hissing sounds.

He glanced around the camp one more time. Other than the three dead miners, the only occupants appeared to be these animals. He looked more intently at the otter closest to him. There was something odd about it. Its lower jaws were slack, exposing its sharp teeth—teeth dribbling pink, frothy saliva just like the first dead miner. His mind raced. Then his words came in a faltering speech.

"Dead miners?—Otters?—Rabid?—What the devil?"

Johansson started to utter something more, but it turned into a stifled scream. He stumbled backward a few steps on the icy terrain, this time somehow remaining on his feet. It couldn't be. He'd heard stories by the Natives who'd had one drink too many in the Juneau bars. He had only laughed—never believing them. The Tlingit Indian stories were about the

Kushtaka, the river otter people, which ate your flesh and stole your soul.

Blood drained from his face as Johansson turned from the horrific scene and ran for his life. The raised pitch of their menacing yowls filled his ears. Fear racked his body knowing that the river otters would be on him if he fell. He scrambled back down the icy trail to where Ollie waited with the boat and the dead Chinaman. Behind the beauty of the Grotto lay only horror and a mystery.

Chapter 1

A Small Town in Southeast Alaska

The gray clouds were so low they drifted like smoke among the forested ridges encircling a long, narrow bay and the tiny Alaskan community of Chatham. The dark water and exposed tidelands melded the sky, the bay, and the land into one damp and dreary scene like gray paint smeared on a canvas by an artist's brush. Twice daily with the receding tide, the bay's muddy shoreline yielded souvenirs of forgotten times. Rotting wood piling, chunks of machinery from a failed industry, and derelict fishing boats that stood out on the mudflats like giant tombstones. More recent artifacts of a throwaway society like discarded appliances, engine parts, oil cans, rusting wire cable, and someone's broken plastic chair littered the beach zone.

On a point of land jutting into the bay, an expanse of midden piles, consisting of bleached shells, lay naked on a stretch of beach, recalling a time when an Indian settlement occupied the shore.

Sentinels of the present, flocks of hungry ravens and gulls, were oblivious to the artifacts. They scratched in the mud for anything edible. Their raucous calls echoed across the narrow inlet, signaling their delectable finds or, often as not, their insatiable hunger.

The feeding birds ignored a young girl trudging

along the sinuous roadway just above them. Her name was Brooklyn and her colorful appearance was in sharp contrast to her drab surroundings, from her calf-high rubber boots, painted with flowers, though presently spattered with gray mud, to the bright orange streaks in her shoulder-length hair. On her head, she wore a striped knit cap. On her shoulders was a blue backpack covered with embroidered flowers and danglers. She liked bright colors because Chatham was a drab place to live. Even the old army jacket she wore had embroidered daisies and sunflowers on the sleeves and pockets.

One would have thought Brooklyn would have a cheery disposition to match, but there was not even a hint of a smile on her round face. Part of her ill temperament was due to the weather, which was exactly as predicted—early fog followed by rain showers throughout the day, just like yesterday and the day before.

The girl picked her way along the rutted, muddy road, which ran the length of her hometown. She circled around the larger puddles and waded through the rivulets that trickled off a steep bank into the ditches before cascading onto a narrow, rocky beach to meander across the tidelands. It was mid-September, and she was tired of the constant rain even though it had been a regular part of her life for sixteen years. Brooklyn was born in Ketchikan, where the annual rainfall was over 150 inches, something most Alaskan visitors couldn't fathom. At least in Chatham, where she lived with her single mother, some precipitation was snow. Chatham sat in the lee of a vast mountain range on Baranof Island. The mountains offered the benefit of semi-decent summer weather. Still, in the winter months, those same mountains often resulted in more than four feet of snow.

Above Chatham Strait, a strip of pale blue sky peeked between lines of clouds streaming along the eastern horizon. It offered a glimmer of hope for a brief Indian summer—short because buckets of rain had already followed an early and very wet snowfall. Brooklyn measured rainfall in buckets because her mother used one by the back door of their home as a rain gauge, and it always needed emptying.

Walking anywhere in Chatham meant wearing boots, and she had to walk everywhere. She walked to school, to the cafe where her mom worked, and to the community center, where she could get on the computer, her favorite pastime. In Chatham, there were only a few means of accessing the Internet, one of the more exciting things in her life. It offered a window to the world away from Chatham—a world without boots, puddles, or buckets of rain, a world full of exciting things to see and do.

Chatham was an Indian town, and some of its residents thought the village had been there on the bay's shore for over a thousand years. Nine hundred and eighty people lived in Chatham during the summer months when the commercial fishing season was open and a guest lodge was operating. Almost a third of them left when the season was over. Brooklyn thought they were the lucky ones. She had to stay. At Chatham's only café, she listened to people talk about leaving for six months in sunny Arizona or Hawaii. Their trips, even if they were just to Seattle, sounded like wonderful and exciting adventures. But the computers in the school's two classrooms and at the community center were Brooklyn's only escape.

The isolation was encouraged by the Native leaders of Chatham. They were a traditional people and didn't like change, preferring the old ways. For example, the construction of a cell tower was not permitted, an exasperating circumstance to Brooklyn, who would have chosen a smartphone over a public computer any day. Anyway, her mom, who was about as independent as the elders in Chatham, told her they couldn't afford cell phones. Why call someone in such a small community when news spread almost as quickly by word of mouth? Her mom, Flo Whiting, heard all the information and the gossip at the café.

Brooklyn found chatting with her classmates was awful. It was either dull or gross. The Tlingit people kept to themselves and were often unfriendly to outsiders. Away from school, most of the young people watched movies or played at home with their Nintendo or Xbox games or in a small game parlor next to the Frontier Pub. Some of the adults spent their idle time getting drunk at the Frontier or the town's other bar. Native towns in Southeast Alaska were often dry, where the sale of alcohol is prohibited. Oddly, Chatham wasn't. On some weekends, the rowdy bar crowd would spill into the street, disrupting whatever else was happening. Even during the Fourth of July parade and fireworks, patrons partied, mesmerized by their alcohol and the twang of country music blasting on the jukebox.

Brooklyn considered herself an outsider, for she was only half Alaskan Native. Her mother was Caucasian, and her father was a full-blood Tlingit, the largest Native tribe in Southeast Alaska and British

Columbia. Because the Tlingit were also a matriarchal tribe, kinship was determined by your mother's family, or you had to be adopted into the tribe. Since her mother had never married her biological father, that wasn't going to happen. So, she wasn't a member of the moieties, or clans, in Chatham—the Raven, the Wolf, and the Eagle. As a result, most of the Native women, particularly the girls her age, shunned her.

The boys in Chatham didn't care. She was sometimes harassed because she was prettier than most of the other girls. Brooklyn had her father's black hair, but she kept it fairly short instead of long, like the Native girls, and she added color streaks, which she changed with the seasons. This month, the streaks were red-orange in honor of the leaf color of the wild blueberries growing along her favorite forest walk.

Brooklyn's father disappeared before she was born, and she had never known her mother's relatives. At Christmas, they usually received a card from one of her mom's two sisters who lived in Portland. They never heard from the other. Brooklyn had also given up urging her mother to tell her about her father. She refused to speak about her lover, although Brooklyn overheard her say his name once in a moment of disgust while arguing with a customer at the cafe. Her father's first name was Vince. There was no one living in Chatham or the nearby communities by that name. Only two people she had asked admitted knowing a person by that name. One was a retired fisherman in his nineties, and the other was her age. She wondered if people were telling her the truth, as they wouldn't look at her when they answered her question. She had found her birth certificate in the bottom of her mom's dresser, but it was no help. Her mom had marked out her father's name. Oddly, she had no last name on the birth certificate. Her mother refused to put down her father's name or her name of Whiting. So, Brooklyn was simply called Brooklyn. It pleased her. Her name was another thing that made her different.

The only road into and out of Chatham followed the bay through the town's small business district. It ended at the boat harbor and the site of an abandoned cannery at the southern edge of town. If you went north, there were a couple of single- and double-wide trailers and a few nicer homes scattered on the waterside of the road. Beyond that, the road climbed over a low summit and followed a valley to Hoonah, some thirty miles away. A four-wheel-drive vehicle was advisable as the only roads led to mining camps or logging sites.

Along the business stretch, was the town's general store owned by Sid Jackson. It sold groceries, hardware, sporting equipment, and lots of rubber boots. He also rented DVDs and video games. There was a marine fuel dock with another pump on the road in front of the building where people could gas up their ATVs. There was a bakery, but it was only open three days a week, and a small commercial office building where two partners ran a hunting and fishing guide business. Chatham had two churches for every bar. Brooklyn couldn't quite figure out how four churches survived since not many people in town admitted to being churchgoers.

While the town of Chatham was showing its age—roofs covered in moss, buildings with peeling paint, and abandoned buildings overgrown with blackberries—the townsite was quite beautiful. The bay was narrow, and directly across it was a magnificent view of the forest and snow-covered mountains. Brooklyn could look in any direction and spot her favorite bird, a bald eagle, either roosting on the top of a piling or riding the air currents.

At the end of the town near the old cannery was a small boat harbor. There was a rock jetty on the windward side built for storing logs for a lumber mill that had burned down long before Brooklyn was born. The boat harbor had space for close to fifty boats. It was used by folks who lived along the shore away from town and for long-term moorage of commercial fishing boats, seiners, gillnetters, and trollers, some over forty feet in length. Several boats moored in the harbor were derelicts. Brooklyn wondered how they remained afloat. They were so decrepit. A couple of them were live-aboard residences.

In the summer, Brooklyn liked to wander around on the docks in the harbor. She would read the names of the home ports of the boats—Juneau, Bellingham, Anacortes, Roche Harbor, Vancouver. One time she had seen a gorgeous yacht with the home port of Tucson and laughed, wondering about a homeport in the desert. Still, the boats were like her use of a computer, offering the possibility of escape to faraway places.

Brooklyn was headed to the community center. She planned to meet with the center director Reginald Boyd about learning software programming. Reggie was a really intelligent guy with degrees in social work and computer technology from the University of Alaska in Anchorage. He'd convinced her that having computer programming skills could land her a fantastic job. She did an Internet search and found there were great jobs just about anywhere.

The Chatham Community and Recreation Center was on the main road close to the boat harbor accessed by a long flight of wooden stairs up the hill.

Three teenage boys loitered at the bottom of the stairway, blocking Brooklyn's way. Her shoulders slumped and she slowed her pace.

"This is going to be triple trouble." She said under her breath. "Just what I don't need today."

One of the boys was Tony Jackson, son of the general store owner and a student in her sophomore grade. The other two were older, and she considered them the town's little band of Native delinquents. Jake Bischoff was the oldest and a well-known bully. Joey Hickman was stocky, and his unkempt, long hair and beady eyes made him look creepy. She would have to squeeze by them to climb the stairs to the community center.

"Hey Joey," said Jake, who was several steps up the stairway. "Look who's here. It's Miss Smarty Pants. I heard Mr. Hendricks gave her an A+ on the science test he handed back today."

"Huh, I wonder how she wrangled that grade." Joey snickered. "Stripped to her panties in the supply closet? My older sister did that for Mr. Hendricks last year and she only got a B."

Jake and Tony laughed. Brooklyn ignored the crude remark and tried to slip by Jake. She climbed several steps, but Jake moved to block her path with his body inches from hers. She could smell his rank breath as he spoke. "Hey, Brooklyn, how about we go down to the boat Tony's father keeps at the harbor and party a little?"

"Oh yeah," said Joey as he put a hand on Brooklyn's bottom. "Have some real fun."

Brooklyn stared at Joey with a disgusted look and tried to brush away his hand, but he was too close. Tony, who held back, intervened and pulled Joey away from Brooklyn. "I...ah... I'm not sure my dad would like us messing around on his boat. There's—"

"Aw, come on, Tony," Jake said. "Don't spoil a little fun. Brooklyn wants to party. Right, Brooklyn?" He grabbed Brooklyn's wrist and started to pull her down the stairs towards the road. His grip was firm and she couldn't break loose.

"This isn't one of your stupid games, Jake," said Brooklyn. "Let go of me."

At this point, Brooklyn began to panic. Her mind raced, and she tried to figure out how she could pull away. What was it her mom had said? If a guy had a hold of her, stomp on the top of his foot, then kick him in the knee. If that didn't work, go for his eyes with her fingers. Hearing Tony's hesitation, she wondered if he would intervene if she fought with Jake. She glanced at Joey. She could shove a fist in his fat stomach, kick Jake in a knee, and then dash up the stairs to the safety of the community center. Brooklyn was about to put her plan into action when a man's voice boomed from the far side of the road.

"Move away from her, you punks!"

A man appeared from behind the rusted hulk of an abandoned pickup truck. His feet were spread, and he was jabbing his right hand in the air directly at the boys. All three of the boys and Brooklyn were startled and turned to see who it was.

"Leave her be, or I'll pound the daylights out of all three of you." The man's gruff voice was enough to get Joey and Tony moving away from Brooklyn and stumbling down to the foot of the stairway. The apparition, tottering on the edge of the road, was a mountain of a man. In Chatham, everyone knew him and gave him a wide berth, as much for how he smelled as for his drunken, brawling reputation. He was strong enough to take on three men and still be standing even when drunk, which he was much of the time.

"We didn't mean no harm, Bingo," said Joey. "We're just teasing Brooklyn."

"I heard what you said to her," the man said. "Now get out of here before I decide to use parts of you boys for crab bait." He pointed down the road towards town.

Jake was still holding on to Brooklyn and hesitated for a few seconds, then released her and raised a fist. "My father will hear about this. He's on the town council, and he'll refuse to let you stay at the boat harbor."

Bingo took another measured step towards the trio. The anger on Jake's face turned to fear, and he nearly fell as he scrambled down the steps and into the road. The three boys kept their eyes on the man as they backed off another few yards, watching to see if Bingo was going to follow through on his challenge.

With balled fists, he took another measured step towards the center of the road. The boys turned and ran.

Brooklyn hadn't been able to move. She was frightened—both by what Jake and Joey implied with their crude talk and by the man who now stood looking at her. Brooklyn knew very little about Bingo Bob, or Bingo, as most people in Chatham called him. His appearance and his reputation scared her just as much as they did all the rest of the kids in town.

The man doffed his cap and stood in the middle of the road, reeling a bit. He was smiling, though, apparently pleased with himself. His long hair was unkempt, his grizzled beard tobacco-stained. His clothes were filthy and worn, and she could smell booze on him from where she stood, gripping the rail on the stairway. She glanced towards the boat harbor down the hill. Brooklyn knew as everyone did that Bingo lived by himself on a derelict boat permanently moored at one of the docks.

Bingo put his hat back on with a bit of flair and did a quick turn to his left like a well-drilled soldier. Then he marched, with a military swagger, down the road towards the harbor. Brooklyn stood at the bottom of the steps, staring after him and trying to register what he had just done.

Chapter 2

The fishing boat *Sherry J* was anchored for the night in a small cove just inside the entrance to Idaho Inlet. The three men on board had tossed back several six-packs of beer the night before and were still sleeping soundly when an alarm went off at 5 am. The skipper, Vince James, managed to get out of his bunk, silence the alarm, and then start a pot of coffee on the propane stove in the small galley. He shoved aside shoes, jackets, boxes of ammo, and beer cans to sit and listen to the early morning NOAA weather report on the radio. The day's forecast was for calm winds and a heavy fog through the late morning for several days. He nodded with satisfaction.

While the coffee finished brewing, he donned a jacket and went out on deck. True to the report, a thick blanket of fog had enveloped the boat, obscuring the shoreline in all directions. If they couldn't see the shore or another boat, then no one could see what they were about to do either.

Vince lifted a hatch cover in the center of the deck and checked the hold below. A dozen silver salmon caught yesterday lay nestled in a bed of shave ice. Before the day was over, the ice and salmon would hide their real catch, a much more profitable cargo than this meager one. Back inside the cabin, he poured three cups of strong coffee. It was time to wake the others.

"Hey, guys, out of those bunks. It'll be full daylight in few minutes." Vince hollered. "We've got to pull the anchor and get the boat into position. We're about to make some big bucks, guys."

His partners, Tom Waters and Ronnie Waltrip moaned and groaned as they struggled to put on pants and shirts. Both had drunk way more beer than Vince during their planning session the night before.

Like Vince, the two men drifted from one seasonal job to another, a typical situation in Alaska where those who chose to live there year-round took what work they could find. A logging accident left Waltrip with a permanent limp, noticeable because of his short, stocky build. Waters was about as opposite as could be from Waltrip. He was tall, gaunt, and suffering from early arthritis from years of hard labor on fishing boats. Waters was like Vince in two ways—both were Tlingit Indian, and neither had finished high school.

They had been friends for years and been introduced by a man called Johnny Kwan. Kwan bought illegal seafood, something that both Vince and Tom saw as easy money. Their similar past and their willingness to break the law to make a quick buck brought them to this place on this foggy morning.

Thirty minutes later, the *Sherry J* cruised slowly to the center of the inlet. Vince shut down the engine and let the boat drift with the incoming tide. Vince stood in the pilothouse, scanning the calm, glassy surface of the bay behind the boat.

The sounds of the bay seemed amplified by the fog—the screams of hungry seagulls, the splash of a sea lion, the lonely call of a raven somewhere along the shore. His partners sat up in the bow with their backs to him, smoking their first cigarettes, 0.222 automatic rifles across their laps. It was now a waiting game.

The dense fog kept the visibility to less than 500 feet, obscuring everything except for what floated close by with the incoming tide. Just to be sure, Vince checked the radar for the second time since leaving their anchorage. He had set the range for five miles. There were no other boats nearby.

A pair of sea otters drifted by the boat, maybe fifty feet from the port side. They lay on their backs, grooming themselves with their front paws. A single adult and a pair of juveniles drifted by on the other side of the boat. It would not be long before many more would follow.

Vince and his buddies had been scouting the inlet for several days under the guise of trolling for salmon. They found vast rafts of sea otters—possibly as many as three to five hundred that let the tide carry them into shallow water at the head of the inlet where they would dive for shellfish.

A fully-grown sea otter consumed nearly 25 percent of its body weight every day to match its high metabolism. Without a layer of fat, sea otters relied on their dense fur for warmth. This unique characteristic made their furry pelts highly desirable.

Vince spoke softly to the other two men, not wanting to spook the drifting sea otter or causing them to scatter.

"Let these first few go on by."

He scanned the water's surface behind the boat again for more of the animals. "The big raft of sea otters is right behind them. We'll wait until they are alongside us."

They waited patiently as more sea otters drifted or swam by, ignoring the presence of the motionless boat. Five minutes later, Vince yelled as he picked up his rifle.

"Ok, start shooting."

All hell broke loose around the boat with the first shots. It was a slaughter. Within minutes over one hundred dead animals floated around the boat.

After two days of killing, retrieving the carcasses, and icing them down in the boat's hold, Vince was in a good mood. The second day's hunt was even better than the first. He estimated they might each clear thirty thousand dollars after expenses. He could make a substantial loan payment on his boat.

When they got within cell coverage of Juneau, Vince placed a call to Johnny Kwan to arrange for the buy. The exchange had to be carefully planned. A recent article in the *Juneau Empire* mentioned a Native near Ketchikan who had been convicted for selling otter pelts to a non-Native. He received heavy fines and lost his boat.

Vince and his partners needed to work quickly to get the otter carcasses to their hidden camp, skinned and dried, before delivering the pelts to Kwan. It would take time to process the animals, all the while at risk of discovery, even though Vince was pretty confident no one could find their camp near a place he called the Grotto. Few people even knew the Grotto existed.

Kwan answered the on the first ring. "Vince! Do you have something for me? Your loan payment is overdue."

"Yeah, at least I will soon. We had a good hunt," Vince replied. "Gonna take me three, maybe four weeks to process the pelts, but I could have part of the agreed amount available in a few days."

He heard Kwan mumble something unintelligible, most likely in Chinese, followed by a sigh before the man responded. "Okay, I'll agree, but it goes towards your loan payment plus interest. I'll have my pickup man contact you."

"Okay. You're going to like these pelts—all big adults and no holes. Killing shots were in the head."

"They better be good quality. The auction price in Shanghai drops nearly by half for a damaged pelt."

"I…I understand. How am I to—"

"I said my pickup man will be in touch."

Kwan disconnected.

Chapter 3

The morning after the incident with Tony and his disgusting friends, Brooklyn sat in her usual spot next to the front windows of the café, having breakfast with her mom. It had been a cool night, and the windows facing the bay were heavy with condensation from the warmth of the large kitchen grill, now covered in sizzling hash browns, bacon, sausages, and eggs. Under normal circumstances, it was a pleasant spot to start the day. In addition to the familiar smells emanating from the kitchen, there was a picturesque view of the bay and conversations of locals lingering over a second cup of coffee before heading off to work. This morning though, Brooklyn's mood couldn't have been farther from such pleasantries.

Her mom sat across from her, taking a fifteen-minute break from her hungry customers. She had propped up a copy of the Juneau newspaper from the day before in front of her and absently sipped her cup of coffee. Even though she had hardly begun her shift, she looked tired and her dark brown hair, drawn back in a ponytail, was frazzled and dull. Under different conditions, Flo might be a beautiful woman. Instead, at 40, her twenty years of physical work as a waitress was taking its toll.

Brooklyn pushed her hot cereal around in the bowl, slowly mixing in a heaping spoonful of brown sugar.

She hadn't slept well either and wasn't looking forward to going to school where she was sure she would have to face the boys again. Stories flew through town, and all the girls her age probably knew about her rescue by Bingo Bob, the last person on earth one expected to be a hero. She had lain awake for hours, imagining the things they would say.

"Hey Brooklyn, we hear Bingo Bob is waiting to walk you home," or holding their noses, they'd sing a little jingle like "Woohoo, here's Bingo."

Flo peered over the top of her paper. "Something bothering you?"

Brooklyn glared back. "I hate this town. We don't belong here. We're outsiders."

"That's what you said last month and the month before. What happened this time?"

"And I hate you for making us live here. We never go anywhere, like on a vacation. We never do anything together."

"That's putting it differently. So, are you going to tell me about it?"

"Tony and his buddies tried to rape me."

Flo nearly spilled her coffee and stared at her daughter with a look of concern. "What? When did this happen?"

"Yesterday, on the road near the boat basin."

"They tried to rape you in the middle of the road?"

"It was just talking. That's all. They tried to force me to go aboard a boat Tony's father has down at the harbor. Only Bingo Bob chased them away."

"Bingo did?"

"Yeah. Bingo yelled at them and threatened to use parts of their bodies as crab bait. Then they ran away. I was scared. What's weird, instead of being a dirty, freaky person, he seemed like a harmless man. He was very polite." Brooklyn sighed and shoved her bowl of oatmeal aside but decided the orange juice was okay and took a sip. "Mom, what is the story about Bingo?"

Flo checked the dining room. The few customers still there were busy eating. She looked up at the big clock by the door to the kitchen and sighed, knowing she'd better spend a few minutes talking this through with her daughter. She set aside the newspaper and looked at Brooklyn.

"I think it was about seven or eight years ago when Bingo Bob showed up in that old boat of his. He kind of staked out his spot on the dock and has stayed put. I don't recall ever seeing that boat leave the harbor since then." She shook her head. "Brooklyn, there are men like Bingo in pretty much every Alaskan town. They choose to live alone, sometimes on derelict boats, again like Bingo, or in a tumble-down cabin. I guess you could call them hermits. I think the wilderness of Alaska has a certain appeal to men like them. Maybe it's the frontier idea where they can be alone, and they don't have to interact or talk to anybody. Or maybe, it is because they had to run away from something in their past. Some of them are grumpy old men or alcoholics who just want to be left alone in their misery and probably should be left to themselves. Some of them are fairly harmless and, I guess, kind of like puppies. When Bingo dresses up and comes to the monthly bingo nights at the community center, he's a perfect gentleman. That's how he got his nickname."

"That's what I thought about Bingo—a lost little dog or frightened kitten. I've always been afraid of him, just like all the other kids in town. But when I thought about what he did, I felt sorry for him."

"Well, don't let a bit of sympathy affect your judgment. I'd leave Bingo be. He did a good thing, but that doesn't mean he's friendly. Men like him can be very unpredictable. They like their alcohol and can just as easily change from a puppy to a bulldog. Violence can be part of their nature."

Flo gathered up her newspaper and glanced at the clock on the wall again. "You need to get to school. We'll talk some more about this tonight, okay?"

"Alright, but what about Tony and—"

"We'll figure out how to deal with them. Just promise me you'll not linger on your way home. It's probably best you don't go to the community center for a few days."

The door to the café opened as she stood up, and two men entered. Flo glanced at them, letting her newspaper slip from her hands back onto the table. She hurried towards the kitchen. To Brooklyn, it seemed like her mother had suddenly turned pale like she had seen a ghost.

Chapter 4

A month earlier

There was a splash as the anchor dropped into the bay, followed by the rattle of the anchor chain as it fed itself over the bow roller.

"You sure this is where you entered that cavern?" Tom Waters said to Vince James as they anchored the *Sherry J.* off a small stream. "There's nothing here but a gravel beach and a salmon stream that is darn near dried up."

"Just wait," said Vince. "There's a second stream. Its mouth is hidden in the rocks and only visible when you're right on top of it. The cavern is around a corner and not visible from out here in the bay." He looked at his watch. "We can use the inflatable to go through, but we'll have to wait a few hours for the tide to come in a bit."

"How come?"

"The water level changes with the tide. At low tide, there is not enough water depth for a skiff or small dinghy, even if we used oars instead of the outboard motor. At high tide, there is not enough clearance for us to pass through."

Vince and Tom took down the dinghy strapped to the top of the cabin. It was a small inflatable Zodiac with an aluminum bottom. Vince used a hand pump to add some air and then attached a 2.5 Hp outboard motor he kept stored in a locker. Then they made some sandwiches and drank a couple of beers. While they waited, Vince described to Tom how he found the site.

"I discovered the location purely by chance. I was working during the summer tourist season as a deckhand for a skipper who ran an eco-charter out of Sitka. The boat took twelve to fifteen guests on a seven-day tour that included kayaking, whale watching, and brown bear viewing. The skipper pulled into this bay to let his guests paddle around for a few hours in their kayaks and enjoy the scenery. He called it the Grotto, and it was his secret. He never revealed its location to anyone or identified it in the travel itinerary posted on his website. The guests had no idea where they were either. They were simply thrilled to paddle right into the Grotto to take pictures. I offered to take a guest further into the Grotto in a double kayak, where I noticed what looked like the remains of an old dock just upstream from the cavern."

"So, why would there be an old dock on this stream?" Tom asked.

"I got to wondering about that too," said Vince. "One day, when I was in Juneau, I started checking some old records the State of Alaska keeps on a database for mining claims. Turned out there's a pretty large one right here. Yup, somewhere around here, there was an operating gold mine. It was a good producer of gold and some silver but for some reason ceased operation after only a few years. That was about a hundred years ago. Maybe it couldn't compete with the big Juneau-Douglas mines, or maybe the owners ran out of money. A lot of the mines around this part of

Alaska couldn't put together enough investors and had to shut down."

Tom stuffed the sandwiches and a couple more cans of beer into a backpack as they talked. "So, we're looking for an old mine shaft?"

"I think so. The State's records indicate a lode claim, which means they were extracting ore from a vein. I found the patent claim. It was still active and held by an old couple living in Anacortes. They were pleased I was interested in it, and when I offered them fifteen thousand dollars, they accepted. So, now I'm broke, but I own a gold claim."

"In that case, maybe we ought to be looking for gold rather than a place for processing otter pelts," said Tom.

Vince laughed. "Digging gold out of a mountain is hard work. Shooting sea otters and selling their fur pelts is a lot easier. Besides, if there is any gold, maybe I'll make enough money to hire someone else to dig it out."

When they motored into the cavern, Tom couldn't believe his eyes. The ceiling, walls, and bottom of the stream glistened. "You said that skipper you worked for referred to this place as the Grotto. Is that marble?"

"Yeah. Pretty impressive, huh?" He didn't bother to elaborate as he was busy keeping the craft in mid-stream to avoid some rocks that could damage the motor's propeller. He kept glancing upstream, looking for the dock site that he had seen.

"See those stumps in the water up ahead? They look like the tops of old pilings to me."

Tom shifted his gaze from the channel's marble bottom to look upstream. "I'll be damned. Those sure do look like rotten pilings."

Vince slowed the small motor and kept going until the tidal influence ended and the stream was too shallow to go any further. They would have to continue their exploration on foot. He gently pushed the inflatable into the bank next to the old pilings. Tom jumped on shore with a line to secure the boat.

Vince took a moment to focus on the dense woods and further up the small stream. The forest all around them was strangely silent and almost eerie. The only sound was the muffled gurgle of the stream's riffles and a small waterfall. There were no signs of human activity—no road, no trail, not even a blaze on a tree or marker for an old trail.

"There's no obvious sign of any mining activity, but a place can change a lot in a hundred years. Maybe we can find a path or an old building foundation. Gonna have to bushwhack and work our way up the valley. According to a topographic map I looked at, this stream flows out of a lake not far to the west of here—maybe a mile inland. So, I'm thinking we concentrate our search between this spot and the lake."

"We'd better stick together," Tom said. "There could still be bears around. I saw quite a few salmon in the stream as we passed through that Grotto."

"You're right. And that might work in our favor. There could be a bear highway right along the stream." Vince took a minute to open his pack. He took out a 0.357 Magnum pistol with a leather holster and attached it to his belt. "Okay, I'm ready if we bump into a brown bear. Let's explore."

Sure enough, the two men found a bear trail right away along the north side and followed it for over a mile until they reached a waterfall. They had not seen any signs of human activity. After searching along the edge of the escarpment away from the waterfall, they found a place to climb up. They reached the lake and, while they discovered a primitive Forest Service shelter, there were still no signs of an old mining operation.

"I think we're doing this wrong," Tom said as he scratched his head. "We need to think like a gold prospector. We need to look for clues in the streambed. A prospector typically finds gold by looking for gold-bearing gravel. There was a definite change in color to the streambed when we crossed a small side stream close to where we left the boat. We could also try to get up above this damn timber and study the terrain."

"I hear you. We could wander around in here for days and walk right past something because the trees and underbrush are so dense."

They backtracked to the small creek and followed it. In a few minutes, they arrived at the base of a cliff and found what they were seeking—mine tailings piled at the bottom of the slope. Tom searched the thick brush and soon discovered a rusty ore cart, some cable, and then a section of steel rail. They followed the twisted rail, and it led them to the mine entrance. Only there wasn't any entrance. The wood bracing had rotted, and the tunnel had collapsed.

"Well, this must be your gold mine," said Tom sitting down on a boulder. "You're right about another thing, too."

"What's that?"

"Becoming a gold miner would be one heck of a lot of backbreaking work."

"Place looks promising, though," said Vince. "I

mean for us. We don't need a building. We could put up a couple of tarps for shelter from rain and eat and sleep on the boat at night. All we need is to drop some of these trees and construct some A-frames to give us a covered area for skinning and drying the pelts. The old mine shaft might prove useful too. If we can dig it out, it could be the perfect spot for getting rid of the carcasses. Toss them in it and when we clear out, set off some dynamite and seal it up again."

"There you go," Tom said, and they smiled as they shook hands.

****

A week later, on a trip into Juneau to buy materials and supplies for their new camp, Vince and Tom decided to grab lunch and have a couple of beers at the Arctic Bar. It was a hangout for commercial fishermen, miners, and loggers who drank and brawled almost nightly. The Arctic had a reputation as one of the more notorious bars in downtown Juneau with sawdust on the floor and an old western saloon motif. As they settled into a booth, Tom noticed a man with messy blond hair sitting alone at the bar.

"That you Ronnie?" bellowed Tom.

The man turned and squinted in the dim light to see who'd yelled his name. A slow grin exposed two missing upper teeth.

"Tom Waters, you old ridge runner, what are you doing in these parts? I heard the State Troopers were looking for you up in Anchorage. Something to do with a missing seaplane?"

Tom laughed. "All a misunderstanding. The owner was too drunk and forgot he loaned it to me. Come on over here. I want you to meet my new partner Vince."

Ronnie grabbed a long-neck beer and strolled over, a bit unsteady.

"Vince, this is Ronnie Waltrip. He and I have partnered a few times. Troopers arrested us once for catching king crab out of season. Ronnie, this here is Vince James. He's got an idea that's gonna make us enough money, that we won't have to worry come a cold winter."

Two hours and three or four beers later, Waltrip, who was also unemployed, became the third partner in their little venture.

****

With Ronnie's help, it took them a few days of hard work to clear the old site, clear a trail, and build a small dock at the stream. It took another few days to dig out the mine entrance. They all agreed that the mine was the best option for disposing of the carcasses. Dumping them in the ocean was too risky, and digging a pit and filling it in would be a lot more work. As it turned out, only the timbers in the first ten feet had rotted and collapsed. At one time, Ronnie worked at a silver mine for a while. He showed the other two how to use logs to replace the posts and a section of missing ceiling beams.

With the entrance to the mine shored up, they used lanterns they planned to keep in easy reach just inside the mine entrance to explore the old underground workings. About a hundred feet in, they discovered where part of the workings had been abandoned and closed off. Further into the mine, another hundred feet or so, they found what must have been the active drift. To their amazement, all the mining tools were still in place, as if the miners had just walked off and never returned.

Ronnie liked what he saw. He picked up a piece of the rock, rubbed it with a shirt sleeve, and then let out a low whistle. "Whew, this stuff is mighty promising gold ore. You need to have a few pieces assayed, and if I'm right, you might want to work it. I can't believe nobody has been in this mine in a hundred years."

Vince nodded. "Yeah, but that takes lots of money. Right now, we still need to figure out how to dispose of the otter carcasses. Let's check that other shaft." He let the other two men lead after sticking a few pieces of the ore in a jacket pocket.

Retracing their steps to the boarded-up side shaft, Vince held up a lantern while Tom and Ronnie dismantled the old barricade. Vince held a lantern ahead of him and took a few steps into the second shaft. "Whew, something stinks in here." He backed up. "Let's get some fresh air."

Back outside the abandoned mine, Tom pointed to a coating of white dust on their boots.

"I think it is bat guano," replied Ronnie. "There must be a bat colony in the closed-off section of the mine. Maybe there's another entrance or an air shaft."

A week later, as the three men processed sea otter pelts from their first hunt, he was proven right. Each evening at dusk, they observed hundreds of bats flying out of the mine entrance and spreading out in every direction into the forest.

The men continued their work, sometimes sleeping on the boat, but most days, they were so tired, they slept in a tent at their camp. They processed over a hundred pelts and stored the finished ones deep in the mine to stay dry. The carcasses were thrown in the abandoned mine shaft with the bats.

The first delivery of pelts to Kwan's buyer went as planned. On the agreed-upon day and time, a nondescript boat arrived in the bay. Vince and his partners were waiting on the *Sherry J.* They had brought five bundles from their cache in the mine each containing ten tanned pelts. The bundles were kept hidden in the hold until Vince could confirm that whoever was on the arriving boat was working for Johnny Kwan.

An older man, possibly in his early sixties, hailed them as the boat approached the *Sherry J.* He wasn't the usual rough-edged guy Vince knew Kwan liked to employ. The man facing him seemed out of place. He was slender, a bit stooped at his shoulders, and his clean-shaven face was pale. He looked more like an office employee or desk jockey than a fisherman or skipper of a fish packer. He was also as nervous as a cat near a kennel of energetic dogs. He kept averting his eyes to check the entrance to the bay like he was expecting the State Troopers to come speeding around a point in a patrol boat, lights flashing.

Vince was suspicious of the guy and the arrangement, but he confirmed he worked for Kwan. He asked Ronnie and Tom to show the man the pelts. Tom was a little slow removing the hatch covers, and he stumbled as he helped Ronnie lift the bundles out of the hold and pass them over to the other boat. Vince watched Tom for a few minutes. His partner was sweating and as pale as the skipper of the fish packer. Vince frowned but said nothing. Tom had been working harder than either he or Ronnie the last couple of days, so Vince passed it off as fatigue. Maybe Tom needed some rest. He knew he sure did.

"Ease up, there, Tom. Ronnie and I can take over."

"I'm okay. Just awfully tired all of a sudden. Let's just get this job done."

With the first fifty pelts on their way to Kwan, Vince and his partners went back to skinning and drying the rest of the 300 pelts they needed to deliver. As they finished each bundle, they stashed them in the deepest recesses of the old gold mine shaft.

Tom's symptoms worsened, and it was apparent to Vince and Ronnie that he wasn't well. His sweating increased and he drank bottle after bottle of water, his thirst seemingly unquenchable. The following day he began moaning and complaining of pain throughout his body. The moans turned to screams. Nothing Vince or Ronnie could do made a difference. They were not even sure he would live through the night.

Chapter 5

With patches of blue sky poking through high clouds and serving as a backdrop for a flock of snow geese heading south, the improvement in the weather did nothing for Brooklyn's disposition. After leaving the café and plodding down the road, she was in no hurry to get to school even though the teachers would be taking roll, in fifteen minutes.

Her school had just two classrooms and two teachers who taught multi-grades since there were so few kids.

Graham Hendricks was the senior teacher, and he taught science, math, and English. Sara Greenblum handled social studies and history. It was rumored Mr. Hendricks was retiring at the end of the school year. He was an okay teacher, but sometimes Brooklyn was uncomfortable around the man. She found him kind of creepy. She would catch him looking at her sometimes when he thought her attention was on a book or when she was helping the younger students.

The way Mr. Hendricks dealt with administrative stuff also sucked. When Ms. Greenblum started teaching at the Chatham school, he turned over the controversial issues and student discipline problems to her. Brooklyn couldn't understand the logic of this. Ms. Greenblum was young and had been teaching for just two years. She was from New Jersey, well educated, as well as a nice person, but not very good at handling discipline. While she was responsible for teaching American history, she had no knowledge of Native culture. A majority of the students were Tlingit Indian, including Tony Jackson and the others who had tried to molest her. So, Brooklyn knew that anything short of outright harassment in class in front of the other kids was not going to go well if Ms. Greenblum had to deal with it.

Soon after her arrival in Chatham, Brooklyn had witnessed Jake and one of his buddies telling Ms. Greenblum about totem poles possessing evil eyes. Even though the boys were just teasing, she didn't know anything about totems and believed them and avoided looking at totems. They had her buffaloed which wouldn't help her case.

As she reached the boardwalk that led to the school building, Brooklyn got the urge to keep walking. Tony's little brother, Bobby, and his friend Sam were approaching the main door. She stopped and watched them enter, unable to follow them. Back towards the center of town, several more middle-grade kids were walking her way. In the other direction, the road was clear. Brooklyn turned and picked up her pace. She walked towards the boat harbor at the end of the road.

Skipping school did not bother her. She got good grades and spent most days teaching herself. She used the satellite education channels that the State of Alaska broadcast to villages and small towns in the Bush, a collective name for Alaska's rural communities. But like the other older kids, Brooklyn was supposed to tutor two of the younger ones. Bobby Jackson was one of her charges, but he would just have to get along without her today.

Her step was lighter and her mood brighter now that she did not have to worry about running into Jake or Tony. She slowed as she approached the home of Gladys Tussock, a widow whose husband Floyd drowned years before when he fell off his fishing boat in Peril Strait. Mrs. Tussock kept herself busy gardening, which was no easy task in Southeast Alaska. While the summer days were long, the growing season was short. Gladys knew just what to grow, and her yard sprouted flowers of every color and size in every possible corner. She had hanging baskets that she moved out of a small greenhouse when the days got warmer. Along the top of a white picket fence that faced the road, Gladys had placed dozens of old teapots. Some were plain and some whimsical. They served as planters for her annuals, pansies, and nasturtiums that cascaded over the fence.

She even had a vegetable garden and sold produce to Mr. Jackson at his general store. This morning, with the weather looking dry with a little bit of sunshine, she was in her front yard pruning and fertilizing her rose bushes. Brooklyn enjoyed the roses most of all. They, and the myriad of other flowers Gladys grew, created the prettiest spot in Chatham.

Gladys Tussock was also a gossip. Her best friend was the town's postmistress. The two women knew everything about the residents of Chatham and the surrounding logging and mining camps, even as far as Hoonah. There was no way Brooklyn was going to get by her without being stopped for a few words. So, she took the lead, hoping to control the length of the inevitable conversation.

"Your roses sure have been beautiful this summer, Gladys."

The older woman was bent over, trimming the older branches in the center of one of the bushes. She straightened up, put her hands on her broad hips, and smiled at Brooklyn, who stood just outside the picket fence Gladys had erected to keep stray dogs out. Dogs wandered all over Chatham and were a problem if you tried to have a decent yard. People with their four-wheelers were a problem, too, as they tended to drive where they pleased. If that meant infringing on another person's property to avoid a big pothole or mud puddle in the road, they did so.

"Why, Brooklyn, that's such a nice thing to say. I do love my roses. Bingo Bob, and now you are the only two people who seem to appreciate my hard work." She shook her head. "Though some people keep sneaking in and picking them. Why are people so terrible these days?"

"I—ah—don't know. Your flowers are just too tempting, I guess. Why not put a little sign here on the fence to just admire and don't pick the flowers?"

"Humph! If people in Chatham would bother to read. I doubt most of them can read." Gladys pushed up her sleeve and looked at her watch. "Speaking of learning, why aren't you at school? It's after 8."

"I...I was at the community center yesterday and left my American History textbook there. I need it today. Ms. Greenblum insists that we have our textbooks handy."

"For a young woman, she's certainly a fuddy-duddy. Sarah showed up at the community bingo game last week and refused to take a seat at the table where

Bingo Bob always sits. And he was cleaned up and sober. We had to squeeze her in next to Bertha Johnson, who plays ten cards. Bertha was put out at having less room."

Brooklyn laughed. "That's Ms. Greenblum, all right. She cleans her hands with waterless soap at least ten times a day. Some kids giggle when she uses the bathroom just to fart."

"Brooklyn, that's an awful thing to say about someone." But she laughed anyway. "Well, you'd better be on your way. She's sure to record your absence."

"Yeah, no doubt. And make me stay after the last period. See ya." Brooklyn adjusted her backpack, waved, and headed down the road.

"Take care. Nice chatting with you, Brooklyn." Gladys called after her and then went back to her pruning. Later she would call her friend at the post office to gossip about Sarah Greenblum.

****

Nearing the foot of the long wooden stairway up to the community center, Brooklyn hesitated for several minutes. She had lied to Gladys about forgetting her textbook. The center wouldn't open until mid-morning since, with better weather today, Reggie was probably working on his cabin on the other side of the bay. Reggie's girlfriend had moved in with him and had complained about how primitive the place was.

She pictured Jake and the others standing on the first three steps, blocking her path and rubbing up against her body. She trembled and blinked several times, trying to make the image go away. She turned her head to stare at the boat harbor. Was Bingo Bob, the little-known man who had shown her an act of kindness, down there on his boat? Using her jacket sleeve, she wiped a tear from her cheek and continued down the road.

Chapter 6

Chatham's small boat harbor appeared deserted as Brooklyn reached the top of the metal ramp leading down to the float docks. She saw no activity anywhere. A few seagulls stood in a row near a fish cleaning table at the bottom of the ramp, perhaps waiting for an easy meal from a lucky returning fisherman. A bald eagle perched on one of the pilings, undisturbed by Brooklyn's sudden appearance, stood on watch.

The boat harbor was laid out to handle a variety of types and sizes of boats. Closest to the end of the ramp was a transient dock meant to serve small boats loading and unloading people and gear. Beyond it was a series of three long floating docks—extending like skinny fingers trying to grab hold of the stone breakwater on the far side of the harbor.

Two of the dock fingers had signs designating them as B Dock and C Dock. The farthest one, C Dock, was reserved for larger commercial fishing boats. At the moment, there was only one boat moored at the far end—a squalid fishing trawler that Brooklyn had never seen before. The name on the bow was *Sherry J.*

B Dock was reserved for recreational boats, and several were now moored stem to stern along both sides. Brooklyn scanned these boats, one at a time, trying to determine which one might belong to Bingo. There were three small boats with tiny cabins and big outboard motors that probably belonged to residents who liked to fish or used them for quick trips to Juneau to pick up groceries or supplies. Opposite the small outboards were a sailboat and the larger cabin cruiser that belonged to Tony Jackson's father. Beyond the Jackson boat, was a derelict sailboat covered with a blue tarp. Next to the sailboat were two other boats notable for their peeling paint, layers of green algae, and general state of disrepair. Their decks and tops of cabins were littered with old lumber and rusting parts. One had windows replaced with plywood. Water hoses and electrical cables ran to each of them like lifelines attempting to stave off their inevitable demise.

One derelict boat differed from the others. Its hull had once been light blue, but now the fiberglass was faded and stained with an oily residue. Below the waterline, it was covered in stringy green algae. What set this one apart was something that reminded Brooklyn of Gladys' roadside garden. Along the rails in the stern and on the cabin roof, flowers were growing in plastic buckets and coffee cans. Amongst the well-cared-for planters was a large tin teapot overflowing with nasturtiums. The other thing that caught her eye was a skiff tied along its side with crab pots neatly stacked in the bow. Bingo had said he was fond of catching crabs. The boat covered in flowers must be his.

Brooklyn stared at the boat for several minutes, watching for any sign of someone on board. She was about to start down the ramp when the resident eagle, perhaps nervous from her presence, spread its wings and flew further down the bay. She watched as it settled on one of a cluster of old pilings, all that was left of a salmon cannery that had once been the major employer in Chatham.

Brooklyn put one hand on the metal railing and took a step down the ramp. The aluminum gratings rattled as she walked, scattering the seagulls. Three took flight, and the other two waddled down the dock a safe distance and stood there watching her. Brooklyn turned left at the bottom of the ramp and walked towards the slip where Bingo's boat was moored. The water under the floating dock was clear. A school of thousands of fingerling salmon swam slowly under it. On the bottom, she could see anemones waving their tentacles in the tidal current and an enormous, multi-arm starfish attached to a big rock. A large crab scuttled away from an unseen predator. With her eyes on the larger-than-life aquarium, she tripped over some of the junk tossed on the dock next to one of the derelict boats.

When she got to Bingo's boat, Brooklyn stopped. The dock lines that secured it were in good condition, as were the fenders that kept it from bumping against the concrete dock. Everything was tidy—what a mariner would refer to as *shipshape*. However, the long strands of algae attached to the bottom were a sign that the boat had not been moved in a long time or hauled out so the bottom could be cleaned. Her mom had said it hadn't moved since Bingo arrived in Chatham and Brooklyn saw that she was right.

She stood a safe distance away and called out. "Hello? Are you onboard, Bingo?" There was no answer and no sounds of anyone on board. She walked closer to the stern with its neatly arranged flower pots, reached over, and rapped on the top of the boat's cabin.

"Hello?" She said it a little louder this time.

Brooklyn jumped as someone answered from behind her on the dock. "How are you, Brooklyn?"

She raised a hand to her chest. "Oh! You startled me." She could feel her heart thumping.

"Sorry, I didn't mean to surprise you." Bingo removed an old knit seaman's cap, exposing his snarled white hair. "I was watching you from the hill above the road. You didn't look up, or you would have seen me. I thought for sure you saw me follow you down the ramp to the dock."

"No. I…I thought you would be inside your boat. I wanted to thank you for what you did yesterday. I was scared, and…well, thank you."

Brooklyn studied the man, who stood a few feet away. He was blocking her way back to shore, but she relaxed when she saw he looked different. While he still looked disheveled, he stood tall and steady and appeared to be sober—not at all like he had been the day before. He was a big man, well over six feet tall. The hands holding the cap were rough and calloused. His fingernails were clean and well cared for.

Bingo put his cap back on and stepped back to give her space. "What those boys did was inexcusable. I spoke to Tony's father about it later while he was working on his boat. Mr. Jackson and I are friends of a sort. I'm a regular customer at his store, and we were both in the Navy for a few years."

Brooklyn remained standing next to Bingo's boat. She glanced over at the Jackson boat, no more than fifty yards away on the next dock. "Mr. Jackson knows?"

"Don't worry, Brooklyn. He was quite upset with his son's disrespectful actions. I'm sure Tony received far more abuse from his father last night than I laid on him with my words. I don't think you will have any more problems with Tony. But I'm not sure how much influence Tony has with his friends. Jake and Joey are pretty hardcore delinquents. I'm worried about them. Once they have money, they'll spend it on things like alcohol and drugs, and who knows what will happen. But I'm hardly the one to say such a thing."

What Bingo said made her feel so much better. It was like feeling the warmth of the sun suddenly popping out from behind a fast-moving cloud. Tony might not be a problem at school after all, and maybe she wouldn't have to talk to Ms. Greenblum about the incident. She suddenly had the urge to head for the school building.

"Bingo, I think you're a good man at heart, and so does Mrs. Tussock." Brooklyn shuffled her feet, wondering if she had said too much. "Uh… I'm late for school. I've got to go, Bingo." She brushed by the man and hurried up the dock. She turned to look back and saw that he hadn't moved. "Bye, Bingo! Thank you again, and I like your flowers."

****

No more than an hour after Brooklyn left the dock for school, Bingo stood washing his breakfast dishes in the tiny galley when he saw a flash of color through a porthole over the sink. People were walking out on the dock going towards the *Sherry J.* Two of them were men he had seen go ashore earlier that morning. Now three people were headed back to the boat, and the third person was Flo Whiting. She was helped on board by one of the men. Then he helped the other man, who stumbled and had difficulty climbing aboard. A puff of black smoke blew out the boat's smokestack as the engine started. The dock lines were pulled in, and minutes later, the *Sherry J* and Flo Whiting were gone.

Chapter 7

Johnny Kwan's luxurious 60-foot catamaran was his home and office. It was fast— nearly thirty knots in choppy water. That pleased Johnny because time mattered in his line of work. Pickups, deliveries, shakedowns—all depended on showing up on time and sometimes unexpectedly. There were very few roads in his turf. Of course, he could use a plane like many Alaskan businesses. He owned a five-passenger jet kept at the Juneau airport. Cruising at 250 miles per hour was fine for a trip to Anchorage or Seattle. But, most of his rather nefarious clients, the ones who provided him with seafood products, were nowhere near an airport. They often operated in remote villages and bays. And the yacht had other advantages. It offered a comfortable salon, a bar, plus living quarters for his trusted henchmen and boat crew.

It took him just under two hours to reach the no-name bay Vince James was using as his processing site. Vince had refused to disclose the bay's name. However, Kwan's pickup man had written down the GPS coordinates and passed the information on to Johnny's skipper.

Vince James was a nagging concern, a risk. It wasn't that Vince had a history of dishonesty and breaking the law and had an urgent need to make easy money. There was something about Vince's past that showed up in his hesitancy to go against his Native culture. Kwan knew Vince had been banned by his Native community. Maybe his wounded pride had festered to the point that he wanted to make amends. Kwan could not afford anything going wrong with the delivery of the sea otter pelts and their ultimate shipment to Shanghai, for he wasn't at the end of the chain. Vince agreed to deliver 300 pelts and received a nice advance. But Johnny's business operation depended on no one welching on delivering and everyone reaching their quota. As a member of a Tong, Johnny Kwan had quotas of his own. When Vince asked for a delay in delivering the remaining pelts, Johnny was not happy. Then there was Vince's boat loan. His current payment was late, making Vince a severe problem in his business ledgers. A personal visit was definitely in order.

It mattered little to Kwan that buying and exporting sea otter pelts was illegal. There were ways to obtain them. Vince, an Alaskan Native, seemed to be one approach. Natives could possess pelts for their personal use, but selling them and then exporting them to China carried a heavy fine and jail time.

But it was all part of the game. Kwan thrived on risky business ventures, and they made him lots of money—as long as people like Vince James didn't screw things up.

****

Johnny was annoyed when he saw that Vince's boat was not in the bay. He and his men would have to go ashore and search for the processing site. He looked at his watch, then at the two men lowering a dinghy into the water. Their slowness didn't help his impatience any. He turned to the skipper, watching his navigation displays and the radar for any other boats in their vicinity.

"Keep one eye on the beach, too, okay?" Johnny said. "Someone might walk out after hearing the racket those guys are making."

"Yes, sir, boss. You going ashore with them?"

"Yeah, I may be wasting my time. If I am, it's going to cost someone extra."

The sound of an outboard motor coming to life caught Kwan's attention. He grabbed a jacket and hat as he headed for the back deck. In the salon, he flipped up the top of a coffee table, revealing a stash of weapons. He grabbed an automatic pistol, checked for a full magazine, and stuck it in his belt. he hated not knowing what he was walking into and he hated the Alaskan wilderness even more.

Kwan and two of his men motored slowly along the shore, searching for signs of a trail to Vince's hideout. There was nothing along a stretch of pebble beach. The rest of the shoreline was steep and rocky. It was beginning to look like a fruitless search when Lee, one of his henchmen sitting in the bow of the small craft, spotted something—a school of salmon swimming in a current coming from a corner of the bay.

"Hey, will you look at that?" the man in the front said. "It looks like there is a stream flowing from behind those rocks." The man at the tiller increased his speed to compensate for the outflowing current. He followed the stream to where it appeared to flow out of a cavern. Only as they continued did they see that it was not a cavern and it was open at the other end. Ahead of them was a crudely constructed dock. The tillerman shoved the dinghy up to it, and Lee jumped out and tied up the boat.

"Looks like a trail going into the trees, Boss," Lee said.

"Okay, follow it and let me know what's up there."

Lee returned fifteen minutes later. "There's a camp, all right. Saw some pelts stretched out under a big tarp. Looks like this is the place. But I don't like it, Boss. The smell is worse than the slums of Kowloon. And there's a tent with a dead man inside."

Kwan frowned. "Was it Vince James?"

"I don't know. The face was all contorted, and the body was wrapped in a sleeping bag."

Kwan led the way back up the trail, trying to avoid the big muddy spots. In the worst places, boards had been placed over the muck. By the time they reached the camp, his shoes were well caked, and his pant legs well spattered.

As Lee had said, under a large blue tarp, there was a makeshift table for skinning and a large rack made from rough-cut wood poles for drying pelts. There were several pelts in various stages of being finished.

On the far side of the clearing were two tents, and beyond them was a mine entrance that had been recently reinforced with new timbers. Much of the campsite was a mess with piles of cut brush and tree limbs, rusty cables and mining equipment, and garbage was strewn everywhere.

Kwan motioned to one of the men as he gave him an order. "Check that mine shaft. Might be someone working in there."

He walked toward one of the tents. The first tent was empty except for tools and supplies. Approaching the second tent, he smelled something. He pulled aside a flap and saw a man's body partially covered by a sleeping bag. He studied the man's face for a moment.

Lee was right behind him and drew the collar of his jacket over his mouth and nose at the smell of death. "Is it Vince James?"

"No. Must be one of his partners."

The third man came back from the cave. He was covering his nose and mouth, pulling his shirt down to tell Kwan about what he'd found. "Not much in the cave, Boss. There's a bundle of pelts just inside the entrance. Too dark to go very far and it stinks worse in there. I think it's infested with bats. Heard some squeaking and rustling around."

"Okay, go back and get those pelts and take them to the boat. Then we'll bury this man. I shouldn't bother but it's the only decent thing to do. There are shovels in the other tent. And hurry, we don't want to be here at dusk when those bats come out of there. I've seen this kind of death before. It can be very unhealthy if we stay here very long."

"What do you mean, Boss?" Lee asked as he glanced at his partner hustling back towards the entrance to the mine.

"I mean, it's a nasty way to die—rabies."

****

Brooklyn didn't encounter any trouble with Tony the rest of the day. Tony glared at her once when she got to school but had nothing to say. It must have been true what Bingo said about talking to Mr. Jackson. She decided to let the matter go. But she made a mental note to be careful in the future about putting herself in a difficult position with boys, and men in general, when she didn't have a means to back away.

She spent an hour with Tony's younger brother on math tables. The boy was a slow learner. She suggested some exercises with things to memorize that would help him add big numbers. But the time in class still passed slowly, and she was anxious to get home and tell her mother about meeting Bingo Bob.

Their house was cold and dark when she got home. Her mom always turned off the heat when neither of them was home. Fuel oil was expensive and had to be delivered by Pete's Heating Oil, a company in Hoonah. Rather than turn on the furnace, Brooklyn headed to her room. She flopped on her bed, pulled a blanket around her shoulders, and grabbed her earphones hanging on a bedpost. After the tension of the last twenty-four hours, she quickly fell asleep to the lyrics of one of her favorite pop songs set on replay.

It was dark when she woke up. Her music was still playing. Maybe that's why she didn't hear her mom arrive home. She stretched. The house was still cold, so she grabbed an oversized sweatshirt and slipped it on. Then she headed out to the kitchen to see what her Mom was cooking for dinner. But neither the radio nor the TV was on—something she always did when she returned home. The door to her mom's bedroom was closed, too.

"Mom? Are you in there? Are we going to have supper?" There was no answer. Brooklyn opened the door. The room should have been neat, but it wasn't. There were clothes piled on the bed, and several bureau drawers were open.

She whipped around, searching the rest of the house for anything else out of place. Then she saw a piece of paper on the kitchen table. It was her mom's handwriting.

"Brooklyn, I have to leave town for a few days on an urgent family matter. Mr. Wilson has given me a few days off, and he said it's okay for you to come by and eat at the café while I'm gone. There's some leftover mac and cheese in the fridge for your dinner tonight. Love, Mom"

Brooklyn grabbed her jacket and dashed out of the house, slamming the door behind her. She ran to the café. It was closed, but lights were on and Leroy was still there, stacking chairs and getting ready to mop the floor. Brooklyn rapped on the front window and waved. Leroy came over to unlock the main door.

"Where did my mom go? She left me a note which I just found at our house."

"She didn't say. Just that she needed a few days off."

"But Mom never said anything to me about planning to go somewhere. When did she let you know?"

"Right after breakfast was over, I guess. Flo seemed nervous about something but wouldn't tell me what it was. This fella was hanging around like he was waiting to talk with her. They spoke in the back, and Flo's voice got kind of loud. But she seemed fine and was calm when they left."

"Were they the two strangers that were here this morning?"

"Yeah, them." Leroy shook his head as he stacked another chair on top of a table. "You know, there was an odd thing about those fellas. She refused to wait on them and asked me to do it. At the time, I thought it was the way their clothes smelled. Kind of like fellas who have been fishing for several days? Don't know why she suddenly changed her mind about them."

"Did you hear any names mentioned? Was one of them called Vince?"

"Can't say I did, but I was pretty busy and didn't pay them any attention."

Brooklyn slumped down in one of the chairs that Leroy hadn't stowed. She buried her head in her arms and moaned. "I don't understand. Why did she just leave me and not wait and talk to me about having to go somewhere?"

Leroy walked over and laid a hand on her shoulder. "I… I don't know. Your mother is a strong woman. I wouldn't worry about her."

"But she's always so methodical and likes to think things through for a couple of days." Brooklyn raised her head and looked at Leroy. "Did you say these guys had a boat?"

"I don't know. The two men smelled like they had been doing some fishing."

"There was a fishing boat down at the dock. It was the…the *Sherry J*. That was the name. Do you think the Coast Guard in Juneau could find a boat with just a name?"

"I suppose. But there has to be a reason for the Coast Guard to do that. Your mom wasn't kidnapped or anything. Then again, maybe it wasn't their boat either. They could have come here on the Hoonah road. If I were you, I'd just do like she said for a day or so. It's possible when she gets to wherever she's going, she'll get another message to you."

"Maybe you're right. I guess I'm just worrying too

much. But this isn't like my mom."

"Tomorrow, you could ask around. Maybe someone saw Flo leave town. You know, getting in a truck and driving off? Or like you thought, leaving on a fishing boat."

"Yeah, someone could have seen her at the dock. Maybe Bingo Bob saw her. His boat was pretty close to where the *Sherry J* was moored."

"I don't know how reliable Bingo would be. If he was drinking, a cruise ship could come in here, and he wouldn't notice."

Leroy stuck his mop in the bucket, swirled it around, and then wrung it out. He paused and scratched his chin. "Still, the guy was mighty anxious to leave. He didn't look too good, either. Kind of sick like."

Brooklyn raised her head again. "What?"

"Yeah, when they left, he almost fell down the steps, and his pal had to grab him. So, ask around tomorrow." Leroy started mopping around a couple of the tables. "Sorry, Brooklyn, but I have to get this place cleaned up and head home. Tomorrow starts early for me."

Brooklyn got up and slowly walked over to the door. She was about to leave when Leroy spoke up again.

"I do remember overhearing one thing they said while they were eating their breakfast. It was about having to leave a sick friend at someplace called the Grotto. Never heard of a place with that name around here, so I assumed it was a place they had given the name. Maybe somebody knows about it. You might ask about that too."

Chapter 8

The *Sherry J* had traveled several hours from Chatham and was approaching False Point when the engine RPMs dropped, and their speed suddenly slowed to less than five knots. Ronnie was at the helm, and Vince, who had collapsed into a bunk as soon as they left the dock at Chatham, was asleep.

Flo woke him up. "Vince, Ronnie needs your help. There's a problem with the engine."

"Huh? Okay, I'm coming." As Vince sat up, he could hear the engine laboring. The boat was also rolling quite a bit. When he got to Ronnie, who was struggling to maintain course, Vince knew why. Ronnie had changed course. The boat was now heading into a strong wind. Waves were breaking over the bow, and spray was hitting the windows in a steady pattern.

"We've lost RPMs. Got any idea what's wrong?"

"Yeah, I think so," Vince said. "It's probably a clogged air filter. The engine is an old Detroit 71, and it scavenges part of the exhaust air for combustion. I've got a spare, but we will have to turn off the engine to replace it."

"Well, I got worried about the engine quitting completely. We're heading to Angoon just in case things get more serious. No marine services there, but if we need replacement parts, they can be flown in from Juneau."

"That's probably the best option," Vince said. "We can't just call the Coast Guard."

"Why not?" Flo said.

"There might be a problem with—" Vince's explanation was cut short by a cell phone ringing in his pocket. He frowned. He hadn't realized they had cell coverage. It had to be because they were close to Angoon, the Native village on the east side of the strait. He fumbled with his cell phone, trying to pull it out of his jacket pocket—almost dropping it as the boat shuddered from the impact of another swell.

"Vince" was all he said.

The caller said nothing, and Vince knew who it was. He frowned again and turned away from the others.

"We found your little hidden camp. Quite a setup and you should have been there, Vince. I had to waste my time and take risks encountering the Fish and Game or State Troopers."

"Sorry, I…ah…I had a slight setback. One of my buddies got sick, and I had to find help."

"Sick friend, that's a good one. I don't care about your friends, alive or dead, Vince. I care about our deal. You were supposed to deliver 250 pelts. My men took another bundle of pelts you had ready. I'm going to consider those to be freebies for my time. With the 50 earlier ones, that's only twenty percent of what we agreed to."

Vince was puzzled. What was he alluding to about not finding the bundles of otter pelts, and what did he mean by friends sick or dead? If Kwan had only taken one bundle and not gone deeper into the mine shaft, then maybe he hadn't found the rest of the cache.

Almost two hundred pelts were stored at the far end of the mine. If he could make another hunt and get another fifty pelts, then his contract would be filled.

"I...I'm going to need more time to deliver the rest. Gimmie a week, maybe?"

Kwan laughed. "I can't do that, Vince. You have a pretty serious problem on your hands."

"What...what did you say?"

"The man you left at your camp, he's dead. That's what. Take my word for it. You don't want to go back there. I saw the bats come out of that old mine shaft, and I'm betting your sick friend died of rabies. It's not a nice way to die, Vince. If you were there, I'm sure you saw the suffering your friend went through. I've seen people dying from rabies in my own country. As I said, it's not a pretty sight. So, if I were you, I wouldn't go near that place. Oh, and the law enforcement folks are going to have a field day when they find it. So I don't believe you when you say you can fulfill our little contract. As to the delivered pelts, I figure they account for maybe the 35,000 that I advanced you for the pelts, but you still have the loan for the boat. Either come up with the rest, or my men will end your crummy life. Have a good day."

Vince shook his head and put the phone on a ledge next to the pilothouse windows. Ronnie looked at him, a question in his eyes.

"Kwan found our camp," Vince said with a sigh. He was sweating as he glanced at Flo. She didn't look happy.

"The man I just talked to visited our camp. Our partner Tom is dead. The man believes he died from rabies. Doesn't that result from a bite by a rabid animal?"

Flo frowned. "Yes. A dog, maybe a raccoon or a fox, but what does…"

"How about bats?" Vince asked. "There's a bunch of bats in the mineshaft we've been using for…for storage. Bats carry rabies, right? And a larger animal is a possibility too. When I was helping Tom, he said something about encountering an aggressive critter down by the stream. So maybe it wasn't a bat. Maybe it was a fox or something. We can…"

Flo interrupted him. "Hold it, Vince. What's going on? You lied to get me to come with you, didn't you? If your friend has died of rabies and you're sick too, you need treatment immediately. It doesn't matter whether he was bitten by a bat or another rabid animal. You probably got it from your friend, and rabies can be fatal if not treated right away."

Vince hung his head and dug out a handkerchief to wipe his brow.

"Vince, listen to me. If it is rabies, I can't help you. I can't. You need a doctor, and you need to be where a doctor can treat you with a special vaccine."

"Seriously?" Vince said. "I…I didn't know there was any danger of rabies in Southeast Alaska. I've read about rabid dogs biting people up north, but…"

Flo didn't let him finish. "You said your friend Tom noticed an animal acting strangely? Rabies can be endemic with lots of small mammals. Did he say what it was? A fox? Or maybe a mink?"

"There are some river otters on the creek, just above the Grotto not too far from our camp," Ronnie added. "They've been pretty aggressive. But, I figured we were just intruding into their territory."

"Did either of you enter the mine? Maybe disturb the bats? By the way, what do you mean by the Grotto?" Flo said.

"Yeah, I've been in the mine," Vince said reluctantly. "Had to, since Tom got sick. Tom made lots of trips into the mine. It's been abandoned for a very long time, maybe a hundred years. I don't know for sure. When we dug out the entrance and explored inside, we found a shaft that had been boarded up. When we checked it out, the floor of the mine was covered in this white dust. We assumed it was bat guano and didn't take the presence of the bats seriously since we seldom needed to go inside."

"So the mine is a grotto?" Flo wasn't going to let this go.

"No, not the mine. It's just a place, the Grotto, the White Grotto. It's sort of a cave—who cares? Some guy I worked for a while back called this hole in the rocks the White Grotto."

While Vince explained about the Grotto and the mine, Ronnie did his best to keep the boat on a steady course. The wind and waves were hitting the boat pretty hard. Every fifth wave sent a heavy spray over the bow and against the windscreen. With their reduced speed, the combination of wind, wave, and tidal current had slowed their progress. It would be several hours before they reached Angoon.

Flo was furious with Vince. She was getting tired of being bounced around in the rough seas, and now she regretted that she even agreed to go with him. But things were what they were, and she knew she had to come up with some way to help.

"Okay, so whatever caused your friend Tom to die

has now made you sick. We're running out of time." She shook her head. "As I said, if it's rabies, you need proper medical attention. You should have taken Tom and gone directly to the hospital in Juneau. You still need to do that for yourself. Your friend's body can wait."

"It's too late to head to Juneau today," Vince said, shaking his head. "Might take us a couple of hours just to get this engine repaired. I guess we can stay in Angoon, repair the engine, and try heading there first thing in the morning. But, it would still take us at a full day to get to Juneau."

"That will delay you getting treatment."

Vince didn't answer and was nodding off again.

"Look at me, Vince. You need medicine now. Here's what we can do. We need to go back to Chatham, where there is a doctor. Doc Perkins is just a family doctor, but he is also a friend. Maybe he can treat you. If he doesn't have the vaccine, he can have it flown from Juneau. We'll get your treatment started. It takes three or four weeks, and you have to be quarantined."

"I don't have four weeks. I mean I…"

"Yes, what do you mean? You have to be treated, or you'll die. What else is going on, Vince?" Flo couldn't keep the anger from her voice. "What were you doing at that mine? Was it something illegal?"

"I…I can't tell you about it, Flo."

She grabbed his cell phone and stared at it for a minute, realizing she didn't know how to use one. She only had an old landline phone at her home. Ronnie, who was busy steering the boat, noticed her hesitancy. "If it's got three bars," he said in an almost apologetic tone, "that's a good signal. Dial your number and push the green button."

She started punching in a phone number. "I shouldn't be doing this, but I'm calling Wally Perkins right now. It will give him time to be prepared when we get there. We're going back to Chatham as soon as we can."

Vince didn't try to stop her from making the call. He was too tired and weak to care.

****

Bingo Bob was anything but calm as he sat in the cabin of his boat. Towards evening his anxieties steadily increased. It was enough to take out a bottle of whiskey and set it on the galley table in front of him, where he sat down and stared at a photograph taped to the wall. It was of a young girl on her bike. He'd given her that bike for her birthday. He stared at the photo and then at the bottle for a long time while he recalled the events of the last twenty-four hours. It had started with chasing away the town boys who were harassing Brooklyn. He had never done such a thing because all he usually wanted was to be left alone. Then she visited him to thank him. That was unusual too. No one in Chatham had ever thanked him for anything. He never went out of his way to help anyone. Well, there was the time he was walking by Gladys Tussock's house, and she was struggling to move a couple of big rocks in her front yard. He asked if he could help, and she nodded. Afterward, Gladys smiled and, nodding, gave her approval. After that tiniest thing, Gladys always made sure he got an early opportunity to select what bingo cards he wanted on bingo night at the community center.

Then in the late morning yesterday, he saw Brooklyn's mother leaving in a hurry to get on a boat with two strangers, but without Brooklyn. None of them were carrying a suitcase or a bag. Something didn't seem right. Flo wasn't smiling either. In fact, she looked downright unhappy. As he watched, Flo and one of the men helped the other man climb aboard the *Sherry J*, which quickly left the harbor. He didn't know what to make of it.

Then there were the memories these events were triggering—things that had haunted him for years, things he thought he had put behind him by running away. Bingo removed the screw top and took a long drink from the bottle. The alcohol burned his throat, and he exhaled. He wiped his lips with his wrist, then a tear from his cheek as he relived some of his life before Alaska.

His real name was Robert Fuller. He had been a successful engineer for Boeing Aerospace in Seattle. He had a wife and a 10-year-old daughter Emily, who was the love of his life. He was happy, but then he began having a hard time dealing with production schedules and setbacks on the job. He started drinking. He lost his job and couldn't get another, not even the most menial kind of work. No one wanted to employ a 52-year-old aeronautical engineer who was an alcoholic. Their savings were wiped out, and he couldn't pay the mortgage or the bills. His wife finally had enough and left him. She took Emily. He had failed his family, and he had lost the opportunity to be a father to Emily. But he still had his boat, and it became his home until he couldn't pay the moorage fees. So, he decided to go to Alaska. Or rather, he escaped.

He took another drink, and the warmth from the alcohol surged through his system. Tears rolled steadily down his cheeks. He ignored them. Bingo knew why he had stepped in to help Brooklyn. He had pictured Brooklyn as his Emily, and she was facing trouble. While he had failed to take care of Emily, he could help Brooklyn.

Over the next hour, he finished the bottle. The alcohol didn't help him forget his past, and it only magnified his failure with his daughter's life. In a drunken stupor, he struggled to his feet, knocking the empty bottle to the floor, and collapsed on his bunk. As he passed out, his mind was filled with the image of a little girl with dark hair, smiling, as she sat on her new bicycle.

Chapter 9

A mile upstream from the Grotto, a family of river otters had a den in a stream bank near a lake. The stream eventually flowed through the Grotto. It was an idyllic location for such playful creatures. With summer days giving way to fall, the otters should have enjoyed feeding on the plentiful stock of fish in the lake. But in recent weeks, their activity had greatly diminished. The two adult otters were emaciated and weak. They were nervous and jittery.

Two people, a man, and a woman paddled a canoe across the lake and beached their craft a few hundred feet from the stream where the otters were hiding and watching. The animals chirped to one another as the man pulled the canoe up onto the shore. He heard the sounds and glanced in their direction.

"Do you hear that, Donna?" the man said. "I've never heard a sound like that before. I wonder what it is. A grouse or a ptarmigan or some other type of small animal?"

"I don't see anything, Jim." Donna listened and peered for a few minutes in the direction he was staring.

"It must be pretty small or well-hidden in that brush."

She walked a few yards along the beach towards the stream.

"You know, we've been a week on this camping

trip and only seen one large animal, that moose on the shore. However, it's been a comfort not seeing a bear." She stopped and peered again into the brush. "Where's the Forest Service cabin that's supposed to be at this end of the lake?"

"In the trees to our left." Jim pointed into the woods.

Donna walked back to the canoe to help unload their gear. Avid adventurers, they'd decided to spend their honeymoon on a backcountry trip in Alaska. They found a company called Eco Wings that flew people into remote lakes with all of their supplies. A floatplane would drop clients off and pick them up a week or ten days later. Jim and Donna selected a lake with several forest service shelters that were primitive, bare-bones cabins. The floatplane pilot dropped them and a canoe at the west end of Evans Lake, where there was a cozy cabin. They were to meet him at a second cabin at the east end in seven days. Despite a day or two of rain, their trip had been idyllic with beautiful scenery and satisfying nights as newlyweds. The pilot warned them that this was brown bear country. He told them that as long as they avoided the major streams in and out of the lake, they shouldn't have any encounters.

They heard the chirping sounds again as they finished unloading. The sounds were louder this time. A splash in the stream attracted their attention, and both of them turned to see a dark, lithe form dive into the water from the brush.

"Oh, Jim. You know, I think it's a weasel! I've never seen one in the wild."

"I think it's an otter. Too big to be a weasel or a mink."

"I want a picture," Donna said as she dug into her pack. "We don't have any pictures of animals at all on this trip. I've still got the telephoto lens on my camera. It would be a beautiful animal to photograph, don't you think? Just look at this setting." Donna took her camera and started walking back along the lakeshore.

"Be careful, Donna. Remember what the pilot said about bears hanging around the streams." While waiting for her, Jim opened a waterproof bag to find his information on the forest service cabin.

Donna ignored his warning and used the high brush to remain out of sight of the creature. She had to get closer to the spot where they had seen it enter the water. She was twenty feet from the location when another otter lunged from the brush and grabbed her left arm with its sharp teeth. Donna screamed and lashed at the squirming form with her camera. It let go and dropped to the ground, but it didn't run away. It stood in front of her bobbing its head yowling at her. Jim heard her screaming and ran to her. He picked up a broken tree branch to use as a club and stood in front of her trying to hold the otter at bay. A second otter emerged from the stream and joined its companion in yowling and hissing at them.

"Back up very slowly," he said as calmly as he could muster. "The cabin is in the trees just beyond the canoe to the left. When I say run, you run as fast as you can for the door. I'll be right behind you."

Sobbing, Donna held her arm close to her body, blood dripping from near her elbow. She did as Jim said and backed slowly away, keeping Jim between her and the threatening otters. These animals were not the cute creatures that Donna had seen in a zoo or expected to photograph in the wilderness of Alaska. Their eyes were wild and bulged. White foamy saliva dripped from their sharp little teeth.

When Donna and Jim were thirty feet away, he hollered. "Now run!"

The two reached the cabin, rushed inside, and Jim slammed the door and slid the latch into place. There was a thud as one of the otters slammed into the exterior of the cabin door.

Donna became hysterical. "Oh my God! What are we going to do?" She held out her arm for her husband to examine. The bite on her arm was bleeding profusely.

Jim wrapped his handkerchief around the wound as he tried to comfort her. "If they leave, I'll get our packs and the first aid kit from the canoe. There's nothing else we can do. We're going to be trapped here until our pilot flies in tomorrow morning."

Donna continued to cry. "It hurts, Jim. My whole arm is tingling and burning. Why did they attack me like that?"

"I'm not sure, but did you notice their faces? There was froth dripping from their mouths. I think they may be rabid. We've got to wash the wound with soap and water and put some antiseptic cream on it right away. It's all we got in our first aid kit, which happens to still be in the canoe. We'll get you to the hospital in Juneau as quickly as we can. I'm afraid you're going to need the rabies vaccine."

Jim hugged Donna, but she went on sobbing. "Oh my God! What if—they don't—have any vaccine? What if the pilot—can't find us?"

Chapter 10

Leroy Wilson had been no help in getting new information about Flo's unannounced departure. Heading back home, Brooklyn was determined to spend the next day trying to learn whatever she could. Someone in town must know something—like who owned the *Sherry J*. That would be a start. It was not like her mother to leave suddenly and without her. Going to school just didn't seem all that important at the moment. It was a feeling Brooklyn rarely had. She enjoyed learning new things, and it was easy for her. But Brooklyn couldn't put her finger on why she should be so fixated on her mother's absence. At breakfast, she had told her mother she hated her for never doing anything together. She wished she could take that back, but it had been said. Maybe it was because they had never been separated before. This new feeling was unsettling.

The house felt lonely without her mother's presence. So rather than spend the night in her own room, Brooklyn slept in her mother's bed. She kept her clothes on and pulled a heavy quilt over herself. She lay there for a long time, reading her mother's note over and over. It was about as bland as a shopping list with no hint of any problem. It was like their conversation had been this morning, a matter of fact—*I've gone to the store and will be back in an hour. Dinner's in the oven. Help yourself.*

Even lying in her mother's bed with the light on, she had a restless night and kept waking up thinking about her mother, hoping she would come home and be lying beside her in the morning. She slept late and when she woke, true to the words of the note, her mother had not come home.

Brooklyn forced herself to have a bowl of cold cereal at home rather than face Leroy at the cafe again so soon. In the silence of the house, her restlessness turned to worry. While she wanted to believe her mother's request and not be concerned, she couldn't help feeling that things weren't okay. The fact that the note didn't mention anything specific may have meant just the opposite. Something about her departure had to be serious.

The two of them had lived their entire lives in this small town without a major incident. No family deaths had come their way. There were no major illnesses. The town of Chatham was like dullsville. Nothing ever happened. No shootings, no disturbances except for the drunks at the Frontier Pub on the Fourth of July. They didn't even have a law enforcement officer. The nearest State Trooper was in Hoonah, nearly two hours away by a lousy road.

"Hoonah!" Brooklyn said aloud. "Leroy said she could have gone to Hoonah. Maybe Mom didn't leave town on the *Sherry J*. Maybe she had to go to the medical clinic. Doc Perkins should know."

Doctor Wallace Perkins maintained a small medical practice at his home in Chatham for the benefit of the community. He was the only doctor for over 30 miles. If someone was seriously ill, they drove to the clinic in Hoonah or hired a seaplane to Juneau. Wally, as everyone in town called Doc Perkins, actually had two degrees—an MD in medicine and a doctorate in public health. His true passion was virulent disease epidemics throughout the world, as he frequently served as a consultant to the World Health Organization and the Center for Disease Control. He lived in Chatham because that was where his parents retired, and he liked it. His father had been a doctor with a practice in Juneau, while his mother was the daughter of a mining engineer for one of Southeast Alaska's once-booming gold mines. Wally and his wife Peggy lived at the east end of town above the boat harbor. He was also an avid wildlife photographer.

Brooklyn rinsed her breakfast bowl and left it in the sink. She grabbed her jacket and headed for the Perkins' home. Getting to most places in Chatham, you either needed an ATV or you walked. She considered taking her mom's ATV, but what if she suddenly came home and needed it? Brooklyn decided to walk.

Brooklyn had been walking for several minutes and was almost to Jackson's store when a large truck lumbered up the main street like a tank crossing a battlefield. It was the heating oil delivery truck from Hoonah. She started to wave a polite good morning, then changed her mind and waved furiously to get the driver to stop. The man at the wheel of the beast was Jake Thompson. His daughter Molly was the same age as Brooklyn, and they had become friends through inter-school sports. If Jake could take her into Hoonah, she could check with the health clinic about her mom. Seeing Doc Perkins could wait until she got back.

Jake saw Brooklyn waving at him and stopped his

truck, the brakes squealing like two pigs in a pen squabbling over a scrap of food.

"Hi, Jake. How's Molly?"

"She's fine. Something I need to tell her about?"

"Nope. Just asking. I was also wondering if you've seen my mom?"

"Flo? No. Should I have?"

"If you just came from Hoonah, I thought maybe you might have seen her. She left town kind of suddenly yesterday. She may have hitched a ride with someone going to Hoonah. I'm worried she might have needed to go to the medical clinic."

"Well, I ain't seen her, but that doesn't mean she's not there. I'm headed home after I make a couple more deliveries this morning, one here in town and one on the road back. I can ask around for you."

"Maybe I could go with you to Hoonah and look for her myself? I'm kind of concerned about her."

"You can ride along if you want, but you'll have to find your own way back."

"Thanks, that would be super."

Jake reached over and pushed on the passenger door. It was heavy and stubborn. Brooklyn climbed in and pulled so hard the door slammed shut, rattling the window.

"I think you need a new truck, Mr. Thompson."

"When I bought the company, this old lady was all there was for making deliveries. I think she's been delivering heating oil for over twenty years and will probably go another twenty. She might be a bit uncomfortable but she'll get us there. Doesn't have any seat belts so hang on to something." Jake popped the clutch and the truck lurched forward.

****

Vince seemed no worse to Flo the next morning. He had helped Ronnie as best he could, and they worked late into the night repairing the engine while Flo slept in one of the bunks. Vince was too weak to do much of the work, so he told Ronnie how to remove the old filter and install its replacement. Then they both slept for a few hours before heading back across the strait for Chatham as soon as it was light enough to navigate. There were no further problems with the engine.

Just after 8, Perkins called back on Vince's phone. He had contacted the hospital in Juneau and arranged for a series of rabies vaccines to be flown to Chatham later that morning. He would be waiting for them when they arrived.

They got to the boat harbor just before noon. Perkins had been watching the bay from his office window and rode his ATV down to meet them. The vaccine had arrived about an hour earlier with a pilot for Eco Wings, who happened to have a scheduled trip in the direction of Chatham.

Wally was a tall, lanky man and wore his usual jeans and a long-sleeved flannel shirt. He wore wire-rim glasses, and his dark blond hair was turning gray over his ears. His Errol Flynn mustache made him appear a bit more distinguished than an over-the-hill basketball player.

Flo met Wally at the head of the boat ramp next to his meticulously clean all-terrain vehicle, so out of place amongst the fleet of muddy and often rusted-out ATVs that ran around Chatham. She didn't bother with so much as a "good to see you and how is Peggy" chat.

Instead, she hurried him down the ramp to the dock, quickly explaining Vince's situation.

"Vince used to live here in Chatham, but it was probably well before your parents moved out here from Juneau. He's Tlingit Indian, and he and I were pretty close a long time ago. For the last several weeks, he and two other men have been working at an abandoned gold mine somewhere around here. Apparently, a colony of bats lives in the mine, and one of the men may have been bitten. Anyway, the guy got sick, and we found out last night that he died. Now Vince is sick."

"One person died? And it could have been from rabies?"

"We don't know that for sure. We had engine trouble with the boat and were unable to get to the camp ourselves. Vince talked to someone who was there yesterday who said it was probably rabies. This person had seen cases before. My concern is for Vince. He was trying to take care of his friend, and now he is sick, very sick. He came to me for help because I did some training to be a nurse. I'm surprised he remembered that. Anyway, he turned up at the café yesterday, and I agreed to help."

"He should have gone to the hospital in Juneau right away."

"I know. That's what I told Vince. But it's been several days now, and with the problem with the boat, I insisted we return to Chatham."

"Well, if it is rabies, and it has been several days without receiving treatment, it's a serious matter. Most folks don't recover unless being diagnosed and treated right away. When exactly did Vince get infected?"

"I'm not sure about that either. Maybe three or four

days ago. He only connected his symptoms with the other guy's yesterday."

"I don't know if I can help. I'll certainly try. I've dealt with a couple of rabies outbreaks in Southeast Asia and Africa while consulting with the CDC, but dealing with infected people wasn't my role. I worked on finding the source. This morning, while waiting for you, I read up on the symptoms. If he wasn't bitten and caught it through inhalation, which is less lethal, there's a chance he can survive. Just in case, I ordered an anti-viral medication and the injectable vaccine series from the Juneau hospital. We've got to get him started on them right away. I'll know more after examining him."

Flo and Wally boarded the *Sherry J*. Wally had to stoop to enter the small galley where Vince was half-sitting, half-lying on a bench along the starboard side. Flo poured herself a cup of coffee and stayed on the back deck with Ronnie listening to Wally and Vince.

"Hello, Vince. My name is Wally. How are you feeling? I'd like to examine you and ask you a few questions."

Vince mumbled a response as he struggled to sit up. "I don't feel too good."

"That's what Flo told me." Wally set his medical bag on the table. He opened it and found of pair of vinyl exam gloves and put them on. He took Vince's temperature and checked other vitals. Vince was sweating profusely.

"You the doctor Flo told me about?" Vince asked. Wally poked his chest and then squeezed his arm muscles.

"Ow!" Vince winced.

"Yeah. Do you have any bite marks on your body?

79

"Don't think so."

"Do you recall being around any animal that might have bitten you? Maybe a bat?"

"It's possible, I guess. There are thousands of them living in one of the mine shafts."

"How about your friend, the one that died? Was he bitten and were you looking after him when he got ill?"

"Yeah. He was a good guy, Doc. It was terrible."

Wally shook his head. "Have you been drinking any water?"

"Are you kidding? I'm thirsty all the time."

"You've got a raging fever, young man, and extreme tenderness in your muscles. I suspect you may be infected with the same disease as your friend. My advice is that you get yourself to the hospital in Juneau immediately."

"No!" Vince replied. "I…I can't do that. You…you've got to help me. Flo said you're a doctor. Can't you give me some antibiotic pills or something?"

Perkins shook his head. "I'm a doctor, but not the kind of medical doctor you need. My prognosis is pretty rough and is based mainly on what I have been told happened. I can give you an injection, but it's only the first in a series of injections you're going to need. It's the standard procedure if a person has been exposed to rabies. Rabies is lethal. The medication will get you started on treatment, but you really should go to the hospital."

Opening his bag, Wally removed a syringe and a package containing some small vials. "I have to warn you, you're going to experience a lot of pain, but not nearly as bad as no treatment at all."

"So, I've got a chance?"

"I won't lie to you, Vince. Because the treatment should have started several days ago, your odds are not very good. If I were you, I'd spend the next day or two taking care of any loose ends. Now, roll up your sleeve. You have to have these shots in your deltoid muscle."

Vince winced again as Perkins gave him the shot.

"These shots are nothing compared to the pain people used to experience with the old medication. It was fourteen shots in the belly muscle. The new drug is just four shots."

Vince rubbed his shoulder. "I'll manage, but I hope I don't have to deal with any loose ends. I'm afraid I've got too many."

After tending to Vince, Perkins left the cabin and made a brief examination of Ronnie and Flo. "I've started Vince on a treatment regimen for rabies. Has either of you come into close contact with Vince? Touched his face or been in contact with his saliva? One of you may have been exposed."

Ronnie hesitated before answering. "I helped him on and off the boat, and we were pretty close while doing the engine repair work."

"Well, if you suspect you've been exposed, you have to be treated too, and right away. Also, wash your hands with plenty of soap."

"Do you think you started Vince's injections in time?" Flo asked. "I mean, in time to save his life?" She was tired and sat down on the cover to the boat's hold.

"Well, let me put it this way," replied Wally. "I've been known to wager on Sunday NFL games. But I wouldn't wager any money on Vince's outcome at this point. Let's see how he is in forty-eight hours. There are some signs you need to watch for—lack of appetite, severe aggressiveness, trying to bite something, facial spasms, and of course, drooling. He already exhibits excessive thirst and sweating. So, whatever you do, don't touch his face. For now, he needs rest."

"Wally, Can I speak to you alone?" Flo asked. "I need you to get a message to Brooklyn."

"Sure. I can take you home if you want."

Flo hesitated. "No, I...I need to stay with Vince. He's going to need my help, especially if your odds-making is correct and he doesn't improve."

"Okay, meet me up by my ATV." Perkins jumped onto the dock and started walking towards the ramp.

Vince came out of the cabin and grabbed Flo's arm as she was about to do the same. His grip was as weak as was his smile. "You don't have to do this, Flo."

"You're damn right I don't. But I can't let you die like this either, no matter how foolish you've been or what you've done."

"Yeah, I...I'm in some real trouble," he said rather sheepishly. "If I don't meet my part of the agreement with the man I talked to last night, he is probably going to kill me." Vince chuckled to himself. "Kind of weird, isn't it? If the rabies virus doesn't kill me, he will. He'll try to anyway. Flo, I've got to hide somewhere, and I can't stay here. This is Indian Town. There are people here who know me and would give me up without caring one way or another."

"You might call it Indian Town, but Chatham is a community, Vince. Your life may have just been saved by someone who is a part of this community. You were banned by your people a long time ago, but that doesn't mean there aren't people in this town that would show some kindness and even a little forgiveness. You've never even tried to ask for forgiveness."

Vince didn't respond, but the look on his face told a different story. "I can't ask them to harbor a criminal. That's what I've been all my adult life. I've never been convicted of a serious felony or spent time in jail. But, I'm far from being an upstanding citizen. There's got to be somewhere else close by."

Flo studied his look of pain before answering. "Okay, Vince, here's my offer. I'll agree to help, and once you're situated, I'll keep your location a secret. There's an abandoned logging camp up near a small lake off the road to Hoonah. Several of the houses built for company employees are still intact, or at least they were when Brooklyn and I went up there on a hike last summer. We can use my ATV to get up there. Once this is over, you are never to see or talk to Brooklyn."

Vince nodded and looked away.

"Now I need to talk to Wally and find a way to get in touch with Brooklyn. She needs me too."

Vince was silent as she walked away.

"What are his real chances?" Flo asked when she'd joined Wally in the parking lot.

"Not good, I'm afraid. I didn't find any sign of a bite, either from a bat or other animal. But, he could have been exposed to saliva or other body fluids from his friend. What's unfortunate is that he may have waited too long to begin the treatment. But then again, the disease takes time to migrate to the brain. That can vary from days to months. He'll need another treatment in a few days, but the problem is he says he can't stick around to see me again. He seemed worried about doing that."

"He wants me to find him a hiding place. He's

serious about not wanting someone to find him."

"I remember you telling me you've had some training as a nurse. If Vince is not planning to stay in Chatham, are you going with him?"

Flo nodded and looked back at Vince's boat in the marina. When she spoke, her voice sounded like she was far away. "Yeah. I have to."

"Can I give the medication to you to administer?"

"I think I can do that." Flo sighed and put a hand on Wally's arm as the two of them walked across the parking lot to the ATV. "Wally, I have to ask another favor. Brooklyn doesn't know Vince is her father."

"Ah, that explains a lot for me. I was wondering about your interest in this man."

"Yes. So, you see why I'm doing this. He's in some type of trouble that I don't know much about, but I agreed to help, and I'll see it through."

"What do you want me to tell Brooklyn?"

"Just tell her I'm okay and that I'll be home soon, and I love her. Don't say you saw me but that I called you. Whatever is going on with Vince, I don't want her involved with his problems."

"Are you sure you're okay? I could see the tension between the three of you. I don't want to pry, but how serious is this trouble that Vince is in?" Wally pointed a finger right in her face. "You're not going to be in any danger, are you?"

Flo didn't react and stared right back at him. "I'm not sure. Maybe, but I don't want my daughter to be hurt in any way. Leave it at that. Okay?"

Wally shook his head. "All right, you're a woman with both courage and a heart, Flo, and I won't stand here and argue with you though I am concerned about you." He removed the medication from his bag and handed it to her. He straddled the ATV and pushed the electric start, and it roared to life. Then he backed up the shiny machine, smiled encouragingly. "Take care of yourself, Flo. Any sign of serious trouble, run."

****

No one waved back as the Eco Wings pilot made a circle of the lake checking the surface for landing and looking for the canoe his company had rented to the young couple from Arizona. He landed his float-plane and taxied up to the small beach next to the canoe. Shutting down the engine, he climbed out onto one of the floats to step ashore when he heard shouting.

"Wait! Wait! Don't come ashore. Start the engine!" A man shouted.

A man and a woman emerged from the cabin running towards the plane with their gear flopping wildly.

"What about the canoe?" The pilot asked as they tossed their things to him one by one.

"There's no time," said the woman who was breathing hard. "They could be watching us. We have to leave right now."

"Who's watching? I didn't see anyone when I circled the lake." The perplexed pilot grabbed the woman's hand to help her onto the float and into the cabin, noticing that her left arm was bandaged and held tightly to her body.

"Not a person. A couple of vicious, crazed animals," replied the husband. "My wife needs to see a doctor." He climbed onto a pontoon behind his wife. "We've got to get her to the hospital in Juneau as soon as possible. She could die. She got bit by one of them, and it could be rabies."

"Rabies? Huh, that's interesting." The pilot replied as he latched the cabin door and fastened his seatbelt. "You know, I just delivered some rabies medication to a doctor in the town of Chatham."

Chapter 11

After finishing his heating oil delivery in Chatham, Jake Thompson headed back home on the Hoonah road. The truck neared the upper end of the bay right about the time the *Sherry J* entered the Chatham harbor less than three miles away.

Brooklyn decided this was exciting and enjoyed riding in the monster truck even though she bounced around a bit and the engine was so noisy they had to shout to talk to each other.

Jake steered his large rig right through the potholes and ruts in the narrow road, carefully avoiding the soft shoulders. Except for rides on the back of Flo's ATV, she seldom had the opportunity to ride anywhere, particularly in a highway vehicle. Trips into Hoonah or Juneau were special occasions—like, to see a dentist. Mom had to ask a friend to drive or hire a taxi.

Brooklyn stared out the passenger window. She caught a glimpse of the river meandering out of the trees into the tidelands. Three deer grazed at the edge of the meadow. One of them bounded out of sight at the sound of grinding truck gears as Jake downshifted for a steep uphill grade. He shifted again, and on the downgrade, the truck sped up until they reached the level of the tide flats again. The shady corners of the road were still muddy from the last rain, and it slid and rolled from side to side. It plowed through water-filled potholes large enough to swallow a small sedan. Brooklyn beamed at Jake, feeling secure as the big powerful vehicle surged through a rutted spot and climbed up the next ridge. Here and there, she recognized old logging roads, most of them rapidly becoming part of the forest again due to fast-growing young alder trees.

The truck crossed a small creek that ran through one large, metal culvert after another—the tumbling stream of mountain water disappearing into the dense forest and undergrowth.

She was chatting with Jake about his daughter Molly when, through the trees, she saw a lone house with a green metal roof. The big rig's tires crunched on the road's gravel surface as Jake slowed to make a turn into a narrow driveway nearly hidden by thick brush. There was a rusted metal sign nailed to a post a few feet from the main road. The name on it said "Archie Hutchinson," and below the man's name written in crude letters, "Trespassers Will be Swiftly Dealt With."

As they neared the house, yard, and outbuildings, Brooklyn grimaced. Three wrecked vehicles were scattered about the yard amongst piles of scrap lumber, unidentifiable rusted objects, and piles and piles of trash. The place reminded Brooklyn of the town dump. The only thing lacking was the smell of burning garbage. However, the air had a peculiar odor, which Brooklyn immediately disliked. It smelled like one of her chemistry experiments at school.

Two dogs tied out on chains started barking loudly as Jake's truck approached the main house. They leaped and yanked on their lines with slobber from their jaws flying everywhere.

The main house looked as unwelcoming as the dogs. Someone had started to put up new siding but hadn't completed the job. The rest of the building was only partially painted. Its windows were covered with sheets rather than curtains. There was a jumble of piled logs close to the main house. A few of the logs were in the process of being cut into firewood.

Next to the main house was a single-wide trailer that had seen better days. The exterior siding was green with algae, and the roof was covered in moss. Smoke rose from chimneys on both buildings.

Two men came out to meet them. The younger one attempted to hush up the dogs while the older one came over to Jake's window. He wore a tan hunter's jacket, plaid shirt, jeans held up with a pair of red suspenders, and duck boots. His face was unshaven.

"Hey, Jake, how're things?"

"Pretty good, Hutch. It's wise you fellas getting a delivery now. I hear it's going to be a tough winter. Comes the end of December, there could be three or four feet of snow on the road. I might not get through to this side of the summit."

"That's what we thought. Plus, at the moment I've got money to pay you. In a few months, all there might be is a disability check."

"That's good too. You know I don't take credit. Cash on the barrelhead, so to speak."

The man laughed. "I take it that's an old oil man's joke. I'll guide yah over close to the tank."

He hesitated for a second, noticing Brooklyn seated on the far side of the cab. "Say, you got a cute chick keeping you company this trip, I see. You're a sly bastard, Jake."

"Brooklyn's just riding into Hoonah with me. She's a friend of my daughter, Molly."

"Well, she's welcome to come into the house. Right, AJ? Get yourself over there, son, and help the girl down out of that rig."

Brooklyn guessed that the other man by the dogs was the son. AJ hustled over to her side of the truck. His denim pants were ripped, smudged, and slung low on his hips. His dirty blond, long hair spilled out from under a Mariners baseball cap. His chin sported stubbly whiskers that reminded her of a harbor seal.

"Thanks, but I'm fine right here. I…I'm not sure of your dogs."

"Heck, they just sound fierce," said AJ. "They wouldn't hurt a baby as long as they are familiar with its scent." His smile showed his stained teeth. "Come on in and get comfortable. Jake's gonna be a while filling our big oil tank."

Turning to Brooklyn, Jake lowered his voice. "Shouldn't take that long, Brooklyn. I've got a high-pressure hose. Maybe fifteen minutes at the most. You can stay here in the truck if you want to."

Brooklyn offered a weak smile to AJ and rolled up her window.

"Suit yourself," AJ said with a frown, shrugged his shoulders, and backed off so Jake could move the truck.

Jake drove the truck over to a tank between the house and the trailer. True to his word to Brooklyn, he had the hose connected and finished the job in less than fifteen minutes. While Jake filled the tank, the two men wandered over to the single-wide and stood watching by the door like they were guarding it. The younger one kept staring at Brooklyn.

Jake coiled up his hose, stowed it, checked the meter, and then took a minute to write out an invoice. Hutch pulled a wad of money out of his pocket and paid Jake with twenty-dollar bills. Jake and Hutch talked small talk for another minute, shook hands, and then Jake headed for the truck. All the while, AJ stared at Brooklyn with a grin that made her a lot more uncomfortable than the three Chatham boys.

As he started the engine, Jake turned to Brooklyn and spoke in a low voice. "We're getting out of here. In case you didn't recognize that smell, these guys are cooking meth."

****

It took nearly two hours of riding with Jake on the twisty, unpaved road to reach the Native town of Hoonah. As he coasted down the final grade towards the boat basin, the extent of the community came into view. It stretched around the shoreline road much like at Chatham, only with many more homes climbing up the slope of the hill beside the bay. Hoonah had a thriving fishing industry with a lot of boat traffic. Like Chatham, there was only one main road that ran along the shoreline from the boat harbor on the south end to the ferry landing and an old cannery on the north end. The latter had been converted into a tourist attraction by the Native community. Cruise ships anchored just offshore and disgorged thousands of visitors to experience the tribe's culture, enjoy a meal of fresh grilled salmon, and purchase souvenirs. Today, there wasn't a cruise ship to be seen anywhere. The tourist season was finished for the year.

Jake dropped Brooklyn at the health clinic so she could enquire about her mom. From there, she planned to check with the Harbormaster before finding a way to get back to Chatham. The Harbormaster was responsible for the several boat basins and monitored boat movements with his marine radio. A boat arriving or leaving the Hoonah harbor cleared it with him, except those just there for a short time for fuel, freshwater, or supplies.

At the clinic, an older woman was taping a sign onto the glass window at the door. Brooklyn climbed down from the truck and waved to Jake as he shifted the stubborn gears and drove away. She paused to read the new notice before entering the clinic. It was an alert to be aware of dogs, small mammals, and bats acting strangely. Several cases of rabies had just been reported to medical authorities. She didn't think anything of it until she remembered the two dogs at the Hutchinson place.

The reception area was empty except for two people at the desk, so Brooklyn took a seat and waited. An elderly man and the receptionist were talking about when the clinic would be offering flu shots, then about the weather, then about his kids and hers. They went on and on. Brooklyn figured they must be related. Finally, the man hobbled to the door, and Brooklyn was able to approach the woman. She had resumed handling a stack of paperwork.

"Excuse me. Can you check to see if a Flo Whiting visited the clinic in the last 24-48 hours? We live in Chatham. Someone could have dropped her off."

The heavy-set woman gave her a stern stare over the top of her wire-framed glasses. "Hmm, are you a relation? Can't give out information on just anybody you know."

"She's my mom."

"And you don't know if your mother visited us? Okay, let's start with a name again. You said her name is Flo Whiting? Like Florence—that's her first name?"

"Yes, Florence, ma'am," Brooklyn said politely.

The portly woman punched on the keyboard like she was urging it to spit out the information. She scrolled down a list of appointments on her monitor. "Nope, no one by that name. Is there a maiden name she might have used?"

"Ah, no. That is my mom's maiden name."

"Then I'm afraid I can't help you." The woman grabbed some files and walked over to a filing cabinet like Brooklyn was no longer there. Brooklyn shook her head and walked back to the door of the clinic. It opened before she could grab the door handle. A woman carrying a screaming baby entered.

Outside, the town taxi, once a yellow vehicle but now covered in rust and wired together with parts from other cars, sat with the motor running. Faded letters on the side of the taxi read "New York City Cab Co." Brooklyn barged through the door and down the steps before he could drive away. She was just in time to rap on the side window to get the taxi driver's attention.

"Excuse me," said Brooklyn. "Have you given a ride in the last 24 hours to a single, white woman in her forties, kind of tall?"

"A tall white woman? In Hoonah?" The man snickered. "Nope. Don't recall seeing anyone of that description around here in a while. She one of them tourists? Maybe lost?"

"Ah, she's not a tourist. She's my mom, and we live in Chatham."

"Sorry, girl. Ain't seen her. Can I take you somewhere?" The taxi operator replied—hoping for another fare.

"No. I...I don't have any money. I'll walk. Thanks anyway."

Brooklyn watched him drive off, and then walked towards the Harbormaster's office, kicking at the gravel in frustration.

At the office, she discovered a handwritten scrap of paper taped to the inside of the windowpane of the door. The Harbormaster was away for lunch and would be back in an hour.

Next to the door was a bulletin board filled with offers to sell everything from crab pots to commercial fishing boats, along with a copy of the Juneau-Hoonah ferry schedule. The ferry schedule indicated two arrivals a week, with one that very morning. Brooklyn trotted around the building and scanned the bay. The ferry had just departed and was about out of sight. Brooklyn shook her head, kicked another rock, a larger one this time. She decided to walk down to the docks and find some more people to ask, limping from hurting her foot.

The boat harbor had three main areas, each with its own access ramp. The one closest to the breakwater was reserved for transient moorage. It was empty, and the one farthest away was for small craft. The middle dock was used primarily by the local fishing fleet. The boat closest to her was a large steel hull vessel all painted black and called the *Blackwater*. Its deck was outfitted with an array of stainless-steel processing equipment. It looked familiar, and she thought she might have seen it once or twice at the dock in

Chatham. The boat was a fish buyer. It followed the fleet of smaller fishing vessels and would anchor close by. That way, fishermen didn't have to make long runs into ports to sell their catch.

Approaching the *Blackwater*, Brooklyn saw two men working on the processing equipment. She stopped on the dock and yelled to get their attention.

"Excuse me, but I'm looking for someone. Have you seen—?"

"We just started work, kid," one of them said. "Ask the skipper." He pointed forward towards the pilothouse.

Brooklyn looked where he pointed, and a man stepped out. She started to ask again and suddenly recognized the man. "Excuse me, but have you….Mr. Hendricks? What are you doing here?" Her mind raced. Mr. Hendricks was a school teacher. What is he doing here in Hoonah?

"I should ask you the same, Brooklyn. You're supposed to be in school. As to me, that shouldn't surprise you. Lots of people hold down two jobs to make ends meet. During the fishing season, I captain this boat and buy fish. The rest of the time, I teach school. Now, if you'll excuse me, I have work to do." He turned his back on her and started back inside the cabin.

"Wait!" Brooklyn said. "Have you seen Flo….my mom?"

Hendricks hesitated and then turned to face Brooklyn again. The stern look on his face said he wasn't happy about seeing Brooklyn. As he looked at her standing below him on the dock, his expression changed, and then he smiled. "No, I haven't seen Flo.

Did you come from Chatham just to look for her? You know you're a long way from home." He paused for a moment, then, with a beckoning hand motion, added. "Are you hungry? Come aboard, and we'll get you a sandwich and something to drink."

Brooklyn's stomach growled at the mention of food. It had been a long time since she'd had anything to eat. She was about to respond when the sudden change in the look on his face registered. It reminded her of her recent conversation with Tony and his friends. Mr. Hendricks could be a little too friendly with young girls. She had seen that in his eyes before in class. Brooklyn glanced over at the other two men. They had stopped working and were watching her and listening. She decided it was time to leave—right now. Uneasiness suddenly crept up her spine and she glanced at her watch.

"Uh, that's all right. I don't have the time. I've got to meet my ride back to Chatham. I'm supposed to meet Mr. Thompson up at the store in a couple of minutes." She lied. "Bye, Mr. Hendricks. Good luck with the fishing."

Before Hendricks could answer, she turned and hustled back up the ramp to the Harbormaster's office and the main road. There wasn't any ride waiting, but she had better find one quick. Her desire to continue her search in Hoonah had turned as cold as the breeze off the bay. It caused her to shiver as she stood by the road, trying to decide which way to go.

Chapter 12

It was early afternoon before Bingo Bob woke up. He had a terrible hangover. His head felt like three monkeys were tossing it around like a rubber ball in their cage. Even the sounds of the boat tapping against the dock and the water lapping against the hull were agonizing. He struggled out of his bunk, washed his face with cold water, and then put on a pot of coffee. While he waited for the coffee to perk, he opened the cabin door, wincing at the bright light.

Directly behind him was the *Sherry J.* It must have returned sometime during the night or earlier that morning. Bingo turned off the burner to let the coffee finish and went on deck. He was so unsteady he had to crawl onto the dock, and then grab hold of a light pole to stand upright. He took a deep breath of fresh air and slowly walked over to the *Sherry J.* Pounding on the side of the cabin, he yelled out, "Anybody on board?" He got no reply.

Walking back towards his boat, he was a bit steadier He saw Kenny Sexton coming down the gangway from the restrooms. The town maintained restrooms and a shower building for summer boaters that rented nightly dock space. Kenny was a small man, thin as a rail, and he lived on one of the other boats. He usually avoided Bingo. Maybe being a little guy standing next to Bingo intimidated him.

Bingo managed to catch up with Kenny before he could disappear into his boat. "Hey, Kenny," Bingo hollered. "You see anybody around that white fishing boat this morning? They didn't secure their dock lines very well." He was lying, but he didn't care.

"The *Sherry J*?" Kenny said. "Yeah, been people traipsing back and forth all morning long. Doc Perkins was with them. Then they all took off."

"Huh? I missed all that. What happened?"

"Gee, Bingo, I don't know. I don't like to get nosy. But the doc was carrying his bag. He left, and later, two guys and that waitress from the cafe took off. Ain't seen nobody else."

"Huh, wonder what's going on? Did one of the guys look a little sick, like he was having difficulty walking?"

"Yeah, some, but not as bad as you. You look like hell warmed over."

****

Johnny Kwan spent most of the day working on a plan. He made some calls and finalized arrangements to get his otter pelts shipped to Hong Kong. A Chinese bulk cargo ship called the *Asian Moon* would be leaving Prince Rupert, British Columbia, some four hundred miles to the south, in a week. Using his laptop, Kwan checked a ship database that tracked AIS signals. Commercial vessels typically have transponders and can be tracked in a global automatic information system or AIS for short. The database showed the *Asian Moon* was currently anchored in the Prince Rupert harbor. Kwan knew the ship's first mate. He was on the Tong payroll.

The second thing he did was contact a distant

cousin who was bringing a crab boat south from Kodiak headed for Seattle for re-outfitting at a shipyard in Union Bay. He asked his cousin to make a short stop at Admiralty Cove to take on the pelts. The fishing boat would then link up three days later with the *Asian Moon* in international waters off Vancouver Island. Each captain would receive a ten percent share of the final sale. Fifty percent was the organization's share, with Kwan receiving the remainder. It was a pretty good deal and beat the margin he made on legal export high-end seafood products.

The arrangement with Vince James had started well and should make Kwan a good profit but what he'd seen at the camp was causing a problem. The inability to use the location to finish processing the rest of his order would delay delivery even if Vince could complete it as he claimed. A delay seriously increased the risk not only the discovery of the operation by law enforcement but potentially with his superiors. He had boasted about this new product to his superiors Not delivering a complete shipment could lead to consequences from the organization in Southeast Asia. And a delay in not making a rendezvous with the freighter was a severe risk to him personally, no matter how it played out.

Kwan tried to analyze what he knew about Vince's operation. If Vince was convinced he could complete the job in a week, there must be another cache of pelts. The man was now shorthanded. If he had most of his pelts hidden somewhere, a successful shipment might still be achieved. Kwan worked through the facts and then thought of another complication. Could his threat of bodily harm scare Vince into talking to the authorities? As an Alaskan Native, one could get out of the situation with a fine, albeit a hefty one, but he would not serve time. If Vince gave him up, he would be convicted of a federal crime. If he was lucky, he would be deported. The organization's ire would then fall heavily on him, resulting in loss of face and probably his future in the business.

Kwan walked over to the galley counter to pour a fresh cup of tea. He took the morning paper and his tea over to a comfortable chair to sit and flip through the pages to clear his mind of the Vince James problem. An article caught his attention. A woman was undergoing rabies treatment at the Juneau hospital. She and her husband had been camping on Baranof Island.

Was the incident related to the bats in Vince's mine? What if I could rid the area of the rabid bats by sealing up that mine? I would be a hero. The Fish and Game people might even make the area around Vince's mine a restricted area. There would give be more time to find the rest of the pelts—a win-win.

But he had to find Vince James. Kwan chuckled to himself as he reached for his laptop and pulled up his AIS ship locator application again. This time, he typed in *Sherry J.* When the map loaded, he found the *Sherry J.* The boat was in the Chatham boat harbor. He was a step closer to finding Vince and to finding the pelts.

Chapter 13

Brooklyn's trip to Hoonah was a big disappointment. She was unable to find anyone who recalled seeing her mother and had to accept the fact that her mother hadn't come to Hoonah after all.

Now, Brooklyn didn't know a way to get back to Chatham—something she hadn't thought through when she asked Jake for a ride.

Not a single vehicle was traveling on the road, which either went to the Hoonah airport or to a few remote mining camps back towards Chatham. She couldn't recall seeing but one vehicle earlier on her way to Hoonah with Jake.

She cautiously kicked a few more stones as she walked along the shoulder of the road to the edge of town. It was stupid to try walking back as she would never make it even if she had all day. So, she waited at the road junction where the road split one way to Chatham and the other to the airport. Someone had built a bench, maybe for kids waiting for a ride into school or for the taxi.

While she sat on the bench, she wondered if perhaps she should have gone to Jake Thompson's house. If she had to stay over, she could sleep in Molly's bedroom. It would be fun to chat with Molly and find out what was going on in town. But her concern for her mother kept nagging at her. And another stupid thing—she hadn't left her own note about going to Hoonah. Nobody, but Jake knew where she was.

The sound of a vehicle coming from the direction of town broke her thoughts. She stood expectantly, watching it come into view and move slowly up the road. It was an old four-wheel, drive pickup. Its engine labored as its driver urged it up a short grade. The vehicle might have been a light color years before, but now it was more rust than paint, and the sides were caked in dried mud.

When the vehicle's driver signaled a turn towards Chatham, Brooklyn quickly waved to get the driver's attention and stuck out a thumb hoping for a ride. As it reached her, it skidded to a stop, and the driver cranked down his window. It was an older man, and if Brooklyn didn't know better, she would have taken him for Santa in the off-season. He had a full white beard and mustache, only it was tobacco-stained, and his white hair was straggly and uncombed.

"Can I help you, young girl?" The man said as he leaned out.

"I'm trying to get back to Chatham. Are you going that way?"

"I sure am. Have to deliver some stuff to my sister Gladys."

"Gladys Tussock? Is she your sister? I...I didn't know she had any relatives."

"Yup. Well, we don't get to see each other very often. I'm usually off in some remote part of Alaska looking for gold. And Gladys, she's not the traveling type."

Brooklyn's face brightened. She couldn't believe

her luck. Of all the people to come along, it was Gladys's brother. He had to be—they both were talkers.

Brooklyn rushed over to the side of the vehicle, commenting on Gladys. "I like your sister. She's a nice lady. And I especially love her gardens. They are the prettiest spot in Chatham."

"Hee hee! She sure does like to grow things. As a matter of fact, I've got a new rose bush in the back seat for her garden."

A little white face peered out from under the man's arm. A small dog was sitting in his lap. The man noticed her staring at the little dog. "Climb in. You might as well keep an old man and his dog company."

Brooklyn ran around to the other side of the Land Cruiser and opened the door to a greeting from a tail-wagging Jack Russell.

"This is Duchess. She's gettin' on in her years. Got gray whiskers to match mine. Duchess! Get in the back and give this gal your seat."

Brooklyn grinned as the dog hopped into the back of the rig. The moment she climbed in, Duchess was licking her ear.

"Hey Duchess, that tickles."

Brooklyn offered to shake hands with the man. "Thanks for stopping. My name is Brooklyn. I live in Chatham, but I don't recall seeing you around."

"Oh, I don't live there. I just came in on the Alaska ferry from Juneau. Taking a few days to visit Gladys. Then it's off to check on things at my gold mine. Name's Luther Calhoun, but most folks just call me Cal. Tourists off those big cruise ships look at me kind of sideways and in whispers refer to me as a 'genuine Sourdough.' Hee, hee, I guess I am all right.

"Gladys married my best friend Floyd right after we graduated from high school. Tough old bird, he was. Floyd survived three battles in Vietnam and got a purple heart to boot. Then one day, he fell off his fishing boat out in the strait. Real tragedy. We think it was a heart attack because that boat ran itself right up on the beach. The engine was still running when they found it."

Cal shifted gears and let out the clutch, and the Land Cruiser lurched forward.

"I've been kicking around Alaska for better than sixty-five years myself. Done about everything there is to do up here—commercial fishing in the Gulf, truck driving during the building of the Alaskan oil pipeline, moose hunting guide, logger, trapper, and gold miner. Looking for gold is what I like best, and I'm kind of betting they ain't found it all yet."

The Land Cruiser's wheels slid on the soft shoulder of the road as the man glanced at Brooklyn.

"Oops, a good driver I'm not, and this sorry old rig could use some serious repairs. Even though it's a tough old, four-wheeler, roads on this island will bust up just about anything."

Without a pause, Cal kept on talking.

"Why take this here road between Hoonah and Chatham, now it's a winner all right. If it wasn't for a few timber sales, miners, and bear hunters, Mother Nature would take it back in no time. Don't worry, though. Got me an ax and a chain saw in the back if we come across a tree or two lying in the road. And my old shotgun should make a brown bear shy away. Now, what are you doing this far from home…uh…Brooklyn, did you say?"

Brooklyn smiled and wondered if she was going to be able to say anything about herself.

"Yes, sir. And I think the road is going to be clear, Mr. Calhoun. I rode over this morning with Jake Thompson in his truck. He delivers home heating oil out of Hoonah."

"So you hitched a ride into Hoonah?" Calhoun asked.

"Yeah. I was trying to find my mom."

"Your mom? Is she missing?"

"She had to leave home in a hurry and didn't tell me much of anything. I was worried and thought maybe she'd made an emergency trip to the health clinic. Turned out, I was wrong."

"Sorry to hear that. But this old rig and me, we'll get you home."

The two of them bounced hard as the vehicle hit a pothole, and then the left wheels rocketed through an even bigger hole. "Wow, that was a real noggin cracker," Cal remarked and they both laughed after recovering from being bounced off their seats.

Calhoun shook his head and tried to assure her. "I wouldn't worry. Not many places one can be around here. She's probably back home now and worrying about you."

"I hope so, Mr. Calhoun…uh, Cal." Brooklyn shivered, thinking about her mom. The feeling enveloped her whole body. Duchess seemed to sense how she felt and crept into her lap and settled down. Duchess's little body cuddled in her arms, and Cal's wandering conversation made the long trip home comforting and seem quicker.

Brooklyn and Cal chatted the whole time. They

talked about the island's school system, the people who lived in Chatham and Hoonah, even about Gladys' marvelous roses. She liked the old man and had to admit she had never met a person quite like him. He was intelligent and kind—sort of like Bingo, but different. Like the Juneau tourists, Brooklyn was convinced that if ever there was a person who might be called a Sourdough, Cal was it. She felt delighted that Cal was the person she happened upon for a ride home.

A curious thought struck her. In the last two days, she had made friends with two people. These two people opened her eyes to things that were so opposite to her own self-centered problem. She had met two people who were unselfish and willing to help her.

As to her taking a day to travel to Hoonah, it had been a wild goose chase. She was now pretty sure her mom had never gone there. That meant one thing; she must have left Chatham on the *Sherry J.* So, where did that boat go? That was her next thing to do.

****

Two hours later, Brooklyn said goodbye to Cal at the bottom of her street and walked the short distance up the hill to her home. Reaching the front porch, she saw a note stuck on their screen door. Her spirits lifted as she ran up the steps and snatched it. The message was signed, Wally. All it said was...*Your mom called and said she's fine. Not to worry, and she loves you.*

She slumped down on the steps to the porch and groaned—helpless as to what to do next. She reread the note and wondered why Doc Perkins didn't mention where her mom went. He had to know more than what was in the note.

"Not to worry?" Brooklyn said aloud as she stared

blankly at the empty road in front of their house. Now she really was worried. This was not like her mother. She was never secretive.

Then she had another thought—how could her mom have called Doc Perkins when she didn't own a cell phone. Most homes in Chatham, including their own, had a landline. In her home, the landline was hardly ever used. If Doc Perkins had received the call, maybe he could call her back.

She decided to use her mom's ATV to get to Wally's house. Brooklyn jumped to her feet and ran around the side of the house to where her mom parked it. She stopped and stared at the spot where it should be. The ATV was gone.

She headed for the cafe. Doc Perkins must have been wrong. Maybe her mom was back and at work at the café.

On her way, she passed the Jackson General Store. Sitting on the board sidewalk and leaning against the building was a very old Native woman. She was a fixture—always there, and most people gave her no notice. Brooklyn had never talked to her but would often smile and wave to her. The old woman never smiled back or said anything, but Brooklyn had seen her eyes follow her as she went by.

This time she halted and walked back a few steps curious to find out if the woman would answer a question or two. Maybe she had seen Flo go by on the road on her ATV. Brooklyn stood facing her. The woman had a raggedy-edged, striped blanket around her shoulders held tightly in front with one hand. On her head was a knit hat pulled down over braided gray hair. A small basket sat in front of her with a few coins in it.

The old woman didn't move or react to Brooklyn's presence and just stared like she was looking right through her. Brooklyn wondered if she might be interrupting the woman's thoughts and swallowed, almost forgetting what she wanted to ask.

"Ah, my name is Brooklyn, Ma'am. You probably know my mother, Flo Whiting, right? She works down the street in the café as a waitress? She passes you every day."

The woman didn't respond, but Brooklyn thought there might be some recognition in her gray eyes. She decided to be more direct.

"My mom has a blue and white ATV three-wheeler. It's kind of loud because it's an old one. Do you think you might have seen her today or maybe yesterday? That is if you were right where you are now?"

The woman nodded slowly, then raised her right hand and pointed down the road towards Brooklyn's house with a long slender finger. Then she swung her arm the other way towards the boat harbor. Brooklyn turned her head half-expecting to see her mother. Only the old woman again pointed in the opposite direction. When she finally spoke, her words came slowly, almost in a whisper. "She rode by with a ghost, a bad spirit. I do not know where they went, but they were in a hurry to get someplace."

Brooklyn was still puzzling over the old Indian woman's words when she got to the café. A half dozen people were sitting at the tables when she rushed through the door. Brooklyn scanned the dining area, then the kitchen. Leroy was busy preparing orders and had a row of plates lined up on the serving counter with rolls and fixings to receive hamburger patties from the grill. Her mom was not there.

"Hi Leroy," she said, trying to catch her breath. "Where's Flo? I know she's back. Her ATV is not at the house."

"Flo? She hasn't come back to work. Sure could use her, though. I haven't had a moment's rest since she took off. If you see her, you tell her to get herself back in here."

"But her ATV is missing from the house. It was there this morning. I just came from Hoonah. She wasn't there or on the road."

"I can't tell you a thing. Heck, I've hardly had a chance to look further than the door." Leroy flipped a row of patties, tossed a piece of cheese on two of them, and covered them with a lid. "Keep an eye on these burgers for me, will ya? I need a break. Fix a burger for yourself if you're hungry."

Brooklyn nodded and took the long-handled spatula he handed to her. Leroy hustled himself to the bathroom.

Brooklyn watched the grill and, from time to time, glanced at the people eating or waiting for their orders. Everybody appeared normal. They chatted to themselves and ignored her. She was just another kitchen helper and not someone who was searching for a missing person. She was tempted to holler out to everyone in the café and ask whether any of them had seen Flo.

Bit by bit, the smell of the burgers on the grill made her ravenous. She hadn't eaten anything since her bowl of cereal.

After a cheeseburger and her hunger pains gone,

Brooklyn walked down the road towards the home and office of Doc Perkins. Wally had been the lone doctor in Chatham for as long as she could remember. It had been a long time since Flo had taken her to see him, probably since she had the measles. But she still remembered how nervous she was at the time.

At school, Mr. Hendricks had shared some interesting facts about Doc Perkins with her class. At least once a year, he traveled to some faraway place to investigate a disease outbreak or epidemic. Mr. Hendricks said Dr. Perkins was famous and had published a lot of papers in medical journals. Yet to Brooklyn, he was just an ordinary guy who loved to hike and explore the area on his ATV.

Not far from his home was a secret place where Brooklyn loved to hang out. There was a trail that started near the boat harbor. It led through the forest up to a high rock bluff and a ledge with a great view of Chatham Strait and a nearby shore reef. A pod of whales could usually be seen near the reef feeding on herring. There was also a colony of sea lions on the rocks below the bluff. But Brooklyn's very favorite thing about the viewpoint was a tall, gnarled cedar tree that grew on the side of the cliff just below the ledge. On the top of the tree was a bald eagle nest, and she spent hour after hour watching the nest. There was a single egg that had hatched three months ago. The newborn eaglet was being raised by a pair of eagles that used the nest year after year. The adults knew she watched the nest and didn't seem alarmed by her presence when they flew to and from the tree to feed the eaglet. The week before, when she was about to return home from watching the nest, Doc Perkins had appeared. He had been photographing the nest for several days and showed her some pictures still in his camera. They were incredible. He used a telephoto lens, and she could see the feathers starting to cover the young eaglet's face.

****

Brooklyn could hear music from the Perkins home as she walked across the porch and knocked on the door. She heard footsteps, and Wally opened the door. His glasses had slipped down on his nose, and he peered over them at Brooklyn and smiled when he recognized her. In his hand was a copy of *Science* magazine.

"Hello, Brooklyn. Have you been out to observe our little eaglet?"

"Ah… no, I haven't, Doctor Perkins. Not since we met on the bluff last week."

"Well, please come in. This visit must be for something else. Am I right?"

"Yes. It's about your note regarding my mom. I found it a little while ago. You didn't say where she is."

"I couldn't. Your mother didn't tell me that."

"But aren't you curious? She left so suddenly and hasn't let me know why she left or where she went. I'm worried."

"I'm sorry to hear this, Brooklyn. I was afraid this might happen, and I understand your concern. Your mother is a strong, capable woman. Wherever she is, I'm sure she's okay."

"But why is she being so secretive about it? All I can think of is that she's hiding something. Leroy Wilson told me she left in a hurry with two men, two strangers. Did she mention them to you, Doctor

Perkins?"

Perkins didn't answer right away, but he shook his head. He motioned at a recliner. "Please sit down. There are a few things I can tell you." He sat down on a couch opposite her, laying his magazine on an end table. "Now, about your mom, she asked me not to tell you much for the very reason that she didn't want you to worry about her. Seeing your distress, I can tell that keeping things from you has had the opposite effect. So, as a doctor, I am going against her wishes and will tell you what I do know. I saw your mother this morning."

"You saw her? She was here in Chatham?"

"Yes. She was on a boat down at the harbor."

"The *Sherry J,* right? I knew it."

"I'm sorry, but I didn't notice the name of the boat. She had phoned me from somewhere, I think it was Angoon, to ask for help. She wanted me to meet her at the boat after it arrived. That was mid-morning, maybe around 10."

"I was in Hoonah looking for her. I thought she might have gone to the medical clinic or something like that."

"As I said, she's okay. She's not sick or hurt. She wanted me to help one of the men. That person was sick and in need of some special medication. Your mother knew I could arrange this, so that's why she called me. I, in turn, called the hospital in Juneau and requested the medication be sent out by plane."

"I don't understand. Then why isn't she home now?"

"The man couldn't stay in town, and he needed to have the medication administered several more times.

Your mother knows how to do this and decided to go with him."

Brooklyn stood up and walked over to the living room window that looked out over the bay. She could see the boat harbor just below her. There was a white fishing boat tied up at the outer end of one of the piers. And a couple of miles out, another white cruiser, a catamaran, was headed towards the harbor at high speed.

"But the *Sherry J* is still here. I can see it in the marina. So she's in Chatham?"

"No, she's not, and she specifically avoided telling me where she would be. She was very emphatic about that."

"Why is she helping this man, Doctor Perkins?"

"You can call me Wally, Brooklyn. My wife and I hate being formal in Chatham, and I am a longtime friend of your mother." Wally removed his glasses and moved forward in his chair. "Look, I'm afraid there is not much more I can tell you. She didn't share very much. You'll need to ask that question of your mother when she returns. I examined the man. He's gravely ill, and your mother wanted to help him enough to seek my assistance as quickly as possible. Frankly, the man should be in a hospital."

Brooklyn got up and started for the front door. "Then we have to find her as soon as possible. She must be in town somewhere."

"I don't believe so," said Perkins. "Otherwise, I could administer the medication myself. I gave it to her. This man needs a series of shots. That is if he even survives the next few days. He may have started the treatment too late."

"Treatment? What for?"

"The man may have rabies. It's serious and your mother knows that."

Brooklyn returned to the window, watching the new boat slow and approach the dock. She turned to face him. "I don't know what else to do, Doctor Perkins, I mean Wally. She's not in Hoonah. She's not on that boat, and now you tell me she's not in Chatham and is somewhere else with two strange men. This whole thing feels strange. I have a bad feeling about it."

"She will come back. She promised me she would as soon as it was safer."

"Safer? You mean she could be in some type of danger?"

Wally realized he might have said too much. "What I meant to refer to was the illness of one of the men is a dangerous situation. It could be contagious. Your mom said she was willing to deal with it and would get word to you or me somehow."

"I've got to think about what to do. You know my secret place? It's where I go when I need some time away from everything. Well, I'm going up there to think about this."

"You're a smart girl, Brooklyn. But you need to trust your mom. Be patient. Going up to the lookout on the cliff is a good idea."

"Thanks for being concerned about my mom and now me. I've got to figure what to do next."

Perkins got up and went to the door. Brooklyn followed.

"Stay safe. And, let me know how the eagle family is doing, okay?"

Brooklyn smiled and nodded.

"I will," she said as she hugged him. "Thank you for sharing things with me."

"Take care of yourself, Brooklyn. Try not to worry about your mom. She's determined to do the right thing. I'm sure we'll understand all about that soon."

Brooklyn walked down the road and turned up the trail through the woods towards the cliff viewpoint. She paid no attention to a group of men down on the dock tying up a sleek white yacht.

Chapter 14

Johnny Kwan leaped off his yacht onto the Chatham harbor dock and stretched. He had been bored the whole trip from Juneau and had taken a nap. Now he was anxious to finish the business with Vince. But first, he had to find the guy.

He had used a pair of binoculars to study the town as his boat came up the bay towards the boat harbor. He observed very little activity—only a couple of men near the bottom of the shore ramp.

Kwan considered his resources. He had brought three men with him, not counting those that handled the boat, and figured that would be enough to find Vince James even if he resisted. As two of the men finished securing the dock lines under the direction of his captain, Kwan announced his intentions.

"Okay, we're looking for Vince James. He's here somewhere. That's his boat over there." He pointed at the *Sherry J.* "And, I want to finish business in this dump of a town and return to Juneau as quickly as possible. Lee, go search his boat. If Vince or anyone else is aboard, bring them to me."

Lee nodded and trotted down the dock to the *Sherry J.* A minute later he was back. He shrugged and shook his head. "No one was on the boat, Boss," said Lee.

Kwan looked around the boat harbor. He noticed

the two men, which were Bingo Bob and Kenny Sexton, still standing at the head of the dock.

"Trung, go grab those two guys and hold them until I can ask them a few questions. Somebody has to know where we can find Vince James. I want to be out of here before anyone in the community recognizes us or discovers what we are doing. When we get Vince James, we'll bring him back to the boat and deal with him after we are underway."

Trung, Lee's shorter and much huskier partner, hustled up the dock.

When Kwan needed a show of force, Trung was his muscle man. Minutes later, Bingo and Kenny were pushed up against the fish cleaning table and told not to move. Kwan approached them. He had a long cashmere coat draped over his shoulders and wore his trademark Panama hat and metallic sunglasses.

"Ah, two of this town's finest and better-dressed residents, I see." Kwan grimaced in disgust as he took in their appearance. "I need some information, and you two just happen to be convenient. I suppose both of you live in this backwater town if you can call it a town. So please don't waste my time. Do either of you know Vince James and where I might find him?"

Bingo and Kenny shook their heads and stared at each other with bewildered looks, then back at Kwan.

"Now, guys, that's not being very friendly to a stranger. You can speak, right? Let's try this again real slow if you are stupid and do not understand a simple question. Does—one of you—know a man—by the name of—Vince James?"

Bingo and Kenny were silent as they glanced around to see if anyone else was close by.

Kwan thought for a moment. Then, remembering the telephone conversation with Vince, he re-phrased his question.

"Does—one of—you knuckleheads—know a woman—with the first name of Flo?"

"Flo?" replied Kenny. His eyes gave him away. "You mean Flo Whiting. She's…"

"Kenny," mumbled Bingo. "Didn't your mother tell you not to talk to strangers?"

"What did you say?" Kwan got in Bingo's face, only to quickly back off. "Man, you stink. Your tongue isn't very loose for all that alcohol. Maybe you ought to tell me about this Flo Whiting."

"I've…got nothing to say. Maybe if you had asked—"

Trung hit him in the left kidney with his fist. Bingo doubled over and slipped to his knees. He retched, and vomit dribbled from his mouth spattering Kwan's white shoes. Trung yanked him to his feet and pushed him against the metal table.

Kwan repeated his question. "Where can I find Flo Whiting?"

"That's none of your business. Even if…"

Trung hit Bingo in the face with a fist. Bingo fell again, hitting his head hard on the dock. Bingo groaned and passed out.

Kwan turned to face Kenny Sexton.

"Maybe now you can finish what you wanted to say about this Flo Whiting. Where does she live?"

Kenny stared at Bingo in shock. He was shaking with fear.

"Do you hear me, little man? Where can we find this woman?"

Kenny discovered he could still speak. "She…I don't know where she lives…she works at the café. She's a waitress. I ain't but said two words to her all the time I've lived here. You gotta ask Leroy Wilson. He owns the restaurant. He ought to—"

"Okay, you can shut your mouth. You're polluting my space as much as your friend here." Kwan turned to Trung. "Head into town and find the café. Lee, find some transportation somewhere. I don't want to walk any more than I have to in this filth."

Kwan looked down and carefully stepped around Bingo and the vomit on the dock boards, then followed his men up the ramp to the parking lot. Bingo remained motionless. Kenny slipped to his knees, clinging to a leg of the cleaning table.

Kwan shook his head as he reached the top of the ramp and parking lot. He had dealt with worthless men like these countless times.

Lee and Trung had hustled on ahead of their Boss. Trung headed into town on foot to find Wilson's café. Lee examined several of the ATVs in the parking lot to appropriate one for Kwan.

****

Leroy Wilson was alone and busy in the kitchen when Kwan arrived at the café. At first, he thought he had three more afternoon customers, but instead of taking a table, one man hung back by the front door as the other two entered the kitchen.

"Hey," hollered Leroy. "Customers are not supposed to come back here. Health Department rules, you know?"

"We are the health department," said Kwan. "Your health, that is."

"What did you say?"

"Look, Leroy, we can make this easy or hard. It's your choice. Tell us what we want to know, and you stay healthy. How simple can that be?"

Leroy glanced at the back door, but one of the men anticipated his reaction and moved to cut him off if he ran for it. The man who had been at the front door entered the kitchen, marched up to Leroy, and shoved him against the prep counter.

"That's okay, Trung. Mr. Wilson is going to cooperate with us. Isn't that right, Leroy?"

"You somehow know my name, but I've never seen you guys before. I don't know what you mean by cooperating. Is this a shakedown? Do you want money?"

"Nah, the couple of bucks a day you make in this town isn't worth my time. I want information. Now that is worth both my money and my time. So let's not play games. Where is the woman who works here? Flo Whiting."

"Flo's not here. She left town two days ago. Listen, I don't—"

Kwan got in his face. "You're not listening, Leroy, Mr. Chief Cook, and Bottle Washer. Tell me what I want to know, and you'll stay healthy." He glanced at Trung. "Maybe he needs a demonstration."

Trung smiled. "Like a cooking show demonstration, Boss?" He grabbed Leroy's right hand and held it firm against the prep counter. Then he picked up a knife and pressed it against Leroy's pinky finger.

"No! Don't." Leroy's eyes widened in panic as he tried to pull his hand away. "Okay! I know where she lives."

Trung lifted the knife slightly.

"She lives on First Street just up the hill from the Baptist church. It's a blue and white house with a big front porch. Lives there with her daughter, Brooklyn."

Leroy was sweating as Trung tossed the knife in the sink. "Two guys came into the cafe for breakfast two days ago. One of them talked to Flo. They argued. I think she knew the guy. She asked me for some time off, and I said sure. They left together, and she hasn't been back. That's all I know, I swear."

Kwan nodded, and Trung relaxed his grip. Leroy jerked his hand away and rubbed his fingers, assuring himself they were all still part of his hand. Sweat dripped from his face onto the bib of his apron.

"If you're lying to me, my man will come back here and make a soup with your fingers and toes. He's an excellent cook."

Leroy's legs weakened, and he slid to the floor as the three men left the café. He heard an ATV start and drive away. He sat there for almost a half-hour shaking with fright and hoping the men would not come back.

****

Lee drove the hot-wired ATV, borrowed from the harbor parking lot, through the town. He found Flo Whiting's home without any difficulty.

With hardly a glance to see if anyone was observing them, the three men walked up onto the porch. The door was unlocked. Kwan waited as Lee and Trung entered. They checked all the bedrooms and the kitchen, where they saw only an unwashed bowl for one person. Lee searched around the sides of the house and then went back to Kwan, who was leaning against the porch railing.

"No one here, Boss," said Lee. "Doesn't look like anyone has been here since maybe early this morning. No evidence that a man might have been here, either. During our search, we found Florence Whiting's checkbook and some school papers bearing the name of Brooklyn. That must be her kid. This is the place, but they cleared out."

"That's okay. I have a plan. I think Vince and Ms. Whiting are playing a game with us, and we need to leave a clear message. Burn the place." He turned and walked off the porch.

Lee nodded and went back inside the house. He and Trung gathered up some clothing and threw them on the couch. Next to a sofa was a basket of magazines and old newspapers. Lee used a cigarette lighter to ignite the paper. The flames took off, fed by a draft from the open front door. In less than a minute, the sofa caught fire. The flames leaped to the living room window curtains. By the time the two men cleared the front door, the fire had reached the ceiling, and smoke filled the room behind them.

Kwan turned his back on the house and looked down the street towards the Baptist church. There was no one in sight. He took out his cell phone as he walked towards the main road. No service.

"What a town this is. Can't even make a cell phone call!" he said. "Let's get back to the boat. I know somebody who can find them quickly. I'm running out of time." He glanced back at the house. Smoke was pouring out the front door.

While on the road back to the boat harbor, they could hear the town fire siren begin to wail.

Ten minutes later, he was back at his yacht. He grabbed his satellite phone and tried again to make his call. This time he got through.

"Hutch, this is Johnny Kwan. I've got a job for you."

"Yeah? Good timing. Just finishing up a batch," replied Hutch. You need some…?"

"Meth? No, that's not what I need right now, maybe in a week or two. Just listen. I want you to find somebody for me—the Whiting woman."

"The gal that works at the café in Chatham? No problem. I can send the boys in to pick her up."

"Not quite that simple. She's gone undercover. I want you to mount a search. Find her or her daughter. Name is Brooklyn."

"You should have called earlier this morning. The kid was here on my property. My boy AJ had his eyes on her."

Kwan smiled. "You're kidding me. The girl was at your place? Look, I don't care what your boys do if they find her. Just hold them for me. And there could be a guy with the woman, Vince James. It's him I want. Call me, and we'll make arrangements to meet."

****

Brooklyn heard the eaglet screaming for food before she even reached the overlook and the eagle nest. She got down on her stomach and crawled to the edge. He had grown a lot in the last week, and more of his white downy feathers were beginning to give way to brown fledgling feathers. He was now a splotchy brown and white, which she thought was very funny looking.

She giggled as one of the adults screamed and circled over her head, then quickly landed on the edge of the nest. Brooklyn relaxed and rested her chin on her crossed arms to watch the adult feed the eaglet bits of salmon it tore from a carcass held in its claws. This looked violent, yet it had a calming effect on Brooklyn. Everything was all right. Death happened, a parent cared for its young, and a new life began.

Brooklyn rolled onto her back and stretched. The forest behind her reached for the clouds that were drifting northward. There was no warmth from the sun, but still, she wasn't cold. The chill would come with the wind late in the day.

She wondered where her mother might be at that very moment. Was she staring at the same clouds and thinking about her? It was both a new and a strange feeling that Mom would care about someone else nearly as much as her. Mom had recognized the man when he entered the café but didn't introduce him to her. Now she knew that her Mom had returned to Chatham and purposely avoided contacting her. Wally was the messenger to leave the note on the door. She could have done this herself as she must have gone to the house to get the ATV. If only she hadn't been on a wild goose chase to Hoonah. Now Mom was gone again.

Brooklyn wondered if they left using a different boat. They could be anywhere, and she couldn't follow because she didn't have access to a boat herself. Bingo had a boat. Maybe he could help find Mom. Then again, his boat might not even run. The only other boat she knew capable of assisting with a search belonged to Tony Jackson's father. That would be unlikely due to the incident with Tony, but she could ask. Maybe Bingo could ask Mr. Jackson. Bingo said they were friends.

She rolled onto her side and looked out at the reef

in the distance. There was a boat moving out there, the sleek catamaran she had seen arrive earlier as she stood in the living room at Wally's. She watched it for a few minutes as it rounded the reef turning northward towards Juneau. Then it was gone, obscured by a point of land.

A faint whiff of smoke reached her. She sat up. It was stronger and smelled different from a wood stove or burning garbage, frequent smells in Chatham. Curious whether it could be forest slash burning close to the trail she used, she stood and headed back. As she rounded the hill above Chatham, she heard the fire siren. Because of the trees, she couldn't see what was happening in town, but it usually meant volunteers were being called out for a fire somewhere in town.

A strange feeling came over her. She could not remember there ever being a fire in Chatham. Brooklyn started to run.

Chapter 15

The word "fire" spread quickly amongst the town's residents. Many of the small towns in Southeast Alaska had a history of devastating fires. Brooklyn saw people heading towards the west end of town, where a thick dark plume of smoke was rising into the forest and drifting over the bay. As she reached the first businesses in town, the thick smoke made her eyes water. Passing the café, Brooklyn saw a lop-sided closed sign hanging in a window. Leroy Wilson was one of the volunteer firemen and must have been one of the first responders. She still couldn't see where the fire was but with all of the activity up ahead, it had to be close to her house.

An ATV engine whined as it came up the road behind her and then slowed.

"Climb aboard! I'll give you a lift." Someone hollered her name over the noise of the engine. Brooklyn glanced to her left as she ran. It was Tony Jackson on a three-wheeler. She ignored him and kept running.

"Come on, Brooklyn. My dad is fighting the fire with everyone else. He told me to find you. It's your house that's on fire!"

Brooklyn stopped and looked at Tony. She was breathing hard, and for a second, his words didn't register. She glanced down the road and then back at

Tony.

"No, that's impossible." She shook her head refusing to believe him.

"Brooklyn, I'm sorry what I said to you and how I and the other guys acted. You've got to believe me. Now climb on. I'll take you there."

Without a word, Brooklyn hopped on the back of the ATV and gripped a bar behind the seat with both hands as Tony floored the gas pedal. The ATV sped up the road towards the Baptist church on the corner of the side street to her home. They passed several more people hurrying to gawk at the fire.

Tony had his head down, and as he rounded the street corner next to the church, Brooklyn saw over the top of him for the first time the source of the smoke. It was her house. The flames had been quenched, but smoke still billowed from the front windows and door. Tony skidded to a stop next to the town's fire truck, and she leaped off and ran towards the house.

"Brooklyn! Stay away. It's not safe. You can't go in there." It was Wally.

Wally was helping the firemen and had responded in case there were injuries. He intercepted Brooklyn before she could reach the porch just as two firemen wearing respirators exited the front door and walked towards them. Mark Owens, a new volunteer fireman, pointed at her.

"Do you live here?"

Brooklyn didn't recognize him as she answered. "Yes. My mom, was she inside the house?"

"There's no one inside," Mark replied. "How long have you been away from the house?"

Brooklyn stared at the house, her eyes welling up

with tears. There was charred wood and peeling paint along the entire front of the house and the kitchen side. "I…I've been gone since early this morning." She looked at her watch. It was nearly 5. She had been gone longer than she thought.

"Well, we were lucky," said Mark. "We got here less than ten minutes after the fire started. It's under control now. The doors to the bedrooms were closed, so the fire was confined to the living room and the kitchen." The young man searched the crowd of onlookers with his eyes. "Do you know where your mother is?"

"No. I've been looking for her. I hitched a ride to Hoonah, and when I got back, there was a note on the door from Doc Perkins. I didn't even go inside and went directly to his home." Brooklyn was babbling as she wiped away the tears on her cheeks with the sleeve of her jacket. "You're sure no one was in the house?"

"Definitely," replied Mark. "We've searched everywhere, even the closets. Good thing, because they wouldn't have survived with all the smoke. Looks like the fire started on the sofa, which caused a lot of smoke. It's characteristic of a careless cigarette smoker. Does anyone in your family smoke?"

"A cigarette? Never! My mother would never smoke a cigarette. Her grandmother died in a fire caused by a cigarette."

"Any visitors?"

"I…I don't know."

"Well, if it wasn't a smoker, then it looks like somebody entered your house and started it. There's no other obvious source of ignition. We'll take a closer look tomorrow when we're sure the fire is out and it's safer to investigate. Meanwhile, no one, including you or other family members, should enter the house."

Perkins put a hand on her shoulder. "You can't stay here, Brooklyn. I'm sorry all this happened, your mom disappearing, and now your home catching fire. You can stay with us until Flo gets back, and then we'll help the two of you find someplace to live for a while. It's going to take some time to get this house cleaned up, repaired, and livable."

"Why did someone do this? Why set fire to our house?"

Mark backed away from them and motioned at the house. "Uh... I'll leave you two to talk about that, and as I said, there's still some work for us to do to make sure the fire doesn't restart. We'll be here a while."

Leroy, who had been standing close to the pumper truck monitoring the water pressure gauges, overheard Brooklyn and Doc Perkins talking. He joined them, rubbing his fingers. "Ah...Wally, Brooklyn, I gotta tell you something. The fire could be my fault."

"Your fault?" Brooklyn said. "You started the fire?"

"I might as well have. I told some strangers how to find your house."

"What? When?" Wally said.

"Maybe an hour ago. Three guys, rough-looking Asian guys, came into the café. I was in the kitchen prepping for dinner. They walked right in and pushed me against a counter and started asking questions about Flo and some friend of hers. I refused to answer. They held my right hand on the counter and threatened to cut off my fingers if I didn't tell them what they wanted to know. I panicked and told them where you and Flo live.

I'm so sorry, Brooklyn. I was too scared of what would happen to me. I had to or…"

"Gosh, they were looking for our house. They were looking for my mom."

"I'm pretty sure. I think they headed this way after leaving the café."

They all turned in response to noises from the house. There was a fire hose snaking up the steps and through the front door. Mark and another fireman tossed a soggy, burned sofa off the porch onto the front lawn. Leroy shook his head as he spoke. "I…I'm so sorry all this happened."

"Did you say they might be Asian?" asked Wally.

"Yeah, I'd never seen them before," Leroy answered. "I think they wanted to find the guy she is with."

Wally nodded. "I think given what happened here, it's Flo's friend who is in trouble. She told me there was something or somebody that they needed to avoid. It was one reason the person sought out Flo for help rather than go to the Juneau hospital."

"There were two men and they are not Flo's friends," said Brooklyn. "She only met them this morning. I saw them too at the café. She didn't pay them any attention, which I don't understand because her note said she had an urgent family matter."

An expression of panic on her face changed as she recalled something. "Huh! If it is a family matter, it can only mean that man is my father. One of the guys is named Vince. It was him, right?" Brooklyn looked straight at Wally.

Wally gave a weak nod but didn't have a chance to respond as Brooklyn kept talking.

"If my father is in some kind of trouble, Mom could be in the middle of something that she knows nothing about. Do you think these men might hurt her if they find her, Wally? If they said they would cut off Leroy's fingers if he didn't help, Mom might get hurt."

"And you too, Brooklyn. That's why she didn't want you in any way to know or become involved. She wanted you as far away from Vince as possible."

"Yeah, and you've got to watch out for yourself," Leroy added. "I'm afraid I told them your name."

"But I don't know anything or where they are."

"That settles it," said Wally. "You have to stay at my house. You can't stay here. I doubt they'll come back right away after doing this. But just in case, you need to be somewhere safe." He looked up at the house and mess in the front yard. "I've got to stay until they finish up here. Then we'll go back to my place."

Chapter 16

It was late and State Trooper Dave Williams had just finished a long day on a patrol boat and was minutes from his home near the Mendenhall River in Juneau. As he made the turn off the Egan Expressway onto Mendenhall Road, two small deer sauntered across the road, their eyes shining like diamonds in the headlights of his Durango. Williams and his partner Bill Laughton were the only Alaska State Troopers in Southeast Alaska assigned to a patrol boat. They spent a lot of their daily shift investigating crimes that happened on the water.

The day had been long and spent searching for a 24-foot cabin cruiser stolen from the marina in Auke Bay near the ferry landing. They found it abandoned and grounded on a beach on the west side of Shelter Island. There was a case of empty beer bottles in one of the bunks, and garbage was strewn about the boat, primarily fast-food wrappers. With no residents close by to interview, no witnesses, and no footprints along the beach, they had to assume the perpetrators had used another boat. Williams wrote up his report citing teenagers out for a joy ride. The bad news was that it took several hours to refloat the boat and tow it back to the marina, and he was tired.

Williams had been fifteen years with the State Troopers. For the last nine years, he'd been assigned as a wildlife trooper with the marine enforcement detachment in Juneau. In reality, he handled everything from people poaching fish and game out of season to wild beach parties with drunken teenagers. There were occasional crimes of passion to investigate, mainly when a patrol vessel was required to reach the crime scene. Alaska was well known for its shotgun divorces where a spouse got depressed during long winters and shot their husband or wife. In Southeast Alaska, that domestic violence took the form of the victim being pushed off a boat.

Less than ten minutes from home, Williams got a call from the Juneau dispatcher. For a woman in her sixties, Dolly Collins had a sweet and very sexy voice.

"Where are you?" Dolly asked ever so nicely. "Been trying to reach you for a couple of hours."

"Nearly home. Bill and I located that missing cruiser and had to tow it in. Where we were, the cell phone coverage was lousy to nonexistent. You should have tried the Coast Guard. They could have patched you through to our patrol boat. What's up? You sound anxious. Ate your last chocolate bar?"

Dolly also had a sweet tooth.

"Hey, watch what you say on the radio, or I'll report that as harassment to Supervisor Wallace." She kept her mike on, and Williams could hear her laughing to herself. She added, "You know. I'll forget that remark if there's a yummy chocolate cupcake from Dream Chaser's on my desk in the morning."

Williams sighed, "Ah, chocolate—the way to a woman's heart."

"One bonbon at a time," she replied.

"As to the reason for the call, honey bun, it looks

like you're going to be late for dinner. I got a call from the emergency room doctor, and Wallace said for you to handle it. You need to go by the hospital and talk to the doc on duty and interview a couple. The wife is being treated."

"Treated for what? Someone shot her, or was it something stupid like being knocked overboard by a fish net?"

"Hitting your wife or girlfriend with a fishnet? Do men do that sort of thing?"

"More than once, more than once, like when she grabs your pole and loses your fish, and it might have been a salmon derby winner, or just bigger than hers already in the cooler," sighed Williams.

"Hey, fishing is a dangerous contact sport."

"Yeah, tell me. That's why I have to wear a gun these days. So, why can't the day shift in Juneau handle it? I'm almost home, and it has been a very long day."

"Nope. The doc said it was urgent. Something about a rabid animal running amuck and biting people over on Baranof. That's your territory."

"Okay, but isn't that a case for one of the officers in Hoonah or maybe animal control? Since when do I need to play dog catcher?"

"Not this time. The doc who treated the woman said she was bitten by a wild animal while camping over on Baranof Island. He's keeping the woman in the emergency room for a few more hours for observation. Her husband is with her. Wallace said you're to interview them, find out what happened, and follow up pronto. He doesn't want the newspaper catching wind of an uninvestigated rabies incident and getting the public all in a panic about rabid animals."

"My wife is going to bitch loudly about this. I left this morning before she was awake. She gets upset when I leave her with the dog to feed and walk. Maybe you can call her?"

"Oh no. I'm not getting in the middle of a domestic violence situation. She's going to believe why you're going to be late when she hears a woman's voice?"

"But Dolly, you owe me at least one favor. I'm the only person on the force who gives you a box of candy on your birthday."

"That's because the other officers make you the delivery guy. They're all afraid of being teased."

Williams could hear Dolly's radio in the background—an officer needing assistance in responding to a possible stabbing at a bar downtown.

"I gotta take this, sweetie. Now call your understanding wife and go talk to the distraught tourists. You can always buy two chocolate cupcakes, you know? One for little old me and one for your wife."

Despite his disappointment, Dave had to smile as he clicked off. With a sigh, he turned on his flashing lights to make a U-turn and head towards the hospital downtown. As the car accelerated, he punched the speed dial for home. He flew down the Egan Expressway doing eighty as he passed the airport. He might avoid being in the dog house, just barely, if it was a quick interview and avoid the cupcake routine, as well.

Chapter 17

Brooklyn woke up in a strange bed. The unfamiliarity of her surroundings added to a restless night and upped her anxiety. Having supper with Wally and Peggy Perkins the night before had briefly taken her mind off the destruction to her home and her mother's disappearance, but sleep did not come easy.

She tossed and turned and, finally, just after 6, she got dressed. It was barely light outside, but it looked like it would be a decent day. Throughout the night, she kept going over her mom's situation based on what Wally had been able to tell her. Getting in touch with the State Troopers seemed the right thing to do, but it wasn't like her mother had been kidnapped. She had left town willingly. Now somebody else was searching for her. They had threatened Leroy and set fire to her home. Was that sufficient reason for the State Troopers to launch a search?

The whole town knew her mother was missing. Everyone she saw after the fire while waiting for Wally said how sorry they were for what happened and that they would be watching for Flo. Several people had come by the house and told her and Wally they would be glad to help clean up and rebuild her home. Even Tony had offered to help her. His offer surprised her the most. Tony's apology was starting to reverse her feelings about him.

Her feelings about the whole community were changing. People who she thought considered her and Flo to be outsiders were offering support. Her world had turned upside down. Like the eaglet about to leave its nest, it was a different world.

Brooklyn smiled. It gave her some hope that everything would be all right.

There was a light knock on the bedroom door.

"Brooklyn, are you all right?" It was Peggy. "I heard you moving around."

"I'm fine, Mrs. Perkins. Just restless—too much on my mind, I guess."

"I understand, dear. Wally and I are having coffee in the kitchen. Why don't you join us? I can make you a hot chocolate if you don't drink coffee."

"That would be cool. I'll be right down."

Brooklyn put on the clothes she had been wearing for the last two days. She needed to go by her house. She needed to see what shape her bedroom was in and whether her clothes had been affected by the fire. Her eyes began to get teary again, thinking about the damage. Where were she and Mom going to live? But first, they had to find each other.

As she went down the stairs to the kitchen, she remembered something Leroy had mentioned about the three men who left with Flo. They had talked about a place called the Grotto. That was something she hadn't thought to follow up on. If the men persuaded her mom to accompany them to this place, and a boat is needed to get there, maybe Tony Jackson could help her find it using his father's boat. First, she had to know how to find the Grotto. There must be someone in town who knew where the place was. She would start with Reggie

Boyd at the community center.

****

Flo also had a restless night and woke up shivering. They had found one of the abandoned houses at the logging camp to be still inhabitable. The doors were not damaged, and there were just a few broken panes in the windows. It had a single bed frame without a mattress and a few pieces of furniture in the kitchen. They moved the bed into the kitchen which had a woodstove to provide them with some warmth. The rest of the place was stripped bare. With what they had brought from the boat and her home, they should be okay for a few days.

Ronnie went out to the woodshed and brought in another armload of wood for the old cast iron stove in the kitchen. He left again to use the outhouse. Flo rose, relit the stove, and put on a pot of coffee. The heat helped rid the old house of dampness, and the smell of the burning wood helped mask the musty smell of the old wallpaper. The smoke from the chimney was a dead giveaway that someone was in the house, but it was a risk they had to take.

Flo spent the night sleeping next to Vince, who was restless and having trouble breathing. Ronnie slept on the floor next to the kitchen stove, rolled in one of the blankets they had grabbed at her house before leaving Chatham. He snored all night and likely never even noticed that the fire had gone out.

She went over to a grimy window and looked out at a peaceful lake just beyond the rest of the abandoned buildings. A solitary loon made little ripples as it dove close to the shore. Generally, when she saw a loon, it was a thrill, but not this morning. She felt as lonely as a loon separated from its mate. She missed Brooklyn.

Flo glanced over at Vince. He was sleeping peacefully now, almost as if he was dead. She went over to the bed and laid two fingers on his neck, being careful not to touch his nose or mouth. He still had a steady pulse, but his face was pale. When he woke, she would give him the second dose of the medication.

Ronnie came back inside. "Some damn critter kept moving around all night under the house. It seemed like he was trying to gnaw through the floor right under my ear." He rubbed his right ear like he was making sure it was still attached, and then warmed his hands by the stove. "How's Vince?"

"He's not any better. Maybe he will respond more with the second dose."

"I hope so. Sleeping on this old floor is killing my back. We should have taken the boat and gone somewhere else. At least I'd have a bunk to sleep in."

"Vince said they would find us for sure if we used the boat."

"Well, if we stay here very long, someone is going to wander up here and notice the wood smoke coming from this old shack."

"Sometimes there's a caretaker for the timber company living here," said Flo. "But it's been a while. There are no recent tire tracks and lots of weeds growing around the buildings." She heard a noise from outside and looked at Ronnie, then walked to the window. "Darn, it didn't take long for someone to show up."

A vehicle had entered the old logging complex. Trying to stay hidden behind a strip of the window curtain, she saw a pickup truck pull to a stop where the road split to the old mill buildings and to the housing area. As she watched, the driver rolled down the window and looked at the fresh tracks from her ATV. Ronnie came over and stood behind her, and they watched the truck make a loop around the buildings, following their tracks, then stop in front of the house where they were. Flo could only see one man in the truck. He sat there for a minute.

"What's he doing?" Ronnie asked.

"I dunno. But if he gets out of his truck, darn, he is," said Flo. "We can't let him come in here. Ronnie, you've got to go out and meet him."

"Me? What if he's got a gun?"

"I can't go out there. Everyone around here knows who I am. You're a stranger. Just tell him you're the new caretaker for Fox Timber."

"Fox Timber?"

"Yes, they own this property."

Flo watched as the man got out of the pickup then looked back inside, where a rifle lay propped on the front seat. He let it lay there but left the door to the pickup open and started for the house. Ronnie opened the door and stepped out onto the porch. Flo could hear them exchange words.

"This is private property," Ronnie said firmly, trying to hide his nervousness.

The man stopped and looked around Ronnie at the house.

"Who the heck are you? There's not been anyone living up here in maybe a year."

"Fox Timber hired me to watch the place this winter. Been some vandalism. They don't want to lose any of their equipment."

"Snowden hired you? He told me he wasn't hiring anybody this year. The company took a tax write-off on the rest of this equipment. He said it ain't worth hauling more stuff out of here no more."

"I guess he changed his mind. There's been some vandalism to some of the buildings. I can't guess what those corporate idiots do."

"Well, you tell him AJ is disappointed he didn't offer the job to me first."

"Sure, first chance I get, like next spring. Now you're trespassing, so move that rig out of here."

Hesitating, AJ peered at the windows of the house behind Ronnie. "You got someone in there with you? I thought I saw someone at the window. I'm looking for a man and a woman."

"Yeah, my old lady, and she's holding my shotgun. Now get on out of here."

Flo remained hidden by the window. She could see Ronnie but not the other man. A minute later, she heard him slam a door on the truck, start the engine, and drive slowly back the way he came. Ronnie came back inside.

"Man, that was close. He could have grabbed that rifle and forced his way in here." Ronnie was sweating, and his hands were shaking as he poured himself a cup of coffee. "Someone is looking for you and Vince. He knew some guy at Fox Timber. If he calls and finds out I lied, he could be back with some help."

"Then we leave in a hurry. There's an ATV trail that goes down to the north shore of Peril Strait. The mill had a log storage area there."

"Then what?"

"I don't know."

Chapter 18

Brooklyn's home was a disaster. Walking up the street towards the house, she saw the mud and puddles of water black with ashes. The front yard was littered with burnt furniture tossed out by the firemen. A strip of yellow caution ribbon had been tied across the front porch.

Picking her way up to the front door, Brooklyn peeked inside. Everything in the front part of the house was partially burned or soaking wet or both. The floor was covered with black ash and standing water. Trails of black footprints led into the kitchen and bedrooms. It was impossible to avoid tracking the wet ash and adding more footprints. Entering her bedroom, though it smelled smoky, it was untouched by the fire. The firemen had put the fire out before it got to the bedrooms. She located some clean clothes in her bureau and put them on.

On her way back through town to the community center, she continued asking anyone she met whether they had seen Flo. Some gave her a blank stare like she was crazy. Others just shook their heads.

Passing the game parlor, she heard a steady stream of explosions and machinegun fire. She hardly ever ventured inside because the computer games disgusted her, and it was always noisy. The kids who sat in front of the monitors were generally engaged in violent games like *Call of Duty* and *Black Ops*. Peeking inside, she saw a couple of boys busy at the game stations. A row of pinball machines on one wall sat unused. When her eyes adjusted to the gloom and glowing screens, she noticed Tony standing next to a friend who was blowing up tanks.

Tony saw her and walked over. "Hi! How are you holding up?"

"Okay, thanks to the Perkins, I had a place to stay. Our house is a mess. Thanks for the ride, by the way. And I'm sorry I snapped at you." She glanced at the other young gamers recognizing them as classmates. "Hey, why aren't you guys at school this morning?"

"It's a teacher training day. Hendricks told us last week. It's some state teachers' online webinar thing that started yesterday. Don't you remember?"

"Oh, yeah, I forgot. Too many other things on my mind, like locating my mom."

"Your mom hasn't come home yet?"

"No. I'm worried about her. She must not have heard about the fire, or she would have come home. I'm sure of that. Something must be very wrong. Why can't she come home or send me a message?"

"You don't travel much, do you?" asked Tony. "Have you ever been out of Chatham?"

"Mom took me with her to Juneau a couple of times. Once we got to watch the Fourth of July fireworks display."

"Well, cell phone coverage is almost nonexistent unless you're near a town. It's possible your mom has no way of knowing what's going on and is unable to call to get a message to you. Does she have a cell phone?"

"Are you kidding? We've got one stupid phone plugged into the wall next to Mom's bed."

"Oh. So where could she have gone?"

"I thought to Hoonah. I hitched a ride there. It turned out she didn't do that. My guess is she left for somewhere near here on a boat. Leroy Wilson told me that the guys she talked with during breakfast mentioned they had been at a place called the Grotto. That's all I know. Leroy had never heard of it."

"The Grotto? Me neither. But you know, there is somebody who might."

"Yeah? Who? I was going to ask Reggie Boyd, but he hasn't lived here very long." Brooklyn sighed.

"Hmm, he's smart all right, and he might be able to find it with an Internet search. The Grotto could be a place name. Then maybe it's just an unofficial name for some unusual landmark. You know, a name used just by locals."

"I do know that *grotto* can mean a small cave. That's unusual. Maybe there's a cave around here that's called the Grotto."

"Yeah. That's why I think Old Frank might know about it."

"Who's Old Frank?"

"Oh, sorry. You haven't participated in our Tlingit ceremonies, have you?"

"Nope, Mom and I are outsiders."

"That's not true, Brooklyn. You guys are just as much a part of this community as us Natives. You saw the ceremony last year for raising that totem over by the boat basin, didn't you?"

"Yup, but that was a public…"

Tony didn't let her finish. "Look, some of our

Native events are public, and some aren't. Old Frank Duffy is our shaman, and he's always part of any cultural event. He leads the prayers, does the blessing ceremonies, and often teaches the young people the meaning and importance of the event."

"I think I remember him. He's an older guy, white hair worn in a ponytail, always has a grin?"

"Yeah, that's him."

"Tony, do you think he can help? Maybe the only way to get to this Grotto place is with a boat. There was a fishing boat down at the harbor that morning that I haven't seen before. Based on what Wally Perkins told me, it could belong to the men who took Mom. That's why I think a boat is needed to find the Grotto. If we talk to Old Frank and he knows where the Grotto is, then maybe you can ask your dad if we can use his boat to find it."

"My dad's boat? I guess so." Tony paused, and Brooklyn could tell he was thinking about her request.

"Sure, I'd like to help you, Brooklyn. I owe you that after the way we treated you. But my dad only lets me drive the boat under two conditions. There needs to be an adult on board, and it has to be good weather—like the water has to be calm. Let's start by talking to Old Frank to find out if there is a place called the Grotto, then come back and ask my dad about using the boat." He thought a moment. "There's a women's basket weaving class at the community center this morning. Old Frank usually shows up to do storytelling. Maybe we can talk with Reggie at the same time. He might help you do an Internet search."

"Sounds good. Can you go with me right now?"

"Sure! Let's go."

As Brooklyn and Tony left the game parlor, a young man sitting in a rusty Ford Bronco watched them head east on Dock Street towards the boat harbor. He waited a moment, then started the engine and did a U-turn to head out of town using the Hoonah road.

Chapter 19

It was mid-morning when AJ got home. A big German Shephard barked and yanked on its chain. He gave the dog a tussle and then let him off his chain so he could run a bit. When he opened the back door, Hutch Senior and his brother Will were drinking coffee at the kitchen table. AJ pulled out a chair and sat down with them. He grabbed a fresh-baked biscuit off a plate on the table and took a bite.

"Did you find them?" Hutch Senior asked.

"Nope." AJ chewed on the cold biscuit and answered with his mouth full. "I drove darn near every road from Chatham to Hoonah except out to the Yellow Creek Mine. They've got a guard at the gate, so I figured they wouldn't be hiding out there."

Hutch Senior shook his head. "Huh. She's sure got her head down somewhere. Will talked to the harbormaster in Hoonah, and he said there were no women around the dock area over the last day or two. He located the girl, however. She's in Chatham."

AJ got up and walked over to the stove. He poured a cup of coffee and brought it back. "I ran across one odd thing. Remember me telling you about that caretaker job up at the old Fox Timber camp? Somebody got hired and is living up there in one of the houses."

"You told me they weren't going to have a

caretaker no more."

"I did, but this guy said Snowden changed his mind. He kicked me out and wouldn't let me look around. There wasn't any vehicle, which I thought was strange, but maybe he had it tucked away in a building somewhere."

"See anybody else?" Hutch Senior said. He got up, refilled his coffee, and topped it with a slug of whiskey from a bottle near the coffee maker.

"I think there was someone in the house," AJ replied, tipping his chair back. "I saw movement at one of the windows. He said it was his wife."

Hutch Senior rubbed his chin. "Hmm, maybe you ought to give Snowden a call and confirm that he hired this guy. You wanting that job is reason enough."

"Sure will. I'm a bit teed off about it, you know? I figured he would hire me again this year. I'll call him after I get something to eat. I'm starving" He stuffed the rest of the biscuit in his mouth. On his way to the fridge, he punched his brother in the shoulder. "Got an eyeful of that sweet little chick, huh? Didn't Dad say to grab her if we can't find the woman? When he gives the word, you and I are gonna go into town and grab her, bring her back here, smoke some weed, and have some fun." They both snickered.

****

Flo was dozing next to Vince when she heard the whine of an engine behind the house. It took only a second for her to realize what the sound was. She rushed for the back door but was too late. Ronnie had opened the shed doors and was sitting on her ATV. She ran towards him, yelling for him to stop.

"Hey, that's my ATV. Stop right now."

He didn't even look her way as he put it in gear and roared towards the road out of the camp. She ran after him ignoring the mud puddles in the road, stumbling over some wood debris, and falling on her hands and knees. She lay there pounding the muddy ground and cursing him as the sound of the ATV faded into the deep woods. The silence of the abandoned logging camp returned, broken only by the gurgling croak of a lone raven atop one of the old buildings.

****

Deep in the abandoned shaft of the old mine near the Grotto, the bats were beginning to stir. It was time to go in search of food. They fed on flying insects—mosquitos, midges, and black flies that swirled over the marsh grass, the lake, and along the small stream that flowed through the Grotto. A few of them dropped from the ceiling of the mine, flapped their wings, and flew swiftly towards the mine entrance. They were quickly followed by more and more of their brethren until a black cloud was exiting the mine. The camp area outside the mine was deathly quiet and deserted. In the forest beyond the camp, a large brown bear sniffed and shuffled its gigantic paws along the trail that followed the stream towards the lake.

Not all of the bats left the confines of the mine shaft. Some had died during the day, and their fallen bodies littered the floor amidst the piles of sea otter carcasses. Some were belligerent and fought with one another. Others who left the confines of the mine shaft flew erratically and appeared to have lost their ability to catch their prey. They would soon die of starvation—rabies was taking its toll on the colony.

Chapter 20

Brooklyn and Tony walked side by side to the community center. While it was strange to be walking with a boy whom only days before she had loathed, Brooklyn no longer felt uncomfortable. And, now she had a purpose for finding her mom—she had a plan and a new friend who was willing to help her.

The Chatham Community Center was the center for many different activities. Built well above the bay, it commanded a stunning view of distant snow-covered mountains, surrounding forests, and the bay itself. While there was a road to the community center, it was a winding road well back from the main street to the harbor. People with ATVs didn't mind the extra distance, but those who walked used the long flight of wooden stairs. At the entrance, the two young people stopped after their climb to catch their breath. Brooklyn took the opportunity to ask Tony some things.

"Are you sure Frank won't mind us asking him about the Grotto? I'm a little frightened to ask. The more I think about it, the more the whole idea seems crazy."

"No problem. Frank is a kind man." Tony replied. "You'll see. There's no need to be afraid of him. He is always helping and encouraging people. That's why he's here at the center, to counsel some of the elders."

"What if he doesn't know where the Grotto is or

refuses to tell us?"

"I think Frank will have heard about the situation with your mother. He has a sixth sense of everything. Heck, I think by this morning just about all the folks in Chatham knew that your mother wasn't here during the fire and want to help. Let's see how he reacts to the question."

The main entrance led directly to the largest room of the center. The room was used for every imaginable community function, from school graduation to hot lunches for elderly citizens and traditional craft classes. It had a community kitchen at one end and a small stage at the other. In the center of the room, a group of women sat around folding tables with piles of sweet grass, cedar bark, and spruce roots in front of them. They were making traditional baskets, which brought top prices in the souvenir shops in Juneau. The most sought-after items were Tlingit cedar hats, and the Chatham Native Women's Guild was known for the quality of their hats.

To the right of the entrance was the director's office. Reggie had the door closed. It probably meant that he was assisting someone or involved in an online meeting. The rest of the time, Reggie had his door open, and anyone could ask his help.

Brooklyn heard a man's voice amid the quiet chatter of the women as they entered. Tony nodded at the man as he and Brooklyn stopped just inside the doorway. It was Old Frank.

Brooklyn looked at the man but tried not to stare. He was quite an imposing figure. His age was impossible for her to guess, although every inch of exposed flesh was wrinkled. His long white hair was pulled back into a ponytail. Over faded jeans, he wore a black vest trimmed in red with shell buttons and embroidered with traditional animal and fish designs.

Frank noticed them and smiled. Even from across the room, Brooklyn could see a youthful twinkle in his eyes. Those eyes, his smile, and how he spoke showed why he was loved and admired by young and old alike. The two young people waited and listened until he finished. Frank was in the middle of his storytelling to the guild.

"Raven liked to sit and observe the human beings. Every day, the human beings gathered things to eat from the shore of the Big Water."

Old Frank brought his fingers to his mouth.

"Like the people, Raven, too, gathered whatever he could to eat. But their food was becoming scarce as more people were born, and everyone, including Raven, was constantly hungry. One day the human beings came to Raven with an idea. If the Big Water would recede, they could gather plenty of food. Raven thought about this, and the next night in a dream, he learned that at the edge of the World, an old woman sat in a cave holding a line tightly in her hands that prevented the waters from receding. When Raven woke, he decided that if he could find this cave and the old woman, maybe he could trick her into letting go of the line. He set off and flew for many days until he reached the end of the World. There, in a cave beside the Big Water, sat a huge woman. In her lap, she held onto a line that led to the Big Water."

Frank paused and looked directly at Brooklyn. He winked as he continued holding his hands in front of him like he was trying to pull on an invisible rope.

"Raven sat, cocked his head to one side, and watched the woman for a long time. She didn't move or acknowledge his presence. Then he got an idea and went down to the beach in front of the entrance to the cave. 'Boy, these clams are sure good to eat,' Raven said loud enough for the woman to hear. 'Where did you get those clams?' the woman demanded. Raven didn't answer and proceeded to hop across the entrance announcing once more to the woman. 'I need to gather some more of those clams. They sure were good.' This time the old woman moved a little as she hollered at Raven. 'I said, where did you get those clams?' Raven was silent and as she moved and left her seat in the cave, being so huge she fell over and, in the process of collecting herself, let go of the tide line. As she struggled to find it, Raven realized she was blind. Happy, he flew back to his home and his people. He found them gathering many, many things to eat where the Big Water had already dropped. For days both Raven and the people stuffed themselves with clams and other delicious things from the shoreline. Several days later, the people again came to Raven, proclaiming that everything along the shoreline was dying from not being covered with water. Raven thought about what to do and finally realized that he needed to see the old woman in the cave once more. So, he flew back to the cave and found her still crawling on the beach, trying to find her line and her way back into the cave. 'Raven, Raven, is that you? Help me!' the woman pleaded. He told her he would help if she promised to loosen the line twice a day. She promised, and Raven led her into the cave and gave her the line that controlled the level of the Big Water."

Frank smiled as he finished his story.

"And that, my dear ladies, is how we have our huge tides and the bounty revealed on our treasured tidelands. Now, if you will excuse me for a few minutes, two of our fine young people want to speak to me, I believe."

The man stooped to pick up his walking stick, a handsomely carved piece of wood and, walked over to greet Tony and Brooklyn.

"Hello, Tony. I see you have a new friend." Frank laid a gentle hand on Tony's shoulder as he smiled at Brooklyn. "I'm sorry to hear about the fire, Brooklyn. I want you to know the Native community will help you and your mother any way we can. Have you heard from your mother?"

"No, that's why we are here. Maybe you know about the place where she may be." Brooklyn replied.

"I like Flo. If I can be of help, I certainly will try."

The man offered a friendly smile as he glanced around the room, looking for a place for them to be seated. The door to the director's office was now open.

"Let's go into Reggie's office where we can talk."

****

An hour passed as the two young people sat with Old Frank and Reggie and Brooklyn explained her predicament. Frank already seemed to know much of the story, including the rumor that someone was searching for her mother and about the person who accompanied her.

When Brooklyn pressed Old Frank about who Vince might be, he said it was a cultural situation that he could not discuss. When Brooklyn asked about the Grotto, that was another matter where he seemed reluctant. He knew of the place and was willing to talk about it, but his words were solemn and full of reservation about them going anywhere near it. To Old Frank, the Grotto was associated with one of the fateful Tlingit legends. He told them the story.

"It is a place where one encounters the Kushtaka, the River Otter People," replied Old Frank. His voice was firm and convincing. "No one should go there, and if you do, you could be risking your life and perhaps your soul. My people respect the threat and danger represented by the River Otter People. Their homeland is quite far from here, but bad things are associated with the Grotto. They are believed to be attributed to the Kushtaka."

Brooklyn could see that Tony was getting nervous as Old Frank spoke about the Grotto and its relationship to the Kushtaka. She wondered if he might back out of taking her there. He was Tlingit and had grown up hearing all the Tlingit legends, but it was apparent he had never listened to this one. Brooklyn listened, and while she respected Old Frank and his remarkable storytelling, she did not believe in legends.

The old shaman reminded her of the author Rowling. She had recently researched and written a paper about the author for her English class with Mr. Hendricks. She had written about several famous writers—people who were great storytellers. Old Frank and Rowling both told stories about fantastic characters. River otters were just other wild mammals, like the mink or weasels, not evil characters. On the other hand, she didn't necessarily like river otters since they stole eggs from nesting birds.

After cautioning the young people, Old Frank

reluctantly described to them where to find the Grotto, but he told them on two conditions. "You cannot remain there overnight, and you must have an adult with you."

Both Brooklyn and Tony nodded that they would agree to this. Tony mentioned that being accompanied by an adult was also necessary to use his dad's boat.

Reggie, who had been listening to the entire conversation, turned to his computer to bring up some aerials. Based on Old Frank's directions, he showed Tony and Brooklyn where to find the Grotto. "This little bay is where it should be." He pointed at the screen. "I would love to be the one to accompany you, but I have to be here at the center for the rest of the basket weaving workshop. It's a three-day event. So, whoever goes with you should come and see me. I'll show him on a map."

As they left Reggie's office, Old Frank put a fatherly hand on Brooklyn's shoulder and said something that surprised her. "I've been watching you as you have grown up in our village. I like how you are different from most of the other kids. You have shown an interest and respect for our environment. I know you are only half Tlingit, but you do have Tlingit blood." Old Frank touched her forehead with a forefinger. "And you have Tlingit instincts. You just need to call on them.

"We tell our children about the eagle who sits calmly high on his perch. Sooner or later, he will spot a salmon that swims too close to the surface, and then he swoops down and grabs the salmon with his sharp talons. The salmon falsely thinks it is safe because it is one of many. The eagle sees everything below him and chooses carefully what he must do. You, my child, are like the eagle and understand Mother Earth. Choose with care what you must do. Like in my story to the basket weavers, do not become blind to what is happening around you, or Raven will trick you. He is a lonely and selfish spirit. What he wants comes first. But if Raven chooses to be a true friend, like the Eagle who cares for the young in its nest, he may choose to help you."

Brooklyn thanked Old Frank for his advice. She liked the old shaman and appreciated everything he shared. As she turned to leave the office, she remembered something the old Indian woman had said when she wanted to know if she had seen Flo.

"Mr. Frank, can I ask you a question? It's something I heard and don't understand what it means."

Old Frank lifted his chin but didn't respond yes or no.

Brooklyn decided to ask despite her nervousness.

"There's an old Indian woman who sits in front of the general store every day. When I asked her if she had seen my mom, she said she saw her riding with a ghost. What did she mean by that?"

Frank smiled and nodded several times before replying. "Child, someday you will learn more about our culture. When someone dies, we no longer say their name. The same is true of someone who has is banned from their village. They no longer exist for us. They are a ghost."

Brooklyn noticed that Frank's eyes were both sad and humble.

Brooklyn thought for a moment about his answer to her question. She could have pressed him on whoever was with Flo, but of course, he wouldn't have been able to say the person's name. The ghost must have been Vince.

Using his cane, the Shaman hobbled back into the big room. Brooklyn heard one of the women giggle as he patted her shoulder and whispered something in her ear as he passed.

A tear rolled down Brooklyn's left cheek, then another down the right cheek. Tony nudged her as he walked out of the office, motioning with his hands that they should leave.

They were walking down the wooden stairway to the road when Tony finally spoke. "We have to find somebody to go with us. Whom do you think we should ask? I need someone to help with the boat if we have a problem."

"I know just the person to ask," replied Brooklyn, staring at the boat harbor below them.

"Who would that be?"

"Bingo Bob."

Chapter 21

During the brief walk to the harbor, Brooklyn tried to convince Tony that Bingo should be the adult to accompany them. Tony was not a decision-maker. His friend Jake or his dad was always the ones to make the decisions. Tony was happy just to follow along and have fun.

"We at least need to allow Bingo to say yes or no, Tony." Brooklyn implored as she half-dragged Tony to the bottom of the boat ramp. "He got here in that little boat of his from Seattle. How far is that? Nine hundred miles? Plus, Bingo goes out in his little dinghy with its tiny outboard motor and can be gone all day. The man must have some knowledge of the bays around here. So, can you read navigation charts, Tony?"

"No," answered Tony. "I've never paid any attention to that. Still, can he handle my dad's boat? It's got big outboard motors. They're a lot different to handle than that little inboard he has. I think my dad should have something to say about this."

"You're avoiding the real question on your mind, Tony. I can see it on your face. Yes, Bingo is an alcoholic, but when he's sober, he's a nice person. He's smart, too. Mom told me he was an engineer."

"What if one of the outboard motors quits, or—"

"He worked on jet planes. How much more complicated can you get than that? Look, he has

159

navigation skills, and he is not afraid of rough waters. Besides, there's one other thing." Brooklyn decided to appeal to his ego.

"What's that?"

"Let's be honest. You want to drive the boat, right?"

Tony smiled and nodded. "Yeah, you're right. It could be fun."

As her feet landed on the dock at the bottom of the ramp, she crossed her fingers. Moments later, she hailed Bingo while standing next to his boat.

"Hello? It's Brooklyn."

There was a prolonged moment of silence. She glanced at Tony. He was shaking his head. She raised her voice.

"Are you on board, Bingo?"

Finally, the cabin door opened, and Bingo emerged with his head down. When he looked up at the two young people standing on the dock, he blushed. Bingo had bruises on his face and dried blood caked on his left ear, and his shirt and pants were dirtier than Brooklyn remembered from their last encounter. He was not wearing any shoes, and there were holes in his white socks. Brooklyn stared at him, wondering if bringing Tony here and asking for Bingo's help was such a good idea.

Bingo tried to find the words to explain. "I—uh— I'm sorry. I must have—"

Brooklyn interrupted him. "Bingo, what happened to you?"

"I—uh—ran into some pretty unpleasant guys who showed up here at the dock. They wanted information and roughed up Kenny and me. Kenny lives on one of the other boats."

"Why?"

"I'm sorry to tell you this, Brooklyn, but they were looking for Flo, I mean, your mother. I refused to tell them anything, and they hit me a few times. Kenny and I were just talking over by the fish cleaning table when these guys climbed off a yacht, came up to us, and started asking questions. I was a little slow in saying anything, so they hit me. They asked again, and when I refused to answer, they hit me some more. I must have passed out because when I came to, Kenny was helping me back to my boat. He was so afraid they would do the same thing to him that he told them where your mother worked. I'm so sorry, Brooklyn. Kenny and I, we were no match for those guys."

"That's okay," Brooklyn said. "They would have found out one way or another in this town. They threatened Leroy Wilson too. Then they set fire to our house when they couldn't find my mom."

"They set fire to your house? I didn't know that. Did anyone report them to the state police?"

"Doc Perkins was there. I think he or one of the volunteers reported the fire as suspicious. But no one seems to know who they are. Leroy thinks they are Asian, maybe Chinese."

Tony was listening. "You should file a report, too, Bingo."

"Yeah, it has to be the same guys. But I'm not sure the State Troopers would believe me. I had a hangover at the time, I'm afraid."

"What about your friend Kenny?" Tony added. "Was he hurt too? Maybe he can report the assault."

"I think he's too afraid they might come back."

Bingo hesitated before saying what else was on his mind. "Brooklyn, I saw Flo board a boat with a couple of guys. My mind is pretty fuzzy on that. I think it was two or three days ago. Is she back?"

"No, that's why I'm worried. Mom didn't say where she was going, who she was with, or when she would return. And she probably doesn't know about the house. If someone else is looking for her and did these things, Mom could be in trouble, and she doesn't know it."

"You need to talk to the State Troopers, Brooklyn. File a missing person report or—"

"They wouldn't take me seriously," snapped Brooklyn. "My Mom told both Leroy Wilson and Doc Perkins that she was going away voluntarily. The State Troopers would just file my message and wait to see if she comes home in a week or something."

"You could tell them about the fire. Maybe Doc Perkins could tell them something else that would lead to starting an investigation. Have you learned anything about either of the groups of men?"

"Only about the two men that took Mom. I think their boat is called the *Sherry J,* and one of the men is called Vince. He may be my mother's former boyfriend, but…" Brooklyn choked up a little.

"But what?" Bingo asked.

"I'd rather not say. I don't know for sure. All I know is that Mom would never do something like this unless it is really, really important. Which is why Tony and I came to see you." She stopped and took a big breath. "Bingo, I would like to ask for your help. Tony and I think we know where my mother is, and we need to use his dad's boat."

"You think you know where she went? I thought you just said you didn't."

"I don't. It's just a hunch. The place may not even be on a map. Leroy Wilson heard the two men mention a place called the White Grotto, and Tony suggested we ask Old Frank about where it was. He knew about the Grotto but was reluctant for us to go there. The White Grotto and the Grotto have to be the same place."

"Yeah," said Tony. "He said the place has bad spirits, and we shouldn't be there without an adult. The Tlingit people stay away from it."

"So, you want me to be a bad spirit chaser or something?" Bingo replied with a half-smile.

"We need an adult with us. You know about boats. So, I figured I'd ask you to go with us."

"To the Grotto, wherever that is?"

"Yes. Reggie Boyd can show you on a map where it is."

"We can get there and back in one day. No problem." Tony added. "We'll use my dad's boat. It's fast."

Bingo attempted a smile. "I agree. It is a nice boat." He looked across the dock at the sleek cabin cruiser. "What's its speed? Can it do 30 knots?"

"Sure can. It's got twin 200 horsepower engines."

Bingo turned away from them and appeared to be thinking about the request. He made an effort to smooth his disheveled hair as he turned and faced them. "I don't know, Brooklyn. Why are you asking for help from a worthless guy like me? Why not Dr. Perkins or Tony's father? What help could I be? I can't even stand up to two guys."

"They beat you, Bingo. These guys are bad. That's

why I have to find my mom before they do. You know how to operate a boat. You're familiar with the water and the shoreline. If we show you where we need to go, you can get us there and back."

"Well, I owe it to your mom and to you too. If you want my help, I will. Just give me some time to get cleaned up."

"Great! Can you be ready in a half-hour? Tony will get the boat ready. I want to find Mom as soon as possible. We should leave—"

"Now just a minute, young lady," Bingo said, raising a hand. "You need to know the first rule about setting off on a boat trip in this country. You have to be prepared for anything. We're going to need some food, water, and a few other things, like what if we need to start a fire to keep warm? How much fuel is there onboard your dad's boat? We might have to stay somewhere because of bad weather. A trip of just a few hours could end up being a few days." He pointed at the cruiser. "One other thing—that small inflatable your dad keeps tied to the top of the cabin. Does it have enough air in it to stay afloat and get us ashore wherever we're going?"

Tony and Brooklyn looked at each other. Planning for the unexpected never crossed their minds, and they hadn't given any thought to what to do once they arrived at the Grotto.

"Bingo's right about being prepared," said Tony. "My dad uses a checklist. And Bingo needs time to see that aerial map Reggie showed us at the center. He can do that while you and I talk to my dad and get the stuff we need to take."

They left Bingo to clean himself up and headed for

the general store. Brooklyn dashed home and grabbed her sleeping bag and some clothes. She also left a note for Flo. She didn't expect her mom to see it, but she wrote one just in case they missed each other. Besides, Flo had left her a note, so why not do the same.

It was early afternoon before Brooklyn and Bingo Bob untied the dock lines to let Tony maneuver his dad's cabin cruiser out of the harbor. The cabin was roomy as Tony's father used it to carry things to restock his store. It had an area in the bow that could sleep three people if they got cozy. There was a small bathroom between the main cabin and the forward bunk. The main cabin had a table and a small galley with a propane stove and a tiny refrigerator. Tony and Brooklyn had stocked the fridge with sandwich makings, water, and snacks from the store.

On returning to the dock, she found Bingo and Tony busy with the boat. They had topped off the fuel tanks with gas from cans Bingo kept on his boat and with some he borrowed from Kenny. With nothing left for her to do, she watched Bingo and Tony check the life raft, start the engines, then gather around a navigation chart to work out their course. If she hadn't known them both, she might have mistaken them for father and son.

Brooklyn was pleased by the change in Bingo. He was no longer the hung-over, depressed man she had talked to not more than two hours earlier. The man was cheerful and rock-steady. He also looked younger, and it took Brooklyn a few minutes to figure it out. Bingo had shaved. His stubbly beard was gone, and he had trimmed his mustache and the hair around his ears.

As they pulled away from the boat harbor, a lone

raven and the resident seagulls lined up on the outer pier like friends and family waving to their loved ones on a departing cruise ship. She glanced at the spot where the *Sherry J* had been. She wondered if they would find the boat. Would her mother be aboard it, or would they find her already at the Grotto? Brooklyn thought about what Old Frank told them about the place. That it was dangerous and she shouldn't go there. But here she was—headed for the Grotto with her new friends. She shivered and pulled up the collar on her army jacket in response to a sudden chill on the back of her neck.

Tony steered the boat past a group of rotting pilings, which, unlike the seagulls, made her a little uneasy. They seemed like a warning of something to come, of something sinister trying to grab on to them. Old Frank's stern words had evoked the same feeling when he told her to be careful.

As if breaking free of the pilings' grasp, Tony brought the boat up to cruising speed and sped away from the harbor. The boat's wake rolled out behind them, slapping against the piling and rocky shoreline like someone taunting a spider on its web. As the view of Chatham grew smaller, Brooklyn's uneasiness lessened but didn't go away. She still couldn't understand her mother's motives for leaving town with Vince. What she did understand was the urgency of finding them. They could be in real danger, given what had happened in the last twenty-four hours.

Neither Brooklyn nor the others could imagine what lay ahead. Was some ancient evil residing in the Grotto, or was there something new and horrible hovering over the place? Brooklyn wondered if there actually was any mystery associated with the Grotto like the old Shaman described. Old Frank had been hesitant to tell them about its strange past and the Tlingit legend associated with it. But the urgency of finding her mother made her determined to follow her instincts. She believed the raven at the end of the dock was a good sign and not a trickster.

The gray gloom of the morning sky was gone and the afternoon sun brightened the water surface ahead of them, giving Brooklyn another encouraging sign. The surface glistened like millions of dancing crystals. It was hypnotic and seemed to invite them into a more pleasant realm. As the boat reached cruising speed, the endless band of bleached rocky shoreline below a dark green forest became a blur. Once out of sight of Chatham, they might as well have been a hundred miles away, for there were no more signs of habitation—not a road, house, or dock could be seen anywhere. The Alaskan wilderness swallowed up all signs of human occupation. They had entered the wild homeland of the Tlingit—Tony's homeland.

While Brooklyn was deep in thought, Tony was exultant. He stood confidently at the wheel. From the look about him, she could tell he loved the water and the feel of the powerful engines in his hands He looked like a different boy. For years Brooklyn had considered Tony one of the town's bullies and avoided him whenever she could. She had never given him the slightest chance to become a friend. Now she knew that he only acted the way he had because of the other town boys. Brooklyn smiled. She was glad Tony had asked to be her friend and agreed to help her find her mother.

She glanced at Bingo, standing by Tony's side

studying a well-worn navigation chart and pointing out the course for Tony to take. He held the chart like a treasure map, the "X" marking their destination and the promise of a reward.

The speeding boat passed a group of small rocky islets. One islet had a lone spruce tree with an eagle's nest high in its branches. The other two islets were barren and exposed, their rocky shoreline glistening with mussels and brown kelp. Three harbor seals that had been sleeping on the rocks and enjoying the warmth of the sun slipped into the water as the boat's wake dashed against the shoreline, disturbing their mid-day slumber. Their gray heads bobbed to the surface like rubber balls to stare at the passing boat.

As they passed the islets, Bingo motioned for Tony to swing wide around a reef and head for a buoy about two miles offshore. The cruiser could probably safely pass over the reef, but Bingo knew it was prudent to stay away from the rocks and shallow waters marked by the buoy.

Brooklyn saw a huge splash about a mile away and directly in front of the boat.

"Whale!" hollered Tony. He had seen it too. "Did you see it breach?"

"Keep an eye on that location," Bingo responded. "It could happen again. Sometimes they will breach over and over."

Tony made a slight course adjustment so the boat would not run over the spot where the humpback whale had surfaced. Moments later, it breached again. Its enormous body erupted entirely from the depths, curved on its side, and then hit the surface with a huge splash that rocked their boat.

Bingo let out a whoop in his excitement, raised a hand, and pointed at the whale. "Just look at that. He's greeting us. The humpbacks are usually here in the deep water next to the reef, either feeding or playing. Sometimes they surface right beside my boat."

"They're beautiful, Bingo," said Brooklyn. "I've only seen them from a long way off. This is the first time I have been so close to them. Are they dangerous?"

"They're gentle, intelligent creatures. I've had whales surface and drift right alongside me, and we'd stare at each other eye to eye—like communicating without saying a word. Their eyes are like windows into their lives and memories. I could see their long journeys across the Pacific and how the females raised and cared for their calves."

Bingo stared out the window and scanning the water for another sighting.

"They talk, too. Well, it's actually a sing-song. And when they are bubble feeding for herring, the big fellows will let out a bellow like they are belching from the satisfaction of a good meal." Bingo chuckled to himself. Tony laughed.

Brooklyn smiled as she listened to Bingo chat about the whales. Another one breached with a huge splash. They all whooped this time.

Then it suddenly dawned on her that Bingo considered the whales to be his friends. Bingo wasn't a lonely man. He enjoyed the company of the humpback whales on the reef. They brought him as much comfort as any family. She had her pair of bald eagles and their new chick in the nest on the cliff to visit, and Bingo had his whales on the reef.

Chapter 22

Flo Whiting stoked the firebox of the old wood stove so she could prepare a meal for herself and Vince. Her eyes were red from crying, and she was still furious with Ronnie for leaving with her ATV. Vince stirred on the bed, but at least he was sleeping. While anxious to see if there would be any improvement in his condition, she did not hold out much hope for his recovery. She reminded herself of what Doc Perkins said—the odds were not good. Another dose of the vaccine needed to be administered when he woke up.

She rinsed out a pot, placed it on the stove, and then picked up her backpack, which was lying on the floor where Ronnie had tossed it. She checked to see what was left in the bag. Shaking her head in disgust, she dumped the contents on the kitchen counter. Ronnie had run off with quite a lot of their supplies. They had maybe two more days of food, and then she would have to risk hiking into Chatham to pick up more.

Flo glanced at the counter by the sink where they kept their drinking water. At least Ronnie had left all the water behind. There were two full jugs. She poured some water into a pan, added the contents of a soup packet, and waited for it to boil. After eating what she wanted, she roused Vince.

"Vince, wake up. How are you feeling? You need to eat something, and then I'll give you your second shot."

Vince rolled over to face her, showing a goofy smile as he used to when they were together years before. "You're still here. I heard the ATV a few minutes ago and thought maybe you left me."

He was lucid, which was a good sign. Flo needed to talk with him.

"Ronnie up and left us."

Concern shadowed Vince's face. "Did he go into town for something? If he did, someone might see him and follow him back out here."

"I don't think so, Vince. He might not be coming back. He sneaked out on me while I was dozing." She pointed towards the kitchen. "He took most of our food, too. We might have enough left for two or three days, and then I'll have to go into Chatham."

Vince struggled to sit up, only to fall back. Flo sat down on the edge of the bed and helped pull him up to a sitting position. "I have some hot soup ready. You've got to eat some of it."

Vince let Flo move him and didn't react to her touching him. To Flo, it was another good sign. He hadn't become aggressive, at least not yet.

She went over to the stove and used a rag to pick up the hot pan and carry it over to Vince. His hands were shaky, but he took the spoon and ate a few bites. Flo decided this was a good time to learn more about what Vince and the others had been up to.

"What were you all doing, Vince? I've got a right to know. Especially now that we are in a pretty bad situation."

Vince nodded, thinking about what to say. He took another spoonful. "You're right, Flo. I haven't been treating you fairly. You do have a right to know. I've been in trouble all my life and always found a way out of it. This time it looks a lot worse."

"Why, Vince? Is it the people who are looking for you?" Flo sat on the bed beside him again and put a gentle hand on his arm.

"Yeah. This dude is a bad one, Flo. His name is Johnny Kwan. He's Chinese and a low-level operative in a crime syndicate. He buys illegal seafood—things harvested out of season and exports them to places in Southeast Asia, where they bring high prices on the black market. That's what makes me afraid of him. He's got quotas to meet and has to show his bosses that he's tough with guys like me that do the real dirty work. Two years ago, me and another guy from down by Ketchikan had a little scheme where we would shoot a black bear and take their gallbladders and sell them. Kwan was the local buyer. He ships them to China, where they're used in traditional medicine. Well, I needed a better boat, and Kwan loaned me three hundred and fifty thousand dollars. The loan had a caveat that whenever I had certain stuff to sell, he would be the exclusive buyer—salmon eggs, sea urchin, sea cucumber, or sea otter pelts. About a year ago, one of his goons found me in a bar in Juneau and informed me that his boss had a market for a bunch of sea otter pelts. Maybe you know that as an Alaskan Native, it's all right for me to gather the pelts for subsistence and ceremonial purposes. The thing is, while I can do this, I'm not supposed to sell them to anybody. The guy told me that Kwan would pay top dollar, and besides, I couldn't refuse because I owed him a lot of money. I agreed to deliver 300 pelts. With what Kwan is willing to pay for them, the three of us would have enough money for the winter, and I could make a big payment on my loan. I knew where there were thousands of sea otters, figured out how to harvest them, and had stumbled upon a great hidden spot to process the pelts. It was a perfect little operation." He took another bite of soup.

"Only we got sick. There was something weird about the mine shaft where we disposed of the carcasses. That phone call I got? It was from Kwan, and he wanted his pelts. He took what I had and said I wasn't going to make good on my loan. He called me all sorts of names and said I would die a stupid little nobody. I'm afraid he's right, Flo. If I live, the Alaska Fish and Game folks are going to throw me in jail for a very long time."

"Oh, Vince. How could you kill those beautiful creatures? You've wronged your people and your culture."

"They may be beautiful creatures to some people, but their population numbers are out of control. With their voracious appetites, they're wiping out our shellfish along with sea urchins, sea cucumbers, and clams. Our crab fishery could be gone in a few years—something that has been an important part of Native subsistence and culture. That's two good reasons why we Natives should kill them or at least help manage them. I know that I lost my culture a long time ago when my people banned me from the tribe. The way I look at it, I'm helping to preserve Native culture and making right what I did wrong. Do you recall what I did years ago, Flo?"

"Yes, I remember. You killed several bald eagles

and sold the feathers and body parts to a white man visiting from California, but wasn't it intended to be a temporary ban?"

"Not in the eyes of the traditional elders. They were pretty mad at me. They could have just excluded me from the community for a year, like make me live alone on an island without any family support. But three of the elders said they never wanted to see me again. In their eyes, I had dishonored the Tlingit culture, and I was no longer Tlingit."

After the soup, Vince looked better. Some color returned to his cheeks. Though when he started to stand up, she wasn't so sure about his condition.

"Let me help you," said Flo. "Are you sure you should be on your feet?"

"I've got to use the outhouse. I'll be okay."

Vince was unsteady, but he made it to the back door and then walked slowly to the small building a dozen yards away. While Vince was outside, Flo finished the soup and made some coffee. She assumed Ronnie didn't drink coffee since he had left all of it.

While waiting for the water to heat up, she heard a vehicle come up the road and into the camp. Her fears were confirmed after rushing to a front window. The same vehicle that had checked on them the day before was headed towards them.

The pickup truck stopped directly in front of the house, and two guys jumped out. One had a rifle, and the other was carrying a pistol as they approached the front door. Flo was opening the back door when they crashed through the front. The one holding the pistol fired a shot that hit the door frame inches from her shoulder. She froze, afraid to move, and turned around slowly to face the two men.

The one with the pistol looked her over and grinned. "You're Flo Whiting, aren't you?" He glanced around the room. "Where's Vince?"

Before Flo could answer, Vince rushed into the room from behind the two men. He had gone around the house to the front door. He slammed into the first man, who was carrying the rifle. AJ hit the wall and slid to the floor, dazed. His rifle flew across the room and slid under the kitchen table. Screaming something unintelligible, Vince charged the second man, knocking him to the floor. The pistol discharged again as it fell from the man's hand, with the bullet hitting the linoleum-covered floor and ricocheting into a wall. Before the man could get on his feet, Vince was on top of him, his fists slamming into his body and face. Flo could not believe Vince was capable of taking on the two men. He reacted like a boxer showing a sudden burst of unbelievable energy. AJ leaped to his feet and grabbed Flo as she was scrambling for the rifle. He threw her against a wall. Flo flopped to the floor.

The other man and Vince rolled on the floor, punching each other. Vince landed several hard hits to his ribs, and the man grabbed one of Vince's wrists, trying to control him. Vince was fighting like a crazed person, unaware of any damage to himself. They both struggled to reach the dropped pistol. With one of his hands restrained, Vince saw an opening and butted the man with his head, and then he bit down hard on the man's arm. The man screamed as he tried to yank his arm free, but Vince had clamped his jaws.

Picking up the rifle, AJ charged over to the two struggling men and slammed the rifle butt into the side of Vince's head. Vince collapsed.

"You okay, Will?" he said.

"He bit me!" Will hollered, grabbing his arm, which was bleeding profusely. "He bit a chunk out of my arm, AJ!" Blood soaked the front of his shirt, and he rolled on the floor in agony.

"Shut up, you sissy," said AJ.

Flo ran over to Vince and knelt beside him.

"Is he dead?" asked AJ over Will's hollering.

Flo checked Vince's neck for a pulse. It was weak. "No, but he could die if we don't get him to a doctor."

"That ain't gonna happen," said AJ. "We've got orders from Hutch Senior to take him and you back to the house." He looked at his brother. "Will, get it together, man. Are you goin' to let a stupid bite slow you down? Wrap it up with somethin', and let's get these two in the truck. I'll take her out. You drag Vince out."

Will sat on the floor and began wrapping his handkerchief carefully around his wounded arm, whimpering all the while. Flo knocked AJ's arm aside as he tried to grab her and continued to help Vince. She used a towel lying on the floor beside an overturned chair to wipe off some of Will's blood from around his mouth.

She looked over at Will and then up at AJ. "You might want to think twice about that. Vince was diagnosed with rabies by Doc Perkins in Chatham. You better get your brother to a doctor fast, or he could be dead in a week."

"Son of a…" AJ looked at Will and then at Vince and Flo. He didn't know what to do.

Chapter 23

Wally Perkins carried a cup of hot tea into his home office and sat down at his cluttered desk. He had just finished an early lunch with his wife while waiting for a return phone call from Dr. Frances Collins, a colleague with the CDC. The two had last met in southwestern Arizona concerning an outbreak of the hantavirus, a highly contagious virus found in small rodents. It resulted in the infection of eighteen children at an elementary school. Dr. Collins had led the team, which included Perkins, to identify the host animal and control the outbreak. Collins and Perkins discovered it was the long-eared kangaroo rat, which had burrows in the schoolyard. The infected animals were leaving their droppings on the playground equipment. The children playing on the equipment would rub their noses or eyes, resulting in a non-bite exposure. Wally wondered if a similar situation had occurred with Vince James in the mine shaft inhabited by rabid bats. He hoped Frances's group could provide him with some assistance.

The phone rang. Wally smiled, expecting it to be Frances. But it wasn't. Instead, it was a doctor with the Juneau hospital.

"Doctor Perkins? This is Sam Young. I'm a first-year resident here at the hospital in Juneau. I just learned that our pharmacy got an urgent request to send you some rabies vaccine. Are you presently treating someone with it?"

"Why yes, a male, maybe in his early forties," replied Wally.

"I treated a young woman with suspected rabies yesterday. She and her husband were camping on a lake over your way. She said she was bitten by a river otter that showed signs of being rabid. I got test results back this morning, and the results were positive."

"Hmm, two rabies cases, both on Baranof Island. You said the woman has been infected due to a bite from an otter?"

"Yes."

"The male I examined was non-bite infected, which means there are two different modes of infection. That's not good."

"Something else you should know, Doctor Perkins." There was a change in the doctor's voice that seemed to echo his own concern. "I reported the incident to the Alaska State Troopers while the couple was here at the ER, and they sent over an Officer Dave Williams to interview them and me. Officer Williams said it would be a while before they can look into it further. The couple was camping in a pretty remote spot at a lake with Forest Service cabins, a place called Evans Lake."

"Evans Lake? Never heard of it, but I can look it up."

"Me neither. I'm from Michigan and have only been living in Alaska for six months. I love getting out and exploring small lakes. Except I haven't had an opportunity to get more than twenty-five miles from Juneau because of my on-call hours in our urgent care unit."

"I know what you mean," Perkins said, recalling his overtime hours with the Public Health Service a while back.

"Uh—the husband said they hired a local guide service to fly them to the lake. They were on their honeymoon. The pilot dropped them off at a cabin on the west end of Evans Lake, and yesterday, he picked them up at a second cabin at the east end. Mr. Wilkins said the guide was an owner-operator of an outfit called Eco Wings."

"Hmm, that's probably the same pilot that brought me the vaccine. He said something about being out this way for a pre-arranged pick-up. Thanks for the call about this, Sam. I'll try to reach the State Troopers. They could be unaware of the magnitude of the situation."

"Glad I could help," Young responded. "Hope your patient recovers. I'm giving the woman a good prognosis."

"Good to hear that your patient will recover. My patient should have checked himself into your hospital days ago, and he refused to hang around for my observation after starting the medication. His odds of surviving are pretty grim, I'm afraid."

Taking Sam Young's advice, he called the State Trooper's office in Juneau. They needed to know this required a higher priority than they were giving it. He reached their dispatcher, only to learn that Officer Williams was not in the office. He got the officer's cell phone number, and Williams answered his call right away.

"Dave, this is Wally Perkins over in Chatham. We met when you were here for a community presentation at the school last spring."

"You're the doctor there, right?"

"Yeah, kind of the de facto doctor. I treat local folks when I'm in town. I'm a consultant to the World Health Organization."

"Interesting. I would never have guessed that. How are things over in Chatham? It's been at least six months since I was over your way. We've got a couple of Troopers at our post in Hoonah that cover general law enforcement matters in your region. My partner and I just lend a hand when the situation is a wildlife case. What can I do for you, Wally?"

"I just got a call from Dr. Sam Young, the one you interviewed at the Juneau hospital? I'm treating a man for rabies and he told me about the rabies case you've been assigned. I understand you interviewed a honeymoon couple that had been camping at Evans Lake on Baranof Island."

"Yup, the woman, Wilkins is her name, was bitten by a suspected rabid animal, a river otter, she said. My supervisor has requested that I investigate it. My partner and I plan to head over there, but it may be tomorrow. I'm not even sure how to get to this Evans Lake."

"Me neither. But there's got to be some geographic connection between where your case and my case were infected. The only other reference I have is to a geographic feature called the Grotto."

"That's a new one to me, and I was born and raised here."

"I plan to check with a few people here in Chatham. If I get any more information, I'll let you know."

"Okay, that will give me time to wrap up a drug case we're handling. We should have left this afternoon, but our current case of a simple boat theft got complicated and now involves illegal drugs. It will take at least the rest of today to wrap it up and update our reports. Then we can start to look for a rabid river otter. If we can locate it, and that's a big if, the animal will probably already be dead. We'll try to find the carcass and send it to our lab in Anchorage. The incident will be history. Case closed."

"I'm not so sure about that being the scenario here. This could be a symptom of a bigger problem—like your illegal drug case. With two other incidents of rabies that occurred in the area, they could be related to yours."

"Two cases? I thought you just said you had one case. How come these haven't been reported? Were these folks bitten by a river otter, too? And who are the victims?"

"I don't have all the facts, but one man is reportedly dead. But that's unconfirmed. I was told he might have been bitten by an otter as well. I've never heard of such an incident until now."

"Mrs. Wilkins and her husband were pretty sure it was a river otter. It could have been another small animal, like a mink or weasel. I haven't taken the time to check the state records to see if any similar cases have been reported."

Wally continued to fill Williams in on what he knew. "I can't confirm how my patient was infected. Based on my questions while treating him, he could have contracted the disease from the dead guy, or like your victim, from an animal bite. But there is also the possibility of infection indirectly from a bat. He was working near an old mine shaft."

"Doc, if there is a suspected death, no matter how the person died, I'm going to need a name. I've got to file a report, and the Troopers in Hoonah will follow up. And if there's a connection to the incident that I'm investigating, I need the information. It would save a lot of time if we knew where this man is right now, where he has been, and of course, if there was anyone else with him."

Wally hesitated. "I have no information on the man who apparently died. As to my patient, well, given my professional opinion, he is probably going to die anyway. I suppose I could tell you what I do know. His name is Vince James. He's Tlingit—"

"Vince James? I know the guy. He's got a record."

"I'm not surprised," replied Wally. "When I examined him, there was some reason he couldn't remain in town or go to the hospital. I was told he had to go into hiding somewhere."

"Hold on a minute while I check something," said Williams. He used his laptop to enter the statewide law enforcement database and searched for outstanding warrants. "Well, checking the database, he isn't wanted for anything. My guess is, given the man's reputation, he's probably up to something illegal."

"There was another guy with him who looked like a real nervous Nellie," said Wally. "Like he was about to bolt if somebody even yelled in his direction. I couldn't decide whether he was worried about Vince being sick, getting sick himself, or the fact that someone was looking for both of them."

"Did you get a name?"

Wally thought for a minute. "It was Ron or Ronald, something like that. Ronnie, that's what he was called."

"Let's try that one," said Williams. "Nope. Struck out again. Only one Ronald and he's been arrested up in Anchorage. So again, there's no reason for either of them to be dodging an outstanding warrant. Kind of puzzling for a guy to be so sick that he might die yet avoid proper medical treatment. He has to have a serious reason."

"Sorry I couldn't be a better help."

"That's okay. I appreciate your information. The officers in Hoonah will contact you and check around. If James contacts you again, call them immediately. Use their direct number rather than going through dispatch here in Juneau. Do you have that number?"

"Probably, but why don't I take it from you." He was about to hang up when he thought of something else. "By the way, did you hear about the fire here in Chatham?"

"No, I haven't heard."

"Might have been set intentionally." Perkins didn't want to say that it was Flo's home and that she was with Vince. Then Williams would want to know how to reach Flo for questioning.

"A report of possible arson would fall in the jurisdiction of our Troopers in Hoonah as well. They're going to be right busy. So, thanks for the call, Wally, and keep me advised about anything more on this rabies incident, okay? I've got to file a report with the supervisor and post both of these cases to the State's database."

After he hung up, Wally saw he had a voice mail message. Turned out Frances Collins was on vacation and would not return for another ten days. Even if the CDC could help, it would take them too long to mobilize a team. He would be on his own in addressing a potential rabies outbreak with a strong possibility that more people could be infected and possibly die before it could be stopped.

With the information he'd got from Williams, he was even further from any answers as to the source. How was the disease being transmitted? He needed a lot more information about rabies hosts and how he might prevent a major outbreak.

What's more, Evans Lake was most likely in a wilderness area with limited access, and he had very few resources to get there, let alone capture any animals. He definitely needed some help.

Wally logged into his satellite Internet connection and started searching for rabies incidents in Alaska. Williams was right in saying there were only a few cases every year, but the reports didn't help. They had all occurred in extreme northern Alaska, and all involved an attack by a fox or a domestic dog. In several cases, the victim had died because they were in a remote area without access to treatment or hadn't known they'd been bitten by a rabid animal. One guy had been so drunk he didn't even realize he had been bitten at all. There were no reports of people in Alaska being bitten by a bat. Still, when he searched for incidences in British Columbia, he found reports of rabies infection that all came from contact with bats.

Wally felt frustrated—foxes and dogs in Northern Alaska and bats common in Northern British Columbia.

He decided to explore the bat angle further and expanded his search about bats serving as a host for rabies. He learned the virus took several forms once it was incubated in a warm-blooded animal. The virus then migrated within the host body to the brain. There were two forms of the disease—the furious form and the paralytic. The furious form was what he had warned Flo Whiting about. In this case, the victim could become aggressive, show a tendency to want to bite things, with their mouth producing excessive amounts of saliva. There were other symptoms that he should have mentioned to her, such as sensitivity to light.

After an hour of research, Perkins wasn't any closer to narrowing down a suspected host for the disease. He had a long list. Infected bats could have bitten just about any local species of small mammals—fox, mink, muskrat, weasel, marten, skunk, raccoon, beaver, or otter. Any of these animals could then have bitten a human. The State's online records indicated that foxes were generally the reservoir for the virus up north. But in other parts of the United States, skunks and raccoons often carried it.

He then remembered having read somewhere about Southeast Alaska having quite a few fox farms in the early 1900s. Some smaller islands were used for raising foxes by letting them run free. However, he found no records of fox farms on Baranof Island, although that didn't mean there weren't any.

There was another possibility—one he really didn't want to consider. He had heard Old Frank speak about an old legend—about people being viciously attacked by river otters. Could the otters in the Evans Lake area be a dormant host of the rabies virus? Could the disease be endemic to the area because of the otters? Were there other species of mammals infected as well?

Perkins learned from his research that the furious variant of the virus can lie dormant in the host for years, and then it suddenly migrates to the mouth and brain. When that happened, the animal became crazed and began biting any other creature it encountered, thereby spreading the disease. The phenomenon was one of the reasons that the virus was nearly impossible to eradicate.

Perkins shook his head as he imagined the consequences.

Could the whole island be in danger from another outbreak of rabies? Other animal populations, people, and pets could be in grave danger. The spread of the disease had to be stopped, but how? How many infected animals were there? Was it already too late to have the area quarantined? How big an area should be quarantined—the whole island?

Wally began to worry whether a panic could ensue. He had to start by getting hold of potentially infected animals and samples of brain matter. Suspected animals would have to be killed or trapped then tested by a laboratory. Maybe he should call Dave Williams back or inform his fellow State Troopers over in Hoonah about his fears.

Perkins suddenly realized that he had failed to mention to Williams that several people had just left Chatham to search the Grotto area for someone.

How could I have forgotten to mention the kids to Williams?

He had been too focused on the rabies cases. Brooklyn and her friends could find themselves unawares in a dangerous situation where one of them could be bitten by a rabid animal.

Perkins tried to call Williams back. The only answer he got was to leave a voice mail. He left a message about Brooklyn and her friends, then put the phone down and thought for a moment.

It's gonna be up to me to do something, but what? I don't know the first thing about trapping live animals, except mice, and haven't fired a gun in years. I need some help and fast.

Chapter 24

By afternoon, a brisk southwest wind was whipping up the waters in Chatham Strait. Three-foot swells forced Tony to slow the big outboard engines to avoid taking waves over the bow. Traveling in the boat got uncomfortable during the last few miles before the entrance to the bay where they expected to find the Grotto. Brooklyn and Bingo had to crowd into the cabin with Tony and hold on to anything handy to avoid getting wet.

As they rounded the last point, Bingo checked his navigation chart and announced that he believed they had found the correct bay.

Tony looked at the water surface. It was rough but not as bad as the seas he had been battling for the last half hour. He slowed the engines further and set a course for the far end of the bay, hoping it would get better.

Bingo studied the waters in the bay too, and like Tony, he didn't like what he saw. There wasn't any calm water to use for anchoring the boat. The southwest wind was pushing the seas directly into the bay.

The bay was long and narrow, with a steep shoreline of granite rock on both sides. A dense forest came right down to the coastline. At the very end of the bay, a stream entered and flowed across a pebble beach.

Lifting his binoculars, he studied the area beyond

the bay. A range of rugged, snow-covered mountains lay beyond the nearer ridges. Nowhere were there any signs of human habitation—not a road, roof, power pole, nothing to indicate anyone resided here. It was wilderness as far as he could see.

Brooklyn was the first to break the silence. "Where is the Grotto, Bingo? I don't see anything here."

Bingo lowered the binoculars. "I'm not sure," he said." Based on the information Old Frank gave you, this should be the right place." He scrutinized the shoreline opposite the stream. There was a cleft in the forested ridge above it that indicated the possibility of a second stream. The mouth of the second stream could exist behind several large rocks.

"It could be over there behind those rocks, but we'll need to use the inflatable dinghy to check."

Bingo had another concern which he did not mention.

Why isn't there a boat anchored in the bay? Had the boat used by Flo been here and left, or was someone still here?

The emptiness of the bay bothered him, but it was getting too late to look at the next bay along the strait.

"Tony, Brooklyn, I'm not absolutely sure this is the right place, but we don't have a lot of daylight left. There may be enough time for me to use the dinghy to see if there is an entrance to the Grotto. If this is the right place, I'm assuming it must be in the corner opposite the stream with the pebble beach. I will try to locate it. When I get back, we can try to anchor the boat. If it holds, then I'll start ferrying the two of you ashore one at a time."

Bingo looked directly at Brooklyn.

"Don't get your hopes up. It doesn't look like anyone is here. But we can check if we can get through the Grotto. Right now, that's a big if."

Tony was looking at how close they were to the shore. "It's not very far to the shore. Dad usually allows three people in the dinghy."

"That might work in calm water, but the wind is getting stronger and creating bigger waves," replied Bingo. "They could swamp the dinghy."

They moved the boat closer to the shore just off the pebble beach. Salmon were milling about the mouth of the little stream. Occasionally one would leap out of the water.

"Tony, I don't think the anchor will work here. You will need to keep the motors running and keep the boat in the deeper water. Can you do that?"

"You bet. No problem."

"Okay. Then let's get the inflatable over the side. Brooklyn, I'll need your help."

Tony stayed at the helm while Brooklyn and Bingo wrestled the dinghy off the top of the cabin and dumped it over the side. Bingo climbed aboard and got the oars set. He nodded to Brooklyn, who released the bowline. Bingo looked around and then started rowing towards the rocks in the far corner where he hoped to find the entrance to the Grotto. He had to struggle with the oars in the rough water as the wind pushed the little rubber inflatable around. Spray from his oars soaked his clothes. Finally, he reached the shore and disappeared behind the rocks. He was back in view within a few minutes and rowing back towards them.

The inflatable bounced against the cruiser, and Bingo had difficulty keeping it close while Brooklyn reached for the bowline. "Grab the line and tie it off," said Bingo, hollering over the increasing wind. "We got lucky. This is the place. I found the entrance to the Grotto, but we have a problem."

"What's the problem?" asked Brooklyn. "Can't we go ashore?"

"The Grotto entrance is flooded by the high tide. We have to wait for it to drop. Could be a couple of hours."

"What are we going to do?" hollered Tony. "It will be dark in a couple of hours. I don't think we can make it back around the point, and the water here in the bay is getting rougher."

"There's a big rock sticking out from the shore, maybe fifty feet from the entrance to the Grotto. It looks like it might provide enough protection for a small boat. I think we can ease the boat in there and tie a line to a tree on the shore."

"Are you sure about that?" asked Tony. "My dad will be pretty mad if we damage his boat."

"Since there's not enough daylight to try to get back to Chatham, we have two choices. Find shelter along the shore or put the boat on the beach over by the stream. It will become grounded as the tide drops. That's pretty risky and could damage the motors, and then we would be stuck here until someone sees us. Our best choice is to get behind that rock."

Tony nodded his head reluctantly and extended a hand to help Bingo climb back aboard the cruiser. The inflatable trailed behind them tied to the stern as they motored slowly over to the shoreline.

Bingo was right. The water was calmer, and they were out of the wind when they got right next to the shore. The rocky shoreline was steep, and the water was deep right up to the bank. Bingo stood on the boat's bow and tossed a line over the limb of a tree, leaning out over the water. He hollered to Tony. "Grab the line. Tie it off to that side cleat next to you, but leave some slack to allow for the outgoing tide. We'll have to check it later."

Tony wrapped the end of the line around the cleat a couple of times. The boat was so close to the shore if he stretched his arm, he could touch it. Looking over the side into the water, he could see the bottom. It was deep.

Bingo slid back into the cabin. "We should be okay as long as the wind doesn't change direction and push the boat against the rocks. We'll place all the rubber bumpers on that side of the hull just in case." There was nothing more they could do now but wait until morning and low tide.

Brooklyn stared at the darkening forest above them for several minutes with an occasional glance at the entrance to the Grotto that Bingo had discovered. The scent of the rainforest rolled over them like a blanket of fog wrapping the boat in its timeless grip. The closeness of the silent forest was a strange contrast to the open sea they had experienced for the last several hours. She wondered what they would find in its depths beyond the Grotto. It was dark and not all that inviting. She hoped Mom was here. If she wasn't, this would end up being another wild goose chase like her search in Hoonah. She shuddered a little and turned away, not wanting to stare at it any longer. She dug into her backpack and found a package of Oreo cookies to share as they settled down to wait. Later, they could eat the cold sandwiches and protein bars they had packed.

Tony was adjusting the canvas flap that enclosed the boat's cabin when they heard the sound of humpback whales blowing just off the entrance to the bay.

"Now that's a comforting sound," remarked Bingo as he offered a cheery smile to the others. "Listen, the whales are being friendly and keeping us company."

"Why do you call the whales your friends, Bingo?" Brooklyn asked as she took a bite of a cookie.

"Well, first, they're intelligent creatures. Whales and dolphins are believed to have very high intelligence, maybe close to that of humans. They have excellent communication skills and talk to each other. Sometimes I think they talk to me when I'm out fishing. I know they watch out for me."

"They do?" replied Brooklyn. "Really?"

"Yup. I had trouble with my motor once, and when I finally got it running, it was dark, and I didn't have a spotlight. I was having difficulty finding my way back to Chatham. One of the whales blew and surfaced right beside my boat. I slowed to an idle to avoid the whale, and when I did, I heard waves hitting a pile of rocks right in front of the boat. I think the whale was alerting me to imminent danger. I could have run right into the rocks."

"Wow, you could have died because you didn't see the rocks. Even if you managed to get to the shore, this is remote country." Tony said. "There's no place to go, and you have to hope someone spots you on the shore."

Bingo absently scratched his freshly shaved chin as he went on. "That wasn't the first time the whales came to my assistance. On my trip to Alaska, I got caught in the fog while crossing Dixon Entrance to Ketchikan. My little compass acted weirdly like there was some magnetic interference, and I lost my heading. I couldn't afford to buy a GPS for navigation, and so I was using a chart. If I followed a wrong bearing, I might miss the channel and be heading out to sea. To make matters worse, I had stupidly not topped off my fuel in Prince Rupert, because I was almost out of money. Making a long crossing and being low on fuel is something an experienced mariner would never do. I misjudged how much Alaskan tidal currents can slow down a boat and cause you to use more fuel to maintain speed."

"What did you do?" Brooklyn asked.

"I found myself in the middle of a whole pod of whales, including several babies with their mothers. They kept surfacing all around me. I nearly forgot my predicament and just watched as one and then another would surface, exhale, and submerge. They were traveling, blowing every few minutes, and moving fast. Then I realized that because it was spring, they should be headed for Alaska just like me. So I put my boat in gear and followed them. One big male seemed to understand what I was doing, or maybe he was just protecting the young calves. Anyway, he moved close to the right side of my boat and matched my speed. If I had used an oar, I could have touched his side each time he surfaced to breathe. We traveled that way for at least two hours when the fog finally dissipated, and I saw my landmarks and the entrance to the channel. I put the engine in neutral and relaxed."

Bingo opened the little onboard refrigerator, pulled out the sandwiches they had stowed there, and handed one to Tony and one to Brooklyn. He took a bite of his sandwich and continued his story.

"I hadn't realized that I had been worrying so much about my situation. My shirt under my sweater and windbreaker was soaked with sweat, and I was chilled. I pulled off my wet shirt and found another in my bunk area. By the time I put my sweater back on and returned to my seat at the wheel, the whales had moved on. As they were swimming away, the big male did a full breach. I think it was his way of saying welcome to Alaska."

"Wow!" Tony said with a mouthful of sandwich.

Brooklyn was entranced by Bingo's description of the incident, but there was something else she wanted to ask him. "Bingo, could you tell us why you decided to move to Alaska? I have heard rumors in Chatham, but I don't believe them."

Rather than look at her, Bingo stared out one of the cabin windows into the gathering darkness and didn't respond for a minute or two. When he did, the excitement in his voice when he had spoken about the whales was gone. His words came more slowly, and Brooklyn could hear some sadness in his voice.

"About the things said about me in Chatham, I'm afraid the rumors are probably pretty close to the truth. I came to Alaska because I was running away from my previous life. It was a good life too, up to a point."

"What happened, Bingo?" Tony asked. "And is Bingo really your name?"

"No, I got that name after living in Chatham for a while. My real name is Robert Fuller or Bob Fuller, whichever you prefer. But it's a name attached to my previous life and its destruction. I had a good job, but it had a lot of stress. I started drinking at lunch and after work. My wife talked to me about it, but I ignored her. It got worse, and I started forgetting things like stopping to pick up bread and milk when she asked me. Then one day, I was supposed to pick up my daughter's dance outfit at the dry cleaners for a performance that evening. I got to the cleaners too late, and as a result, she didn't get to dance. She was devastated, and my wife was furious and made me move out." He sighed.

"I lived on my boat at the marina for several months, but my drinking got worse until one day I woke up and discovered I hadn't gone to work for nearly a week. I lost my job, and after my money was gone, I couldn't afford to pay the moorage and utility bill at the marina. So, I decided to set off in the boat for Alaska."

"Have you seen your family since then?" Brooklyn asked.

"I've tried many times, but my wife refuses all contact. She even returns letters I've written to my daughter. So, the whales are my family now."

"Thank you for telling us, Bingo," Brooklyn said. "I'm sad about your family, but now I know you have a new family, the whales out there."

As they settled down for the night, Brooklyn reflected on Bingo's life. It was not just the first things she noticed—shaving his face and trimming his hair. He stood more erect. His vision was steady and focused instead of being dulled from alcohol. His eyes were no longer watery and they shone with the same excitement of adventure as Tony's.

Just before they left the dock, Bingo told her he was proud she'd asked him to accompany them. Ever since his arrival in Chatham, Bingo had been shunned by the residents of the tiny town. Few people in Chatham wanted anything to do with him. He was the town drunk left to live alone on a small derelict boat in the harbor. He thought he had escaped an unbearable situation in Seattle only to find himself imprisoned on that little boat. He told Brooklyn that he made himself a promise. When they had found her mother and returned to Chatham, he would not go back to his old life. Chatham could have a better life for him—he just needed to be open and accept it. No more living like a hermit on a derelict boat and constantly drinking himself into a stupor. He was going to either burn that boat or sink it and find an apartment or a house in town.

****

A steady rain began late in the evening. The beat of raindrops on the cabin roof and windows drowned out the wind and waves hitting the rocky shore. The boat rocked every few minutes as a larger swell entered the bay and deflected off the shore. Each rise and fall of the boat caused the tie line to the tree limb to go taut, then slack. Nobody remembered to check it.

The trio settled down in sleeping bags and blankets and finally nodded off to sleep one by one. Brooklyn lay awake longer than the others, thinking about what Bingo had shared. They were very personal memories, and she was glad he shared them. The man didn't deserve to be known as the town drunk or whatever the people in Chatham made him out to be. Yes, he did drink, and often he was seen drunk. She had witnessed it herself. But when he was sober, he was a kind person. She hoped the goodness in him would finally win out.

Meanwhile, the constant jerk of the tie line gave her a sense of security that they were safe, making her drowsy. Eventually, she fell asleep.

None of them noticed when the jerking stopped, and there was a change in the boat's movement. With each jerk of the line, Tony's poor tie of the line to the cleat loosened. Inch by inch, the end of the line worked its way off the cleat. It was after midnight when the line freed itself, and the boat began to drift. The fall of the tide pulled the boat from the shore, and soon it was drifting into the center of the bay then pushed broadside by the wind and waves.

Bingo was the first to notice the drastic change in the boat's motion as it rolled from side to side. He scrambled to his feet, brushed aside the cabin's canvas enclosure, and nearly fell onto the back deck when a big wave hit the boat. His first thought was the inflatable. A soft bump against the hull told him it was still there. Still, they were in big trouble. In the rain and the darkness, he had no idea how far they had drifted.

He went to the helm and turned on the ignition key. Nothing happened. The engines didn't start. Bingo swore to himself and hollered. "Brooklyn, Tony, wake up! We're drifting!"

Suddenly, the boat pounded hard against something solid and lurched violently, knocking Bingo down. He grabbed the gunnel and peered into the misty darkness. He could hear a stream somewhere close and surmised the boat had to be grounding on the gravel beach on the far side of the bay. At least he hoped that was where they were and not on a rock out in the strait. He shielded his eyes from the rain, squinted, and was relieved to see the shadow of beached drift logs a short distance away.

Confused, Brooklyn and Tony wiggled out of their

sleeping bags and struggled to put on their coats. The rolling and pounding of the boat required them to crawl rather than walk to join Bingo on the deck. As Bingo tried to decide what to do, each successive wave pushed the boat further onto the shore.

"We've drifted onto the beach on the other side of the bay. At least, I think that's where we are. We have to get off the boat. It's too dangerous to stay onboard. It's tilting badly and could roll over on us. We have to jump over the side and wade to the beach."

"No!" Screamed Tony over the wind whipping at his jacket. He grasped a rail and looked over the side. "Dad's boat! We've got to save it. Push it off, or I'm going to be in real trouble."

"Too much wind. We can't push it off the beach. It's far too heavy. We'll try when the tide comes back in. Right now, we have to get off. Our weight will only make the damage to the bottom worse. You two head for the beach. I'm going to rescue the dinghy and drag it onto the shore."

Tony was upset, but he and Brooklyn did what Bingo asked and jumped into the water. The shock of the cold water took Brooklyn's breath away. Still, the seriousness of their situation was foremost in her mind, and survival took over. She'd had the foresight to grab her backpack, which was fortunate. It contained a flashlight and most of their remaining food. Minutes later, all three were pulling the inflatable dinghy up onto the pebble beach.

"If we flip it over and lean it against one of these logs, we'll have ourselves a little shelter," said Bingo.

"Okay," Brooklyn said. She was chilled and her teeth were chattering.

She dug out her flashlight and used it to help them find a clear area next to one of the bigger logs. Then Bingo waded back to the boat to retrieve their sleeping bags, only to discover that they were soaked.

Meanwhile, Brooklyn and Tony crawled under the dinghy. Being so close to Brooklyn made Tony even more uncomfortable than the uneven ground they were forced to lay on.

"Brooklyn? Are you okay? We're in trouble aren't we?" Tony was shivering from being soaked to his waist.

"Yeah. I'm wet and cold and I'm bummed about what happened. I keep telling myself it was my stupid idea to come here."

"I'm the one who has really been stupid, Brooklyn. First, the way I've treated you, and now forgetting to check how I secured my dad's boat and putting us in this predicament."

"Well, I can agree with half of what you're saying," Brooklyn said as she tried to get comfortable. "You are a jerk to pal around with your so-called friends. They're trouble makers, and you're better than any of them. You're smart, Tony. I was the one to suggest we use your dad's boat to come here looking for my mother. I could have left that to the State Troopers, or maybe the Coast Guard. No, I had to keep up my search, and I let my feelings interfere with good judgment."

"Gee, I don't know what to say other than that I'm truly sorry, Brooklyn. I...I really thought we would find her. Maybe she is here. I guess we'll know tomorrow. But, I'm more worried about the boat." Tony groaned. "I'm going to be in big, big trouble."

Bingo, who had squeezed under the turned-over dinghy with them, interrupted their quiet conversation.

"Hey, you two. Get some sleep. I think the boat will be okay, and as long as we are here, we'll look around, okay? While there wasn't another boat here in the bay when we arrived, there could be a cabin or a camp nearby. Who knows? The camp could be further back from the shore and we can't see it. And someone could have taken the boat to a safer location. There are lots of possibilities to check out. So, see if you can sleep."

Moments later, Bingo, who was lying on the other side of Brooklyn, began to snore. Brooklyn and Tony giggled as they listened to his snores get louder and louder. After a while, Brooklyn got no response when she asked Tony if he was warm enough. Tony had fallen asleep too. But for her, it would be a long, dreary night listening to the soft patter of raindrops on their makeshift shelter. She began to dread what other trouble daylight would bring.

Chapter 25

The Arctic Bar in downtown Juneau was in full swing due to the festivity of a group of locals celebrating a birthday. Couples were dancing to an old rock-and-roll song on the jukebox. Tables were loaded with empty beer bottles and half-empty baskets of popcorn. Though the tourist season was over and the thousands of people from cruise ships were gone, the street outside the bar was busy with local traffic and people shopping or just strolling.

Sitting at the long bar sipping his third beer, Ronnie Waltrip didn't mind the noise. He was feeling pretty good himself. He was sure he was about to make a lot of money—a far cry from his situation just twenty-four hours earlier when he had sneaked out and stolen Flo's ATV. He had driven it back down to the harbor in Chatham and taken the *Sherry J* to Juneau. His first thought was to go south to Ketchikan or maybe even to Seattle. But he didn't have enough money to buy fuel. In fact, he was darn near broke because Vince hadn't paid him. He would have to use a credit card to pay his bar tab and hope it cleared.

He realized that using the boat, other than for the short trip to Juneau, was a bad idea. There was a good possibility the boat would be reported as stolen to the Coast Guard, and he could get caught. During the hours he spent at the wheel, he came up with a great money-making idea. His two partners were dead, or soon would be in the case of Vince, and he was the only person who knew that the rest of the otter pelts were hidden in the old mine shaft back at their camp. Well, maybe Flo knew if she and Vince had talked some.

Ronnie figured all he had to do was negotiate his own deal with Johnny Kwan. Kwan could have Vince's boat too. He didn't care about that old tub. While he wasn't very good at math, he figured on walking away with a hundred thousand dollars, maybe more. Kwan really wanted those pelts and must have agreed to pay Vince a lot for them. He had heard about a guy who made hundreds of thousands of dollars selling otter pelts that ended up being sold for double or triple the price in Hong Kong or Singapore. He couldn't remember the details, but that sounded good to him.

Ronnie checked his watch for the umpteenth time. It had been close to two hours since he had talked to Kwan on the phone and arranged a meeting. He finished the beer and was about to ask the bartender for another when two husky guys entered the bar. From the look on their faces as they walked towards him, their message was pretty straightforward.

The smaller guy did the talking. "You must be Waltrip. Come with us. Kwan said you have some information for him."

Ronnie looked them over. "I prefer to talk right here. Maybe have another beer. Did you bring the money? What I've got to say is worth a lot. Nobody knows where the rest of the stash of pelts is but for me. Heh, heh. Well, maybe Vince's old girlfriend. But she's never been there. So, I—"

"Yeah, we've got something for you. Outside in

the car. Let's go." One of the men grabbed Waltrip by the arm and pulled him off his stool. He glanced at the three beer bottles in front of Ronnie, pulled out a twenty, and threw it on the bar. "Kwan's a generous man. He's paying for your cheap beers."

It was not so much a stroll to the door as it was like a barge pushed by two monstrous tugboats. Ronnie couldn't move in any other direction. The tugboats didn't even slow down or attempt to open the door first, and he hit it with a smack, and pain shot down his left leg as his knee connected with it. Outside the bar, a black SUV was parked at the curb. One of the tugs moved around him and opened a rear door. As the other one pushed him in, the first one took a syringe out of his jacket pocket and jabbed it into Ronnie's neck.

Ronnie yelped. "Hey! What's going on? This ain't part of the business deal."

Neither man answered. One of them went around and got behind the wheel. The other man slid into the back seat with Ronnie. Before the driver could lock the car doors, Ronnie threw open the back door, jumped out, and began to run. The only problem was his legs weren't working very well, both due to his bum knee and the drug surging through his veins. He zigged when he should have zagged.

Next to the bar was an empty area facing the bay with a railing along the sidewalk. Fifteen feet below the barrier in the dark void was water. Parts of downtown Juneau had buildings built on pilings, and the bar was one of them. A group of the revelers from the bar were making their way down the sidewalk ahead of Ronnie. When he glanced over his shoulder and saw his two captors giving chase, he zigged again to go around the revelers. Knocking into the railing in his drugged stupor, he toppled over. The startled revelers stopped, and with barely sober eyes, they saw a man hit the frigid water, sink, and then resurface flailing his arms.

The two men stopped and looked over the rail along with a gathering crowd. The short one took out a cell phone and punched a number.

Kwan answered. "Well? You got him?"

"Nope. He decided to go for a swim, Boss. I guess he didn't like your offer. Maybe he'll appreciate it more after we fish him out of the bay. Got some information for you, though. If Waltrip doesn't talk, we need that woman from Chatham. She may know where the pelts are."

Chapter 26

Flo lay on the floor next to Vince. Her hands were numb from being tied up by the Hutchinson brothers. She was handled roughly when pulled from the truck and man-handled into a single-wide trailer, but at least they didn't hurt her. Vince wasn't so lucky. Will Hutchinson punched and kicked him several times in the ribs and back. Then while he was still unconscious, Will and AJ dragged him into the trailer by his arms.

Vince lay next to her on the hard floor. When he woke, he moaned when he tried to move. There were lacerations and dried blood on his face and more blood matted in his long hair. The two brothers had dumped them on the floor of a bathroom. It was filthy and stank horribly, but there was nothing she could do about it. Both their hands and feet were bound.

The worse discomfort was the duct tape over her mouth. Why did they have to do that? There was probably not another person, other than their captors, within ten miles. She thought she heard a woman's voice while the men were hustling them from the vehicle. So there must be other people around, maybe a residence?

But where were they? Even though she couldn't see where the vehicle had been going, she felt sure it wasn't back towards Chatham. When they got to the main road, they had turned left, not right, which meant someplace along the road to Hoonah. She had traveled that road many times and knew there were only a few residences before the road went over the summit. They hadn't traveled long enough to go over the mountains. So maybe they weren't too far from town. No matter. Getting free didn't look to be in her near future.

Flo squirmed around so she could take a look at Vince. He had stopped moaning, and she wondered if he was dead. The two young men had beaten him pretty badly. She rolled her shoulder until she touched his back. She could feel him breathing. She needed to talk to him. If he was awake, maybe he could pull the tape away from her mouth. She gently nudged his back, but he didn't respond. She rolled further until her face was up against his shirt. She had an idea. Rubbing her cheek along the wool fabric, she could feel the end of the tape across her mouth begin to catch. She rubbed faster. More of the duct tape pulled free of her face and stuck to the shirt. She kept working it, and when she thought enough of the duct tape stuck to the shirt, she jerked her head back, and it came free. Flo lay still for a few minutes, thankful she could now breathe more freely. Next, she had to determine how Vince was doing.

"Vince," she whispered. She nudged his back again with her shoulder. His body responded by shaking slightly, but he didn't answer. She nudged Vince again. His whole body shook again.

"Vince, are you okay?" She had a frightening thought. Maybe he's dying. A tear rolled across her cheek. "Don't die, Vince. Oh God, please don't die."

His body convulsed. He moaned again, then was still. When he finally spoke, his slurred speech, due to his swollen lips, was slow. "Did they—hurt you too,

Flo?"

Flo let out a sigh. "Thank God you can talk." She moved her head closer to his. "No, they didn't hurt me."

Vince tried to move and groaned. "I…I'm…sorry I got…you into this mess. I—"

"Vince, don't try to move. You probably have broken ribs. They kicked you several times."

He relaxed his body and craned his neck back and forth. "Where…are we? I must have passed out."

"We're all right, at least for now. They put us in the back of an SUV and drove us somewhere. We're in a trailer, but I don't think it's a home. It's dirty and smells awful."

Vince sniffed several times, and she could see him begin to focus. He tried to lift himself, but the pain in his side was too great, and he collapsed back onto the floor. He coughed and shuddered once more. His breathing was shallow.

"I know that…smell. It's meth. We're someplace where someone cooks the stuff. Ah—there's only one guy on the island that does that, Archie Hutchinson."

"That fits. I heard a woman's voice. It could have been his wife. She sometimes stops by the café when she's in Chatham to buy a few groceries. She seems like a nice lady, but quiet and a bit timid, like she's afraid to talk to people. She always orders hot tea with milk with a piece of cake and sits in the last booth, so maybe no one will notice her. One time she had a black eye and a bruised cheek. Said she'd slipped on their porch a few days before."

"Her name is Mona. She used to work as a checkout clerk at a supermarket in downtown Juneau. I think she's a drug addict. Mona is Archie's second wife, maybe his third. I don't know." Vince was talking more clearly, and she thought he was a bit more alert. They stopped talking when they heard a door slam and someone laughing. Then a vehicle started up and drove away.

"Now's our chance. There might be fewer of them out there now," said Flo. "If we can get ourselves untied, maybe we can get away."

Vince didn't respond, and he seemed to shrink from her. Flo wondered if he could still hear her. He was not in any condition to run anywhere. It wasn't just the fact that they were tied up hands and feet. He was dying.

It struck her that Vince had been running away all of his life. He had run away from her when she got pregnant. He had run away after being banned by his Native community. Coming back to her for help had been an attempt to stop running. And now it was too late.

"Vince?"

He didn't answer. Flo pressed hard with her back. Still no response. Her hip ached from lying on the hard floor, and her arms and legs were numb. Never the less she had to check on how he was. Ignoring the painful scraping to her exposed skin, she wriggled her body around and put her bound hands gently on Vince's shoulder. The shirt was damp, and she could feel the heat of his body. She hadn't been aware of it in her struggle to free the tape over her mouth. He was burning up. He needed water and, more importantly, a doctor.

Would screaming get anyone's attention? Not very

likely. She looked up at the sink basin. Even if she could manage to stand up and reach it, she didn't know if there was a glass or anything to fill with water. And with her hands bound, how would she hold it while turning on the faucet?

"Flo?" Vince said very softly. "Flo, can you hear me?"

She felt relief. "Yes, Vince, I can hear you."

"I…I'm so sorry I did this to you. It's all my fault. I've been so dumb. Making bad choices is more like it. I've been making them all my life, like leaving you. Now it's too late to make things right. You should have had more than Chatham with a kid to raise. I should have been here."

"It's okay, Vince. I've managed, and we will get out of here. They'll let us go for sure."

"No. You don't understand, Flo. It's not Hutch and his sons. They're waiting for someone else to show up, a nasty guy named Kwan. What Hutch's boys did to me is nothing like this guy's men will do. They'll probably kill me because I owe this guy a lot of money, and now I can't pay him." Vince's shoulders shook as he chuckled. "It's funny. Johnny Kwan wants to kill me, but I'm already dying."

"You can survive this. We'll get you to a doctor."

"Keep thinking that, Flo, but it's not going to happen. I've run out of luck."

"Then tell me about Kwan. You can make things right by telling the State Troopers everything you know about him. He must have partners or someone he works for. Who are they?"

Vince didn't respond right away. Flo was beginning to think she had stepped over the line. Maybe she shouldn't know things about Kwan.

"Okay," Vince finally said as he tried to roll over to face her. He groaned as he made it onto his back. His ribs hurt too much to lay on his side. "But you have to promise that you will not reveal what I tell you until there is a chance for you to speak with a Trooper. If you let something slip with any of the Hutchison folks or one of Kwan's men when they show up, they will kill you or seriously hurt you or Brooklyn."

For the next half hour, Vince told Flo everything he knew about Kwan's operations. He told her what he and his friends were doing at the Grotto, how he found it, and the forgotten gold mine. He described the old mine shaft, the veins of gold left untouched, and the bat colony.

He described who worked for Kwan and who some of his other clients were, like himself, who did the poaching and gathering and sold their illegal products to Kwan.

Vince had met a few of Kwan's people a couple of times, like a cousin who delivered illegal seafood to someone else at an offshore rendezvous point. He told her about Kwan having people working for him who were go-between guys and could also be dangerous. Some of them were desperate men with honest jobs or reputations to maintain. They worked for Kwan for the extra income.

Flo concentrated on remembering every detail. She was glad for something else to think about than their predicament.

Lying close to one another in the semi-darkness, Flo saw Vince manage to make a silly grin despite the pain. There was still some sparkle in his eyes that she remembered from when they first met.

"What are you thinking?" She asked as she punched him in his side.

Vince flinched.

"Sorry, I forgot about your ribs."

"You should know what else is in the mine." Vince finally answered. "Kwan wants my otter pelts, but all he grabbed were the ones I delivered early or hadn't yet stored in the mine shaft. We must have over two hundred thousand dollars in pelts that we stashed in the mine to stay dry."

Vince kept talking, but his words became more and more confused until it all seemed like nonsensical babble. He was tiring, and there were long periods between words.

"Even if…you can't remember everything I've said, remember this one thing…you are a partner in that mine. It's all legal and filed in Juneau—you and me—we could be rich."

"Me? I don't understand. Why me, Vince? We haven't spoken in years." Flo leaned closer to him and was silent for a few minutes. "I wish you had come back sooner. We could have made it work, Vince. You could have been part of raising our daughter. Brooklyn misses not having a father. She talks about it all the time. I've tried to be a good parent, but there are so many things I haven't been able to give her, like a father's love. Maybe you still can. Just hang on. We'll get through this. Oh Vince, please, for Brooklyn and me."

But Vince was finished talking. He turned his head away from her and went to sleep or passed out. She couldn't rouse him. So she remained cuddled as close as she could. Despite the cold and the dirty linoleum floor, it was somehow comforting—like their early days together.

****

A voice was calling Flo's name. It sounded far away, then closer, and then right in her ear. "Flo, wake up! Flo!" When Flo opened her eyes, a woman was kneeling beside her. Flo was groggy and confused.

The woman used scissors to cut the zip ties binding her feet and then her hands. She tried to help Flo to her feet.

"There, you're free. Now come with me."

Flo couldn't stand and crumpled back down. Her legs felt like tree trunks from the lack of circulation.

"Hutch has gone to meet someone, but he could return soon. His sons went into Chatham to celebrate at a bar. You can go, but you have to hurry."

Flo recognized her. "Mona? That's your name, right? I've waited on you at the café, haven't I?"

"Yes, you have. I know you're a kind person. So, I'm letting you go." Mona stood up and started to back out of the room.

"But what about Vince? Aren't you going to help him too?"

"Vince is dead. See for yourself."

Startled by Mona's statement, Flo struggled to get up onto her knees. She turned to Vince and put her hand against his neck to check for a pulse. "No, he can't die. He's taking the medication." Tears welled up in her eyes and rolled down her cheeks in rivulets. "Vince, oh Vince, please stay with me. Don't die." She shook his body.

"No use, honey. He's dead. You've got to come

with me now. I'll show you where an old logging road goes down to the bay and back towards Chatham. It's a shortcut that I use myself."

Flo rubbed the tears from her eyes and tried to stand up. Mona grabbed her arm and helped her to her feet. Flo's legs were still numb. Then it struck her what Mona was trying to do. "You're letting me go?"

"Yes, All I ask in return is that you help my son Will get treated by a doctor. He's not my boy except kin by marriage, but I don't want him to die as Vince did."

Flo looked down at Vince while steadying herself by holding onto Mona and the doorframe. "Poor Vince. He didn't deserve to die like this either. Can you cover him up with something?"

"Sure, and I'll make sure Vince's body will be taken into Hoonah. You can make the funeral arrangements there."

"Funeral for Vince? Oh! I—"

The sound of a vehicle coming down the drive from the road caught their attention.

"Please, follow me," Mona said, anxiety rising in her voice. "Remember, see about Will getting treated for rabies as soon as possible. Will is the only one who gives me any respect."

Mona led Flo through the trailer's kitchen past the meth equipment and a table covered in bottles of chemicals. They hurried out of the trailer and around the far end towards the timber. The two dogs chained near the main house watched them go but remained calm and didn't bark. Behind a high row of blackberry vines was the old logging road. Young cedar trees and underbrush had taken over what had once been a road, but now only a faint trail. It was the one Mona used to get to Chatham.

"I...I've got to get back," Mona said. Flo saw the imploring look in her eyes as she repeated her request. "Remember about Will."

"I promise, Mona."

Flo hugged Mona, turned, and began to run at a hobble, then more quickly, as she disappeared into the forest.

Chapter 27

The Frontier Pub and Grill had multi-color LED lighting strung along shelves laden with liquor bottles and under the front of the bar. It was a sad attempt to transition from a time-worn, Alaskan hangout into something more upscale. Despite the glitz, local patrons still preferred country music on the jukebox and cheap beer over hip-hop and imported microbrews. To label it a grill was also an exaggeration. The menu consisted principally of frozen fish and chips or burgers heated in a microwave oven or fryer. The muted lights softened the aged and cracked leather of the booths and hid spills on the rough wood floor. But nothing short of an overhaul of the mechanical system would rid the bar of the smells of greasy fries, popcorn, and cigarette smoke.

A pool table in the back was occupied by a couple of men too drunk to do anything but stumble around it. They knocked the cue ball about the table, laughing at their missed shots.

In a corner booth, another patron, a white-haired man, sat seemingly oblivious to his surroundings. The soft light from a small laptop revealed both the age lines on his face and a natural brightness in his eyes. He stopped pecking at the keyboard for a minute to pick up a glass of Makers Mark with a liver-spotted hand and take a sip. The remains of a half-smoked cigar lay in an ashtray on the table.

A disturbance outside the pub broke the man's concentration. The front door crashed open. The Hutchinson brothers sauntered in, shaking the rain off their jackets and stomping mud off their boots. One of them hooted at two girls working at the bar.

Stella and Clara, the two cocktail waitresses working the early afternoon shift, looked in their direction. Both young women wore tight black dresses that barely covered their butts along with high-heeled, black leather boots. The owner believed this basic dress code would attract more young miners, loggers, and fishermen. But logging had slowed, and the startup of a proposed gold mining operation had dragged out over a year due to environmental permits. The local business was slow, and Stella and Clara knew they were lucky to have full-time jobs in Chatham.

Stella handled the food orders. It was a boring job and she much preferred working in the bigger Alaskan cities like Juneau or Anchorage. But Stella was naturally lazy and she didn't have to put up with a bunch of temperamental customers in Chatham.

Clara's job was bartending. She tolerated the small town mainly because Will Hutchinson, her boyfriend, always had money, and he took her on trips to Las Vegas every few months. Neither Clara nor Stella ever asked Will or AJ about jobs or their sources of income.

Clara jiggled to the music and gave Will a sexy smile and a wave when she saw him come in. Stella yawned and stubbed out the cigarette she was smoking as she watched them. AJ grabbed a stool next to her, and she didn't bother to react when he pinched her behind.

"How's life treating you, Stella? Been to Juneau lately?"

"It could be a lot better than things are right now," she said, removing another cigarette from her pack on the bar. She pouted. "Be nice if you offered to take Clara and me into Juneau in your boat."

AJ's face brightened. "Hey, Will, what you say we do that? Stella has a great idea."

Will had his eyes on Clara, who moved her lithe body to the music while restocking the beer cooler.

"Just waltz into Juneau," said Will. "Wouldn't it be just our luck to bump into Kwan in some restaurant or bar? I don't want to see him or any of his goons right now. He sounded pretty angry when Dad talked to him on the phone this morning. I heard him shouting. I'm not about to walk up and ask Kwan what kind of day he's having."

"Yeah, but Dad paid us. He must have something arranged."

Clara was drying a couple of glasses she had pulled out of a small dishwasher behind the bar. She paused and looked at AJ. "Who's Kwan?"

"Johnny Kwan? He's a friend of our dad," said AJ. "Well, maybe more of a business associate than a friend. He's a Chinese guy who thinks he's important in the Alaska seafood business. Dad sells—"

Will interrupted. "AJ, shut your mouth just once in a while. What business Hutch does with him is none of our business nor of these nice young ladies. Look, can't you see they're bored to death. So, it's good we're here. Let's liven up the place. Let's have a few beers and a good time. Enough talk about the Chinese dude."

Clara noticed the bandage on Will's arm.

"What happened to your arm?"

"What?" Will replied. "Oh, some idiot decided to bite me in a fight."

"Well, serves you right. I don't understand why you men always want to settle things by fighting. You'll get no sympathy from us gals."

The old man in the corner booth smiled as he listened to their conversation. He scratched the white stubble on his chin and raised his eyebrows at the mention of Kwan. He took another sip of his whiskey. The man was one of a few people who knew his reputation because he made a living at freelance journalism and writing mystery novels. Kwan offered an excellent character study. He was known to be both a shrewd businessman and truly dangerous if you crossed him. He wished these two young men luck if their father was working with Kwan. Now he knew why he'd seen Kwan's fancy yacht tied to the dock. Something was afoot between Hutchinson and Kwan.

Clara turned up the volume on the jukebox. There were speakers spread around the perimeter of the room and the noise level became deafening. Clara resumed her wiggling to a lively country tune.

Sadly, all the noise ended the man's eavesdropping on the Hutchinson boys' conversation.

****

Flo stopped just inside a line of brush bordering the road to listen for sounds other than the pounding of her heart. She didn't know how long she'd been running. After the whine of the truck and Mona's frantic goodbye, her mind had gone blank. She couldn't even remember the slapping of wet tree branches in her face or stumbling and slipping on the muddy trail. Her wet clothes, muddied hands, and scratched face said otherwise. If someone, or maybe one of the dogs, was trailing her, there wasn't any sound to indicate it. The road in front of her was a quiet scene as well.

Flo struggled up a low bank on the side of the gravel road and looked both ways. She could see several houses, maybe a quarter of a mile down the hill to her left. The other way was nothing. Ignoring the increasing downpour and without hesitating any longer, she began to run again, this time down the hill towards the houses that she felt certain were at the edge of town. Reaching the church and the side street that led to her home, she made a turn without losing a stride. It was only another five hundred feet to her front door. The shock of what she saw up ahead caused her to stumble and stop to stare. Her front yard was filled with burnt wood and furniture. Where the exterior paint wasn't scorched and peeling, it was black with soot and smoke. Bits of yellow caution tape waved in the wind.

Wiping the rain from her face, she walked cautiously up the rest of the road and onto the front porch. While the scene was startling, her first thought was about Brooklyn. Had she been inside when the fire started?

"Brooklyn?" Flo hollered as she rushed up the front steps and pushed open the front door. "Are you in here? It's Mom." No one answered.

She entered her living room—her eyes taking in the stark scene. While there were some signs of cleanup, it had been badly burned. Someone had removed most of the wall paneling, ceiling, and doors to the kitchen and bedrooms. One wall was in the process of being rebuilt with new studs already in place.

The smell of cut lumber mixed with the lingering acrid scent of the smoke from the fire. She walked quickly to the kitchen. The ceiling and cupboards in the kitchen were various shades of smoky gray. The blackened linoleum floor was smudged with footprints—small footprints, mixed with larger ones. She checked Brooklyn's bedroom then hers. Both were empty, but there were dirty clothes on the floor in Brooklyn's room and, again, smaller footprints. She concluded Brooklyn had been to the house after the fire and she must be okay.

Suddenly getting clean was all Flo could think of doing. She searched her closet for some fresh clothes that were not too smelly from the smoke, shut herself in the bathroom, and stripped off her muddy, wet clothes. For a moment, she didn't think about Brooklyn, the horrible shape her house was in, or even whether there was any hot water. All that mattered was a shower. She let out a sigh of contentment when she discovered the water was hot. After washing her hair and letting the hot water warm her body, she felt a thousand percent better. Dressing quickly, she was ready to find Brooklyn and learn what had happened.

A moment of sadness for Vince overcame her as she sat on the edge of the bed putting on some clean shoes. Remembering that she had assured Vince that she would inform the authorities about what happened, she looked at the phone by her bed. Picking up the receiver, she heard a dial tone. She dialed 911.

"Alaska Telecom 911, may I help you?" The operator said.

"Yes, now please listen carefully. I don't have much time. My name is Flo Whiting, and I live in

Chatham. I need to report a kidnapping."

"A kidnapping? Who is the missing person?"

"Me, I mean a man named Vince James and me, but he's dead."

"Could you repeat that, ma'am? You say someone who has been kidnapped is dead?"

"Yes. Would you please just listen? I have to find my daughter, who may also be missing. She's not at home, and I don't know where she is."

"What is the name of your daughter?"

"Brooklyn."

"That would be Brooklyn Whiting?"

"Yes. Just let me finish. I was with two men—Vince James and Ronnie Waltrip. Waltrip stole my ATV, and I suspect he is now somewhere aboard a boat named the *Sherry J.* He probably stole it too. Please inform the State Troopers and the Coast Guard. Vince James and I were kidnapped by a man called Archie Hutchinson and his two sons, Will and AJ. His wife's name is Mona. She let me escape."

"Where are these men now?" The 911 operator asked.

"I don't know, but they could be searching for me. That's why I called, and now I have to find my daughter. So I have to hang up."

"Ms. Whiting, you have to remain on the—"

Flo headed for the front door. There, she paused to look around the room one more time. "How did this happen?" Her voice echoed in the empty space and she shook her head dejectedly. Her thoughts were confounded by too many unanswered questions.

How am I going to pay for this? It will take all my savings—money meant for Brooklyn's college education. And where is she?

She turned and quickly opened the door to leave. A man was standing directly in front of her on the front porch. Rain was dripping from the brim of his hat and his right arm was hidden behind his back. She recognized him.

"Why are you here? Is this about—?"

The man's arm came up, and something hit her on the side of her head. He grabbed her body with one arm before she fell and hauled her back inside the house.

Hutch, who had been standing in the shadows near the corner of the house, climbed onto the porch.

"Nice work," he said. "I'll bring the truck around to the back door. You bring her out that way, and we'll take her down to the dock. Did you arrange for the boat to meet us as Kwan asked?"

"Yeah, it should be at the harbor in less than thirty minutes from now. She recognized me."

"Well, what were you going to do? Wear a bandana, like an outlaw?"

The man holding Flo hesitated. She moaned. He hoped that meant he hadn't hit her too hard with the piece of pipe that Hutch had given him.

"What are we going to do with her?" He asked.

"We'll leave that decision to Kwan," replied Hutch. "He's the person who wants information from her. You've got plans for all that money he pays you, right? Are you going to let her spoil them?"

Chapter 28

It was a miserable night on the beach for Bingo Bob and the two kids. It rained constantly, not a downpour, but heavy enough to get everyone thoroughly soaked despite the lean-to shelter Bingo had made using the overturned inflatable. There wasn't quite enough room underneath it for all of them, but Bingo insisted he would be okay lying near the edge. Brooklyn and Tony were too exhausted to argue.

Bingo woke later in the night and waded out to the beached boat to retrieve some of their gear, including several blankets. One he used to cover the young people. He also salvaged a partial package of cookies and several water bottles, put them in a Styrofoam cooler, and tucked it under the big log next to their makeshift camp. Then he wrapped his soaked body in the other blanket and a small tarp he found stored in a locker with some fishing tackle. It smelled fishy, but he had experienced worse. Once his body was warm, he fell back asleep, albeit a fitful one with a disturbing dream.

Bingo again dreamed of a little girl riding her bike. He was lying on his side in a sunny patch of grass, watching as she rode along the paved pathway near a pretty little pond. She wore a blue jump-suit, and her brown hair was tied in a ponytail with a yellow ribbon.

There was an island in the middle of the pond with

weeping willows, stands of cattails, and water lilies in bloom near the shoreline. The warmth of the sun and the setting lulled him into a state of being only half awake.

The girl waved to him as she passed and sped down the path to a bridge crossing over the pond. She started to cross the bridge but stopped and dropped her bike in the middle to watch several ducks feeding under it. To his shock, the girl leaned out over the railing and fell into the water. From his resting spot on the grassy bank, he was roused from his stupor by her screams. He tried to get on his knees and stand up but his body felt heavy, and his arms and legs were numb. Instead, he crawled towards the edge of the pond in slow motion. The sky grew dark, and a mist rose from the surface of the pond, making it difficult to see the girl flailing her arms to stay afloat, her screams pounding in his ears. Why couldn't he stand up and run to her rescue?

Then his hand touched an empty bottle of whiskey lying in the grass and he realized he was drunk. The sky wasn't dark. There was no mist hanging over the pond. His vision was blurred, and he could only watch helplessly as the little girl slipped below the surface.

Bingo woke up again. He was sweating under the tarp. The rain had finally stopped, and in the early dawn light, he stared at the trees beginning to emerge from the dark shadows of the forest. With a sigh, he felt relieved that they were all safe for the time being. He tried to go back to sleep, but his dream had been too vivid about the little girl in the pond. As he lay there on the hard ground, Bingo vowed never to let harm come to the two young people who were sleeping beside him. It was time for him to quit drinking, stop taking from the community of Chatham, and start giving back. His sorrows were in the past. He had to live in the present, and Chatham had so much to offer him if he would only let it. With these thoughts, Bingo fell back asleep.

****

Their makeshift camp was located on a narrow strip of grass just above the pebble beach and the high tide line. It was just the kind of grass that bears loved to eat, and there were a lot of big brown bears living on Baranof Island. But there wasn't much they could do about a bear looking for an early breakfast. There had nowhere else to go the night before, and they were too tired to worry about such a danger until they faced it. Bears should have been eating salmon and berries this time of year, but sweet sedge grass was part of their diet. A bear wandering out of the woods and getting a sniff of them was Brooklyn's immediate thought when she opened her eyes and recognized where they were.

Without disturbing the others, she crept out from under the inflatable. There was not a bear in sight. In the shallow water close to the pebble beach, she saw that the cabin cruiser was still there. It looked out of place. The boat was grounded, listing to one side. She hoped it was not too damaged for Tony's sake. But what else could they have done?

When they abandoned the boat in the middle of the night, Bingo told them that water had flooded the battery compartment. As a result, he could not start the engines, nor could he use the marine radio to call for help. If the radio still didn't work today, they were stranded. They had the inflatable dingy, but it would never get them back to Chatham. To attempt to use it in the open water of the straits was far too dangerous.

Encountering any waves at all would swamp the small craft.

No boats had arrived during the night. They were alone, and it frightened her. Behind them, she could hear the sound of the small stream that crossed the beach. It was only a few hundred feet away. The forest looked impenetrable, dark, and very, very wet. Brooklyn knew from experience that if they entered the forest, there would be rotting logs, downed timber to climb over, and ponding water to avoid. They were in the rain forest. It lived up to its name and did everything possible to discourage a person from entering. The nearest community could be over twenty-five miles away—too far to walk overland. The forest might as well be a high wall keeping them imprisoned on the beach.

Their biggest hope of rescue was someone on a passing boat seeing the grounded cruiser, getting curious, and coming into the bay to investigate. With the narrow entrance to the bay, someone would have to be close to shore to spot a beached boat at the far end. It was a distance of nearly a mile.

These thoughts added to her depression. She had been so convinced that her mother was here that she'd ignored the risks of being stranded in the Southeastern Alaskan wilderness.

Brooklyn made a quick trip into the bushes, then seeing the cooler Bingo must have brought ashore from the boat, she checked to see what food they had left. She also checked her backpack. All they had was a bag of chips, some cookies, a half dozen protein bars, and some very soggy leftover sandwiches. That and four bottles of water wasn't much. Unless the boat was operable, or they were rescued by a passing boater, hunger would soon be a problem. The water bottles could be refilled from the stream a few yards from where they slept. If they were lucky, maybe there were still wild berries to pick or they might be able to catch a spawning salmon in the shallow riffles of the stream.

Bingo finally stirred and sat up. He immediately looked out at the forlorn-looking boat just as Brooklyn had done. There was little change since he had removed things in the night. It was well-grounded on the rocky beach, and it would be hours from being refloated by the incoming tide.

"Are you okay?" he asked her. "Are you warm enough?"

"A little chilled because my clothes are still damp. Moving around helps." Brooklyn hesitated before saying what had been on her mind since waking up. "Bingo, what are we going to do now? I'm sorry I got us into this mess. It's all my fault what happened to us and Tony's boat. I should have let the state police locate my mom. Instead, I had to be a good girl scout and do things on my own. I know now that I made stupid mistakes, and each time there has been trouble. But this is awful. What are we going to do?"

Bingo stretched and got to his feet. "I don't think we have to be too concerned. A lot of boats pass by here—maybe a dozen or more a day. It's the main route to Juneau. Someone will either spot the boat and come to investigate or call the Coast Guard. People report derelict boats all the time."

"Derelict?" There was a muffled response and a groan from Tony. He was still under the blanket and sat up to look at the boat. "My dad is going to be so mad.

I'll never be able to drive his boat again, let alone use it."

"If he's the father I think he is, Tony, he's going to be more concerned about your safety than about the boat," Bingo replied. "The boat is going to be fine. I think we can get it off the beach once the tide is a little higher. That might be a couple of hours from now, but we'll give it a try. Meanwhile, we came here for a reason, to find out if Brooklyn's mother, or anyone else, is here. Since we have nothing else to do but watch the tide come in, we might as well look around."

"Where are we going to look?" asked Brooklyn.

"Let's start by finding the Grotto and see if that gives us a clue. We're not more than a few hundred feet from it right here." Bingo pointed across the bay to the rocks that hid the entrance.

"Remember where I tried to go with the dinghy? The water level should be low enough to get inside it. We'll launch the dinghy and give it a try. First, we need to spread the blankets on top of these logs to dry a bit. We may need them. Then we'll eat our food and drink some water."

While Brooklyn and Tony gathered things up as Bingo suggested, he searched for pieces of wood and dragged them onto the beach. There he constructed a crude arrow pointing towards the entrance to the Grotto, like a road sign to where they were headed.

****

It was late morning when Wally Perkins entered the Jackson general store. He had two reasons for his visit. First, he needed to learn whether Jackson had heard from Tony and Brooklyn. Second, he needed to find out where he could locate someone who was an experienced trapper to help him trap wild animals for rabies testing. Without any mobilized help from the CDC or the State of Alaska any time soon, he needed to take steps on his own. The spread of the virus had to be stopped. Wally knew all too well from his experience with the spread of contagious diseases that quick action was the best solution. Once rabies started to infect a few warm-blooded animals, it was only a matter of days before it spread to other animals. This significantly increased the possibility of exposure to people. If he was fortunate, through testing, he might even locate the source of the outbreak.

As he entered the store, Wally noticed there was no one at the checkout counter. Sid Jackson was back in one of the household aisles helping Gladys Tussock. He overheard Gladys mention the words "rat poison." Wally smiled and remained near the front of the store, turning to look at a drone hanging in the store window. He had never seen a drone up close and was curious how they could be adapted to carry a camera. He was also curious why anyone would want to own and use a drone in this part of Alaska when there was so little open space to use one.

Sid came over to where Wally was standing. "They are the latest thing. It seems everyone wants one. My son certainly does, but they aren't toys. Reliable ones don't come cheap either. This one retails for nine hundred. Although, if you're interested, I could knock the price down a bit."

Wally shook his head and laughed. "I don't know where I'd use it, although it sure would be fun to try one as a part of my wildlife photography. It would be just my luck to drop it in the bay."

Sid laughed too, loud enough to catch Gladys' attention as she studied a rack of garden seeds with the seriousness of a baseball card collector.

"Your boy and Brooklyn make it home last night?" Wally asked.

"Nope. I'm a little worried, too, because of the wind that blew up last night. They had enough food and water for a day or two, though. I insisted an adult go along because Tony has never handled the boat in rough water. You know, I was a little surprised Brooklyn asked Bingo Bob to be the person to go with them. But when I thought about it, he does know how to handle a boat."

Wally nodded. "I wouldn't worry too much. I talked to Bingo for a few minutes before they left. He's a pretty capable person. Most people don't see that side of him because of his drinking binges."

At the mention of Bingo out in a boat with a couple of young folks, Gladys' curiosity was piqued, and she moved down an aisle to better overhear their conversation.

"I have to confess that I've been a bit concerned too," replied Wally. "But it's more about where they were headed."

"Really? Why's that, Wally?" Sid asked.

"This may sound absurd, but there've been several incidents of rabies reported in the last two days. I've been in contact with a doctor in Juneau and with the state police. All the evidence as to the source of rabies points to the location where the kids went."

"Rabies, you say?"

"It's hard to say how serious the outbreak is, but it's definitely rabies. Do you have any way of reaching

Tony, maybe with the marine radio that's on your boat?"

Sid tilted his head towards the shelves behind the checkout counter, where a UHF base station blinked with a green light. "Yeah, if they're not out of my range. There's a radio on the boat, and I have one here in the store that's on all the time. Tony has never used the radio, but Bingo should know. I sure hope they remember to keep it turned on. I use mine to talk to boats out in the strait that want to know about dock space at the harbor or what fresh vegetables or milk we might have in stock. Maybe I should call the Coast Guard and have them try with their big transmitter."

"That would be good, Sid."

Sid hurried over to the checkout counter to try his radio. While waiting, Wally glanced around and saw Gladys staring at him. She blushed at having been caught eavesdropping. But instead of looking away, she rushed over to Wally like a freelance reporter sensing a hot lead.

"Doctor Perkins, did I just hear you say we've got rabies here in Chatham? You know we've got a lot of stray dogs running around. You need to contact the Alaska State Troopers right away."

"Now, don't jump to conclusions, Gladys. Yes, there have been some reported incidents, but not anywhere close to here. I've already talked to the State Troopers, and they said they would investigate."

"Well, they better. And we need someone to start vaccinating people right away, like you. We older folks are very susceptible to viruses. There's a preventative drug available, you know. I read about it in *National Geographic*."

"It's a little early to determine whether people need to do that, Gladys. But I'll be sure to let you know right away. So, can we keep this to ourselves? Don't want to start a panic among the town folk, right?"

"Oh! Certainly not. People around here get riled up about things that are nothing at all. You let me know about when the vaccinations will take place, though, and I'll help spread the word."

Gladys headed for the front door forgetting about the rat poison. She crossed the road and then headed towards the east end of town and the post office. A four-wheel-drive pickup caked in dried mud halfway up its side panels, rattled by, and skidded to a stop across the road. Wally watched with curiosity as Gladys rushed over and climbed in. He didn't recognize the driver, an older man with a full, white beard.

Sid was on the phone with the Coast Guard unit in Juneau and beckoned for Wally to come over to the checkout counter.

"The Coast Guard needs a location where the kids might be. What can I tell them?"

"I'm not sure, Sid. They aren't more than fifty miles from here, but unfortunately, I don't know the place's name. Let me think a second. I was told it's near Evans Lake, wherever that is. According to the doc at the hospital, there are a couple of Forest Service cabins on the lake. Tell them to look for a stream leaving Evans Lake and entering Chatham Strait."

"I've never heard of Evans Lake, but there's a USGS map on the wall at the back of the store. See if it's on the map. There are a lot of the unnamed lakes on the island, but with Forest Service cabins, it might be on there."

"Okay, I'll check the map. When you get off the phone, I need some help myself."

Wally started to walk to the rear of the store, but a passing vehicle caught his attention. He watched a State Trooper SUV stop for an old Indian woman crossing the road. There were two officers in the front and two men in the back with dropping heads.

He heard Sid finish his report to the Coast Guard.

"Okay, I'll call back if I hear from them or have more information," Sid hung up the phone and joined Wally at the window just as the SUV started up again.

"Huh, it's not every day you see someone get arrested in Chatham. Not surprised it's those two, though."

"You know those two men?"

"Most people in town do, at least those who frequent the bars. That was the Hutchinson brothers, Will and AJ. They have been nothing but trouble around here ever since the Hutchinson family moved in maybe five years ago. I heard there was a commotion at the Frontier last night." Sid shook his head as he turned to face Wally. "Let's look at that map."

As they studied the map, Sid repeated his question.

"Now, what kind of help are you looking for?"

"For a pretty tough job. Maybe a mountain man, or an Alaskan sourdough, someone who is an experienced trapper, if there is such a person around here."

"You're looking for a mountain man? Are you joking?"

"Someone with trapping experience will do. Know anyone who does?"

"Well, there might be someone, but he's more like your other option, a Sourdough. His name is Calhoun,

Gladys Tussock's brother. He's a pretty tough old bird. He's been everywhere in Alaska and done just about everything a man can do living in the wilderness by himself. I imagine that includes trapping critters. And you're in luck. He's in town to visit his sister."

"Calhoun? He lives here on the island?"

"Well, sort of," replied Sid. "Rumor is he has a gold mine over near Crab Bay. But I guess he hasn't struck it rich since every spring, he goes off prospecting up on the Yukon looking for the big one."

"I'll be damned. Calhoun sounds like the kind of man I need. Now, if I can just convince him to stay around here a while and give me a hand."

"Well, whatever you plan to use him for, find those kids. I'm worried about them, and there's not anything else I can do about it until I hear from them or the Coast Guard."

"Yeah, I'm worried too, and thanks for the information on Calhoun. I'll stop by Gladys' place and see if I can convince him to help me."

Wally walked out of the store, looked to see if a muddy pickup truck was anywhere in sight and not finding it, hopped on his ATV, and headed back through town. For the first time since learning about the rabies incidents, he figured there might be a chance of preventing a severe epidemic. He hoped Calhoun knew how to trap small mammals alive and that they could get started quickly.

Chapter 29

Just as Bingo figured, the tide level was perfect for entering the Grotto. It was a bit precarious with all three of them in the small rubber boat, but rowing slowly and with no one moving around, they stayed afloat. Bingo rowed, and Tony helped by guiding him through the Grotto and avoiding hitting any rocks or getting grounded. They all took a moment to gape at the beauty inside the Grotto. The smooth, wet surfaces of the ceiling and walls glistened like polished marble. In the hushed silence, broken only by the splash of the oars, Brooklyn could not believe what she was seeing. It was like pictures she had seen in books she'd read—like a secret hiding place for Jules Verne's *Nautilus*. Her thoughts about the Grotto faded when Tony shouted to Bingo that he'd spotted a small dock up ahead. Bingo pushed the dinghy onto the streambank next to it and Tony tied the boat securely to a tree branch. Bingo didn't want a repeat of the night before when their craft broke loose and drifted.

On the shore, they found what Bingo had also guessed they would find—a well-used trail heading up the stream into the forest. Before following it, Bingo took a minute to use a stick to draw another arrow in the dirt pointing where they were headed.

The trail was easy to follow. For the first several hundred feet, it went along the stream. They saw signs

236

that it had been used not too long before by bears maybe to catch salmon in the riffles. At a small side stream, a trail with only human footprints veered off. Bingo led them single file in that direction.

The forest was strangely quiet once they were a few yards from the stream. There were not any raven squawks or squirrel chatter announcing their presence. The morning breeze off the bay did not penetrate this far into the forest, giving the place an ethereal stillness. Brooklyn always felt at ease hiking on trails around Chatham, like the one up to the cliff to her favorite spot with the eagle's nest, but this trail made her feel uneasy. Maybe it was the warning Old Frank had given them that the Grotto was part of that disturbing tribal legend. Brooklyn had never taken any of the Native legends seriously, but the way Old Frank told it made her uneasy. She reminded herself the stories were simply fairy tales—a means to convey or educate young people how to survive. On the other hand, Tony, being Tlingit, confessed that he believed the story.

She glanced back at him. He did appear nervous and kept looking behind them—like he suspected someone or something was following them. Brooklyn's uneasiness increased with every twig snap or rustling noise from the thick brush on either side of the trail. Except for her desire to find her mom, she decided she didn't want to be here. If it hadn't been for Bingo's presence, she would have bolted and run back to the boat, pleading to get away from this spot. She did not doubt that Tony would have readily agreed and followed.

Bingo slowed and held up one hand. He placed a finger in front of his mouth for silence and then turned to watch the trail up ahead while listening intently. Brooklyn couldn't see anything with his broad shoulders blocking her view, and she was too afraid to move to one side to try and see around him. She tried to remain calm by reminding herself that she trusted Bingo. The man had been there for her several times, and he was here now. She glanced back at Tony. He was staring behind them again.

She jumped as Bingo spoke. "There's something up ahead. We'll check it out."

Tony was the first to say what Bingo was sensing. "Something smells pretty awful."

As they reached a clearing, all of their senses reeled from what was around them. Brooklyn had read stories by Edgar Allan Poe where he used the word "macabre," and that was the only word she could think of to describe what she was seeing.

Rough-cut wood poles supported several torn blue tarps. Underneath the tarps, animal pelts were stretched and hanging on frames like wretched prisoners in a medieval dungeon. On one crossbar hung a partially skinned animal carcass that had attracted horse flies and other buzzing insects. The stench of decaying flesh was almost overpowering. On the far side of the clearing were two sagging tents and scattered camp gear. Another tattered blue tarp provided shelter for a table, some tipped-over plastic chairs, and a wood plank nailed to one of the tree trunks holding a propane stove and cans of food. Trash and smaller items were scattered about the ground, perhaps by an animal intruder. Beyond the shelter was an enormous pile of garbage. A raven and a couple of jays were scratching through its contents.

Bingo glanced around the camp. Close to the tent was a fresh mound of dirt. He walked over to it.

"Looks like a grave," Bingo remarked. "It's been freshly dug."

Bingo walked over to the tent, pulled aside a flap, and looked inside. There were three sleeping bags and some clothes scattered around. A rifle with a scope was lying on top of one of the bags. In one corner of the tent sat three wooden crates. His eyes went wide as he read the labels on the boxes. The larger two had labels that read DYNAMITE. A small box next to the two larger boxes read DANGER - DETONATORS. He dropped the tent flap and backed away, waving to Brooklyn and Tony to stay back.

"Looks like three people were staying here. Weird, though. I don't know if they were doing some mining or trapping by the looks of the animal pelts. And that's odd, too, because these carcasses and pelts sure look like they're from sea otters. If that's the case, it would be illegal."

"These were sea otters?" Brooklyn asked in a muffled voice. "Why...why would people kill sea otters?" Like Tony, she hadn't moved more than a few feet into the camp. She was holding part of her jacket over her nose and mouth to avoid the foul smell.

Tony was the first to notice the entrance to the mine shaft.

"What is that over there?" He pointed to it.

Bingo studied the workings for a moment. It explained the presence of the dynamite in the tent. However, the only mining equipment in view was remnants of an old rail track extending from the mine shaft. It was a rusted and twisted relic of some past mining activity and half-buried in brush and dirt. He moved closer.

"I'd say this mine shaft was fixed up recently. The timbers look new and there's a fresh pile of rock and dirt that is probably from cleaning it out."

"Do you think there might be someone in there?" Brooklyn said. "Maybe we should leave. I don't think my mother would be in a place like this. As Tony said, it smells awful."

"Yeah, we've gotta tell the State Troopers about this place," Tony said as he moved to take a closer look at the pelts. "Look, they have white faces. They're sea otters for sure."

Bingo nodded. "Okay, but give me a few minutes. I need to check the mine shaft. If there is no one in there, we'll walk back to the beach. We don't want to hang around here."

Bingo approached the entrance. His guess it had recently been rebuilt and had activity was correct. The ground was well-trodden from the camp right into the shaft. Bingo checked for recent footprints and then studied the entrance and the size of the pile of rock and dirt. There wasn't very much material, which didn't seem to match someone digging it out and doing some mining.

Just inside the entrance, Bingo spotted a couple of lanterns sitting against one of the walls. He picked one up. It was new and battery-operated. It also worked, so he used it to light up the shaft further inside.

"Anyone in here?" He called. "Hello?" His voice echoed back, but there was no other response. He walked a bit further. There was a faint flapping noise up ahead, then nothing. There were old mining tools scattered here and there, and further back it looked like something was stacked in bundles. He was about to investigate when he heard Brooklyn scream, and then Tony hollered from outside.

"Help! Bingo! Come quick!"

Forgetting about the odd sounds, he turned and ran back towards the entrance. The two kids were rushing to meet him while looking over their shoulders to where the trail entered the camp. Bingo immediately saw what had caused them to run.

On the far edge of the clearing was a large river otter standing on its hind legs—its long body bobbing up and down. The animal made menacing noises that could be heard from fifty yards away. He had seen river otters many times. They always acted playfully or were seen searching for something to eat. More than once, he had found an otter on the back deck of his boat in the marina, usually when he left some fish heads in a bucket intending to use them for baiting his crab pots.

The otter facing them was acting much differently. This one was definitely not playful—in fact, just the opposite. It was clearly aggressive. Its eyes bulged like they were going to pop out of its skull. Its jaw was dripping with a frothy white drool. The hissing and yowling sounded frightening even to Bingo. It only took a few seconds for him to realize what was different about this otter.

"Brooklyn! Tony! Stop! Don't run." He shouted. "Very slowly, walk to where I am. That animal is rabid and could very likely attack you. You don't want a rabid animal to bite you."

Tony stumbled over some debris and nearly knocked Brooklyn down as he did as Bingo asked. His eyes were wide, and he was near panic.

Brooklyn grabbed Tony's arm. "Tony, Bingo's right. Don't run." Brooklyn could hardly speak herself. Her words came almost in a whisper. "Walk as calmly as you can to where Bingo is in front of the mine shaft." They moved again, this time a step at a time.

Brooklyn carefully picked a route through the camp, past the tents, and up the slight slope in front of the mine entrance. She kept glancing back over her shoulder to see if the otter was following them and about to pounce on her back. The thought of being bitten on the neck frightened her to the core. The otter had advanced further into the clearing, but it was far enough away that she was pretty sure they could now reach Bingo. But then what would they do?

"What do we do when we get to you?" Brooklyn called to Bingo. "We'll be trapped. We can't get back to the beach and the boat."

"We'll take shelter in the mine shaft and hope it goes away. Maybe it won't stick around. Maybe it is just hungry and came looking for food."

While looking back at the otter, Tony again stumbled over some tools obscured by tall weeds. The otter leaped forward but stopped when Bingo hollered as fiercely as he could and raised his arms above his head. "Hah! Hah! Get out of here!"

The big fellow stood up again on its hind legs and snarled back. It made no indication it was going to run away as Bingo had hoped. It stood its ground, letting Brooklyn and Tony finally reach Bingo's side. While Bingo was deciding what to do, a second otter appeared and looked just as menacing.

"That settles it. Inside the mine!" He shooed them

through the entrance without turning his back on the otters.

"There are a couple of lanterns on the floor just inside," Bingo shouted. "See if you can find one or two that work. With some bright light in here, maybe those crazy critters won't try to come inside."

Brooklyn exhaled and then took a couple of big breaths. She spotted the lanterns and grabbed two of them. She handed one to Tony and fumbled to find a switch on hers. It worked, and the area inside the entrance suddenly brightened. Tony found the button on his and swung it around wildly like he was trying to fend off something unseen.

"Easy, Tony," Bingo said as he joined them inside the mine. "I don't think they will follow us in here."

"Wow, that was close," said Tony as he rubbed his bruised knee.

Brooklyn noticed him doing so. "You okay?"

"Yeah, a bum knee is better than being mauled by those guys. They're scary."

To Brooklyn, his face was a pale white in the light of the lanterns. Her voice faltered as she voiced her concern. "Was that first one really going to attack us, Bingo?"

"Rabies does strange things to an animal," Bingo replied as he walked further into the mine. He motioned for the two of them to follow. "It can make an animal very aggressive."

Brooklyn looked behind them towards the mine entrance. Everything was pitch black outside the circle of light from her lantern and the opening. She didn't see any movement and there was nothing silhouetted by the bright light from outside.

Bingo's voice sounded strange in the confines of the mine tunnel. "I spoke to Doc Perkins before we left Chatham. He told me two people were recently bitten by wild animals, and one died. The other person was able to be treated with rabies vaccine. If one of us gets bitten, we have no way right now of getting medical help. For the vaccine to be effective, the injections have to be started as soon as possible. And from what I have heard, the treatment is pretty dang painful."

Bingo reached the point in the mineshaft where he had stopped exploring earlier.

"You two wait here."

He took the lantern Tony had been carrying and raised it to peer further into the mine. He could barely make out an area where the shaft turned to the left, possibly splitting into two directions. That must have been where he heard the faint noises. He frowned as he sniffed the foul odor, which was now stronger farther into the mine shaft. He had a pretty good idea what caused it as he turned and walked back to where Tony and Brooklyn waited.

"We may have another problem, guys," Bingo said, lowering his voice a bit as if to emphasize the seriousness of what he needed to say. "I think there's a colony of bats somewhere in the mine. That odor comes from where they roost during the day. They're going to want to leave the mine come evening, and we're right in their path. If the bats have rabies, they are a threat, too. We have to be careful. I'd rather we weren't in here very long."

As if on cue, they all sat down and pressed themselves up against the sides of the mine to give the exiting bats more space. The lantern Brooklyn held dimmed and went out. They all noticed it. Bingo clicked off his lantern to conserve its remaining battery life leaving them in total darkness. Brooklyn pulled out her flashlight and turned it on and off. She wasn't at all sure that her little flashlight would fend off a bunch of bats streaking by her for the mine entrance, but it felt better with something in her hands.

Chapter 30

Wally Perkins parked his ATV in front of Gladys' house, opened the gate in a white picket fence, and walked up a path between two rows of rose bushes. Their few remaining blossoms were valiantly showing off, despite the brief snowfall of a few weeks earlier. The roses were well-cared for as was the rest of the yard and house. Knocking on a purple-painted front door, he noticed off to his left the old pickup he had seen earlier near the post office. The front door opened moments later.

"Doctor Perkins, you're here about that awful outbreak already?"

"Well, good morning again, Gladys. No, I'm here to see that old Sourdough brother of yours."

He entered and joined Gladys and Cal who were sitting in the living room having a cup of tea. He joined them. It didn't take long for the conversation to get around to his request.

"Cal, while I was talking to Sid Jackson, he told me you'd spent some time trapping."

"Yup, beaver, foxes, even caught a wolverine one time north of the Yukon. That critter darn near took my hand off when I tried to set it free. I've also done some trapping both here on Baranof. It's been a few years, though. I think there were also a couple of years when Floyd, Gladys' husband, and I ran a trap line together.

Right, Gladys?"

"Oh yes, I sure do. You two made a stinky mess out of my storage shed. You know, I think Floyd's traps are still out in that shed somewhere."

Wally tried to explain his need. "Well, I—ah—need someone to help me trap a few animals. I need to obtain samples for what might be considered a medical emergency—"

Gladys interrupted. "My lord, Dr. Perkins, is this about what I heard you and Sid talking about earlier this morning? About there being a rabies epidemic on the island? Luther, you've got to help him." We can't have rabid wild animals chasing down every loose dog and cat in Chatham. And the children, the children could be exposed to a horrible disease."

Cal raised a halting hand. "Gladys, there's no need to get all concerned about a few rabid skunks or some other critter running amuck around here. Besides, they would die of fright upon setting foot in your yard before they could die of rabies."

"Why, Luther Calhoun, are you inferring that my attempts to keep animals from eating my vegetable garden and digging up my flower beds are overzealous? You need to come around more often and see what they do to my beds."

"But Gladys, I do care about your flowers. Why I just brought you a new rose plant."

"Fiddlesticks, a brother dropping in once in a blue moon bearing gifts doesn't mean you can say anything you want about my hard work. I have a reputation to maintain in this town."

"I…I apologize most sincerely. I—"

"Enough said about that. But, I do like seeing you

more often, especially since my Floyd is gone. Now, you listen to Doc Perkins. He has something important to tell us."

Wally sat patiently listening, hoping he could finish his request for help before the day was over. It appeared Cal was a lot like his sister. They could each talk a blue streak and sure go at each other. He smiled.

"As I told you this morning, Gladys, we don't know the extent of this outbreak. There have been several cases, and all of them were some distance from Chatham. And I'm afraid this is a little bit more serious than a rabid skunk, Cal. I really could use your help. I need to trap some critters and get some brain specimens for lab analysis, and I can't do it alone."

"Well, I think Gladys has just volunteered me," responded Cal. "So, when do we start?"

"How about first thing tomorrow morning? Oh, and one more thing. We're going to need a boat."

"That's not a problem," said Cal. The fishing boat that Gladys's husband used is down at the harbor. It's been a while since I've used it, though. Might take some time to change the engine oil and check things out."

"You could leave right now, Cal," Gladys said. "Jim Boudreau, one of Floyd's old buddies, rented it for the summer fishing season. He just returned it last week, and I haven't had the chance to get someone to winterize it."

Cal slapped his knees to acknowledge his being part of the adventure. "Well then, Wally, if you want to make it an early start, I better get busy and get Gladys' boat fueled up and ready to go."

Chapter 31

Two men carried a semi-conscious Flo out of her house to a van and pushed her into it. One of the men got in the back with her, and the other drove. The vehicle bounced as it sped along on the pot-holed street down to the Chatham boat harbor. Her face scraped on the dirty floor mat rousing her, but the concussion from being hit on the head kept her disoriented. She struggled to get up, but the man shoved her back onto the floor hidden from any onlookers.

At the boat harbor, she was pulled from the van and hustled down the gangway and along the dock to a large boat. It was an entirely black boat with a big array of fish processing equipment on the back deck.

Upon hearing people tromping down the dock, Kenny Sexton peeked out of one of his portholes. He immediately identified one of the people as Flo Whiting, who seemed to be having trouble walking and was being held by two men. He also recognized one of the men holding her and ducked as the man glanced his way.

When the three people got to the black vessel, another man appeared on deck and lifted Flo, who was still struggling, onto the boat while a fourth man looked on from the pilothouse door. He recognized that man, too. Kenny ducked again.

Kenny had heard about Leroy Wilson's run-in and

Flo's home having been set on fire. He didn't want to be part of any more trouble.

There was a low rumbling sound of the boat's diesel engine as it pushed away from the dock. Kenny mustered enough courage to take another peek. The boat was moving out. He read the name on the stern as it slipped by him. The boat's name was *Blackwater*. He glanced down at his hands. They were shaking, and his palms were sweaty.

Kenny sat down for a moment, wondering what he should do. He knew some bad people were looking for Flo, and what he had just witnessed didn't seem right. Flo looked like she was being forced onto that boat. If it was the same men, they might do to Flo what had happened to Bingo and himself. He had to tell someone. He grabbed his cap, leaped off his small boat, and scampered up the dock.

Heading for the café, he would tell Leroy Wilson what had happened. He'd let Leroy decide whether somebody should contact the State Troopers.

Minutes later, a breathless Kenny barged into the café and spotted Leroy clearing a table of dirty dishes. Kenny yelled as the man headed for the kitchen.

"Leroy, they've got Flo! We have to tell somebody."

"What?" Leroy shoved the dishes into the sink with a clatter. "What's going on? You're saying you saw Flo? Where?"

"Down at the harbor. I think it was those guys who were going to cut off your fingers or their friends. Anyway, they have her. They got on this boat, the *Blackwater,* and took off. What are we going to do?"

"Geez, Kenny, you sure about that? You haven't

been drinking with Bingo again, have you?"

"I'm telling you they took her. Two men were holding her arms. They forced her onto this boat. I ain't never seen anything like it before."

Kenny sat down at one of the tables and buried his head in his hands.

"You don't happen to have a beer in that cooler, do you? I need a drink. Maybe you will too when I tell who else I saw on that boat with a pistol sticking out of his pocket."

"What? Who was it?"

"You're never going to believe me. Not in a million years."

****

Wally couldn't help but take a liking to Luther Calhoun. Cal had done as he promised and the boat was ready with everything they might need for the trip already stowed when he climbed aboard just after six the next morning. Gladys had put together several meals for them, including some of her delicious homemade bread. There were also ample supplies of canned goods and snack foods for the days they would spend setting and checking the animal traps.

The galley didn't have a coffee pot, so Wally's first job was making sure there was plenty of hot water for making instant coffee to satisfy Cal's insatiable need.

Once they got underway, Wally accepted the situation that he would have to put up with Cal's storytelling. The man had a hundred stories to tell about his adventures. It eased the boredom of traveling on a slow boat.

Gladys had been married to a commercial fisherman. His old 32-foot fishing vessel was indeed slow and it was slower still towing a 12-foot skiff for getting to shore once they were anchored. Cal handled the boat well, and because of its age, he was cautious not to push it to its top speed. At six knots, they resigned themselves to the fact it would take them over three hours to reach their destination.

As soon as they cleared the harbor and entered Chatham Strait, Cal made a radio call to the Coast Guard to determine if they had received any reports on Jackson's small cruiser.

There was no report to assure them that the kids and Bingo had been found. Wally continued to worry. Overnight, the weather had improved with the rain clouds moving out of the area and the wind and seas moderated. Still, Wally was concerned for what the young people may have endured during the night. Surely Bingo would have sought out somewhere safe, but where?

Wally kept an eye out for the Jackson boat. Like a deer on alert, Wally stood beside Cal, scanning the shoreline and the open water of the strait for any sign of the cruiser while listening to the old-timer's stories of his adventures in Alaska Interior.

Hours later, entering the little bay they believed to be their destination, Wally and Cal immediately saw the grounded boat. They glanced at each other. Without saying a word, Cal increased the boat's speed and headed straight for the beached cabin cruiser. Wally raised his binoculars and glassed the hull. He was pretty sure it was Jackson's.

Wally shook his head. "That's Sid boat all right. This doesn't look good, Cal. I don't see anyone on or near the boat and it's listing to one side. I think they had some serious trouble. You better report this to the Coast Guard. Tell them we found the boat and will investigate. We may need their assistance."

"Right. Do you see anyone on the shore?"

Wally kept his eyes on the boat and the beach as they got closer.

"Haven't seen anyone yet. But someone has used a rope to prevent the boat from drifting into deeper water, and there are some blankets or something on top of a log up in the grass."

He set down the binoculars and headed for the back deck.

"I'm going to use the skiff and check it out. You can hold this boat further out, and I'll signal you whether to drop the anchor. If Sid's boat is okay, I'll try to pull it off the beach and bring it out to you."

Wally watched the shore as Cal put his boat in neutral and let it slow down so Wally could retrieve the towed skiff. As far as Wally could tell, the tide was almost high enough to refloat the grounded cruiser. But where were Bingo and the kids?

He used the skiff they had towed from Chatham and headed directly into the beach. No one rushed to meet him. After checking the boat, he signaled Cal with a thumbs up and planned to pull the cruiser back to the other boat using the skiff. Next, he walked up and down the beach and discovered Bingo's arrow sign pointing to the other side of the bay. Using his binoculars, he scanned the shoreline but couldn't figure out what the arrow might be referring to.

Meanwhile, Cal made the call to the Coast Guard. Then he busied himself anchoring, loading two backpacks, and then getting out his pistol and a 12-

gauge shotgun to take ashore. One pack was filled with animal traps and the other with some essentials in the event they would be gone for most of the day. His essentials included a couple of water bottles and a bag of Gladys' snickerdoodle cookies, his favorite.

Around his portly waist, he strapped on a gun belt and holster containing his old 44-magnum pistol. It showed signs of age with most of the bluing worn off but the large pistol was oiled and clearly well cared for. Having spent over 40 years in the Alaskan wilderness, Cal knew the importance of having a trustworthy weapon close at hand.

"I don't get it," Wally said as he tossed the cruiser's tie line to Cal to secure. "There are a lot of tracks, and someone spent the night up by those logs. Luckily, they left a marker on the beach pointing to the other side of the bay. Maybe, they used the inflatable to get over there. Anyway, it gives us a starting point."

Cal used a pair of binoculars to scan the rest of the bay's shoreline. They had been so focused on the beached boat that they had ignored the rest of the bay.

"Well, I don't see anything, but there are some rocks that might be obscuring our view. It may be there. Do you think we may have missed them heading back to Chatham?"

"I hope they didn't try to do that—not with three of them in that small boat. I would think Bingo would have the sense to wait and see if the tide would refloat the cruiser. Only, why aren't they with it?"

"We should check that spot using the skiff."

"I agree," Cal replied. "The Coast Guard can handle the strait. They could have gone to a location where a passing boat would see them."

"Okay." Wally saw the ruck-sacks lying on the deck. "Are we taking the traps with us?"

"Yup. They're packed along with some snacks."

Wally stowed the packs in the skiff while Cal got settled at the tiller. As Wally pushed off and Cal put the outboard motor in gear, they heard a message on the marine radio. It was a Coast Guard's message to all mariners to watch for a small inflatable with three people on board. He knew they would repeat the message every 20-30 minutes. That should have eased Wally's concern, but the lines on his brow showed that he was still worried about the safety of Brooklyn and her friends.

Cal nudged the skiff's outboard motor into reverse to clear the larger vessel, then into forward as he headed towards the rocky corner of the bay. In a few minutes, they saw the stream flowing out of the Grotto. He followed the current, and moments later, they were inside it.

"Wow!" Cal exclaimed. "Have you ever seen anything like this? I've seen some pretty amazing karst formations down on Prince of Wales Island. There's one place they call Cavern Lake, where a stream flows out of a cave. But here, the tidewater comes right in. Look at that ceiling. Gladys has got to see this. It's beautiful."

Distracted by the scenery, they bumped the skiff into a submerged rock and then careened off one of the cavern's walls. He hollered to Wally. "Grab an oar and push us away from the rocks."

They were almost through the arched cavern and gawking at the marble walls when they saw the inflatable.

"Look, there's a boat up ahead, right where the stream enters the tidewater," said Wally. "See if you can put ours right next to it."

As the bow touched, he grabbed an overhanging tree branch to prevent their boat from being pulled back downstream by the current while Cal shut off the motor. Without the engine's sound, the surrounding forest was quiet except for the soft gurgles of the stream. Cal stood up, grabbed a line to tie up the boat, and stepped ashore.

Cal checked his shotgun and chambered a round of buckshot. "Some years back I was tramping up a stream off of the Yukon carrying a heavy pack in search of a spot to do some gold panning. I walked up on a brown bear in thick brush, like that in front of us. Fortunately, the bear was just as surprised as I was and took off in the opposite direction. Later, I discovered my gun was not loaded."

He handed the shotgun to Wally and checked his pistol.

"That's quite a cannon you lug around, too," said Wally.

"It will do the job of slowing down a charging bear. That is if I don't shoot my foot off getting this hog iron out of its holster. Of course, then the bear has something to munch on while I hobble away."

Wally laughed at Cal's wry humor and looked around them. "It looks like there's a trail into the brush, and someone has been using it. Tracks in the mud look to be the same as the ones I saw over on the beach—must be our group."

"Okay, but let's take it slow and quiet. My right ear itches, and when that happens, I consider it a sign of trouble. Better we see trouble first, meaning a bear."

Wally chuckled. "Then you lead the way. I've got a wife."

"Hey, you're younger than me," Cal replied.

"And more agile and quicker to run the other way, old man."

"Okay, if we get charged by a bear, I'll shoot it, and you take pictures."

Wally laughed again as he handed the shotgun back to Cal. "That's a deal. I'll do my shooting with a camera. We'll need photos to attach to all the paperwork the fish and game people will want if you shoot one."

Following the well-trodden trail and proceeding cautiously, they were still unprepared for what they saw as they walked into the cleared area of Vince's camp. Cal had killed wild game and witnessed Eskimos butchering the carcass of a dead whale on the shore of the Bering Sea. Several times he had come upon the remains of animals killed by bears in the interior of Alaska. Even with all that gore, the sea otter processing camp was bad.

"What the heck is this?" Wally remarked. "We go looking for a couple of missing people and find something out of a horror film."

"That about describes it," replied Cal.

Wally approached one of the drying racks and examined a partially dried animal hide. "This must be Vince James' concealed camp."

"Looks like sea otter pelts to me," said Cal.

"When Vince got sick, he must have left in a hurry. This place is a mess." Wally spotted the fresh pile of dirt. "This must be the grave of Vince's partner. Flo told me about him."

A brown animal came bounding over the dirt pile accompanied by fierce hissing noises causing Wally to step back quickly. Cal saw it too and reacted by bringing up his shotgun and firing. The animal dropped not more than ten feet from Wally—its wounded body writhing on the ground. Cal pulled out his pistol and fired once more.

"Hope you didn't shoot it in the head," said Wally. "This could be the rabid critter we're looking for."

Muffled voices came from the far side of the camp. Both men looked in that direction. Brooklyn and Tony were waving their arms and running towards them. Behind them, a greatly relieved Bingo Bob stood in the entrance to a mine.

Chapter 32

Kwan's yacht was anchored in a quiet cove near the Juneau airport. A very classy Zodiac inflatable, with three people aboard, approached the craft. Moments later, a dripping wet Ronnie Waltrip was thrust through the aft door, but not before one of the other men stripped off his muddy pants, shirt, and shoes. Retrieving Ronnie from the bay had been a messy job.

In his drugged state, Ronnie tried to focus on a man seated in front of him and the voice that spoke. His mind was slow to recognize the man. *Kwan.*

"Have a seat, Mr. Waltrip," said Kwan as he stood up and motioned to Ronnie. "As you can see, my chef has prepared a light dinner."

The imposing figure stood near a long table in the well-appointed salon. From the beautiful mahogany wood paneling and furnishings to the artwork and collection of Chinese weaponry that adorned the interior walls, it exuded money. A fully stocked liquor cabinet sat next to a gorgeous mahogany flight of carpeted steps leading to the pilothouse. A small galley along one side of the salon had black granite countertops sparkling with flecks of gold. A man in a chef's hat was busy stirring a pot on the galley stove. On the table were serving dishes heaped with various Chinese delicacies.

The smell of the food made Ronnie ravenous. He

stared at the platters of food and licked his lips. He had not eaten in nearly twenty-four hours, having not bothered to cook for himself any of the food taken when he left Flo and Vince.

Kwan directed Ronnie's attention to a porcelain washbowl and towel on a side table. "Perhaps you would like to wash up before partaking of a little nourishment?" Kwan shook his head disgustedly. "Oh, I see you have already bathed." He beckoned to one of his men standing near the door. "Find Mr. Waltrip something to cover himself. His appearance is spoiling my appetite."

The man tossed Ronnie a throw that was lying on a side chair. Ronnie slowly pulled the throw around his shoulders and took a seat in a chair sitting in the middle of the room. He shivered uncontrollably. Then there was the growling of his stomach.

Kwan noticed both. "Relax, Mr. Waltrip, I mean you no harm and apologize for how my men may have treated you." He sat back down.

"Now, Mr. Waltrip, you wanted to speak to me about something? You have information that I greatly need for which I am willing to provide some compensation. But you are very much misinformed as to its value. I am a businessman and have a reputation to maintain—both with my associates and with business acquaintances, such as the recently departed Mr. James. I am so sorry to hear about his horrific death. Most unfortunate."

"Vince is dead?" Ronnie uttered. The news cleared his head briefly. He felt a stab of grief even though he'd suspected Vince might die just like Tom Waters. Forgetting his situation, he replied with a weak sneer.

"Yeah, right. I've heard of your reputation, Mr. Kwan. You're pretty ruthless with your associates."

"I prefer to call it being fair, Mr. Waltrip. Vince and I had an agreement, but unfortunately, he failed to keep his part of the deal. Now, I understand that you can offer me something to fulfill Vince's obligations. You said that Vince has a cache of pelts—a lot more than he has delivered, in fact. Well, I already have that information. Vince revealed it before he died. So, why should I pay you for something I already know about?"

Kwan was lying and paused to take a glass of wine from the chef to let Ronnie ponder his situation. Ronnie said nothing and dropped his head to stare at his wet socks.

"Let's get to the point of you being here. I believe those pelts to be rightfully mine. If you can direct my people to their specific location, that information might be worth something. Tell me where they are, and then enjoy a meal." Kwan smiled and waved a hand at the prepared dishes of food. "Usually, it is customary in my country to conduct business after one has shared a fine dinner and a few glasses of wine. But in this case, I am quite impatient, and you and your partners have given me a great deal of frustration. You have been late in delivering the goods, to use an American term. When I recover the remaining pelts, perhaps some minor finder's fee might come your way."

Ronnie sat in his chair, contemplating his next move. He thought having information to sell to Kwan was a stroke of good luck, but the man was a master at negotiation. He would be lucky just to remain alive. The thousands of dollars he'd expected to receive was as much wishful thinking as his attempt to evade

Kwan's men.

As the chef approached the table with a bowl of soup, Ronnie bolted for the door to the back deck. One of Kwan's men tripped him, and he fell to the carpeted deck and slid into a cabinet, banging the side of his head. Then he got a vicious kick to the stomach for his foolish move.

Kwan's voice changed. He no longer offered any pleasantries, just pity, and hostility.

"To refuse my hospitality is an insult to my chef and to me. You might soon regret your actions, Mr. Waltrip. You see, I have another option. Ms. Whiting is now a guest as well. She and my associates are on their way to your former camp. She might be more willing to share the location of the pelts. I believe she values her life and her daughter Brooklyn's more than you do your own."

Ronnie groaned and remained curled up on the floor, protecting himself from another kick. Through the deck, he could feel the vibration of the yacht's engine starting and the anchor brought up. The boat was about to leave the harbor.

His hopes of bargaining with Kwan for a nice sum of money were gone. Now he was hoping to avoid a watery grave.

Chapter 33

When she heard the gunshots, Brooklyn hoped someone had dealt with the rabid otter. It also meant there were people in the camp—rescuers. They could leave the dusty, smelly mine shaft and be free of the tiny denizens of the dark—the bats. However, the gunshots also excited the creatures, and the bats began flying around in increasing numbers.

"Yeah! About time." Tony yelled, jumping to his feet and starting for the entrance.

Bingo grabbed his arm. "Hold on a second, Tony. We don't know who is out there and whether they are friendly. We could be rushing into the hands of the people that operated the camp. We don't know what the shots are about. We'll go see, but stay behind me."

Bingo moved cautiously towards the entrance to the mine. He sighed in relief at seeing Wally Perkins standing in the center of the camp. Another man with a white beard stood over the body of the otter.

Brooklyn recognized the second man immediately. It was Cal.

Before Bingo could even say anything, Brooklyn and Tony surged past him squealing for joy.

"Hello, folks," Wally had a chance to holler before receiving hugs. "We've been looking for you." He ducked as several bats swooped close to his head. He looked up at Bingo with a questioning look on his face.

"Is everyone okay?"

"Yes," Bingo replied. "But any more time in that blasted mine shaft and no telling what could have happened." He took a moment to brush away several bats that clung to his hat and the shoulders of his jacket. "We got inside before the otter could get to us and waited for it to go away, except that put us in the path of another problem—these bats."

Bingo walked over to where Cal stood, examining the otter.

"I'm guessing it wasn't going away." He stuck out a hand to Cal. "Name's Bingo Bob. Nice shooting. Thanks."

Cal nodded and grinned. "Howdy, Bingo. I've heard about you from my sister Gladys. I'm Cal. You and the kids were in a real pickle, all right." Cal pointed his weapon at the carcass of the river otter. "This old guy was madder than a hornet in a Mason jar, I'd say."

Brooklyn stepped back from hugging Wally. Her attention was drawn to the steady stream of bats making their exodus from the mine. Some of them swirled around her, darting at flying insects, while others broke off in all directions and into the trees and foliage. She wasn't afraid of them any longer, despite their ugliness. She studied their swallow-like flying with the fascination of a science student on a field trip.

Wally tried to get her attention. "Brooklyn, what about your mother? Did you find anything that indicated she was here?"

"What? No, we didn't see anything. There's no sign that she's been here."

Tony injected himself into the conversation. "What about the boat? Is my dad's boat okay?"

Wally responded. "The boat's fine, Tony. We pulled it off the shore and left it tied to our boat." He turned to Brooklyn again. "If Flo hasn't been here, there's no sense in us hanging around. Let's get you guys back to the boat. We'll have something to eat and then see if we can get you started back to Chatham. It's gonna be a while before Cal and I can leave. We have to set some traps first. That's why we're here."

To get them moving, Cal stepped away from the dead otter and headed for the trail to the dock.

Brooklyn liked that idea. Not because she was hungry, thirsty, and cold, but because of the lingering stench in the camp and her general uneasiness with the place. While pleased to be rescued, Brooklyn remained quiet. She couldn't shake the strange feeling she had about the area. Just as when they had passed through the Grotto earlier that day, the silence and closeness of the dense woods on either side of the trail made her nervous. While Cal had shot one of the otters, there had been two of them. She kept her eyes peeled for the other otter. It had to be close by—maybe watching them from the thick brush, ready to leap on any one of them. The feeling sent a chill up her back far worse than the ordeal of being trapped in the mine.

As they walked down the trail to the boats, Wally chatted with Bingo. Tony walked ahead of them next to Cal. He was a regular chatterbox. Brooklyn smiled to herself. In all of their classes at school together, she had never heard Tony say so much in so little time. Even Cal had to listen and not be the one not talking. Tony finally shut up when Cal described the condition of his dad's boat, how Wally had got it off the beach and that it was now safe in the middle of the bay.

****

Archie Hutchinson stood on the back deck of the *Blackwater* having a cigarette. Hutch could see Flo through a window, her head and shoulders slumped over the table where she sat. She looked like her will to resist was gone—at least he hoped it was. They needed to learn where Vince's pelts were hidden. Kwan's message was clear. The man was concerned with how long it had taken to find the woman and the limited time left to retrieve the pelts and get them out of the country.

Hutch had been upset with Mona for letting Flo go. Mona had only understood why they were holding Vince, so it was understandable to let Flo leave when Vince died. While she had escaped with Mona's help, he was pretty sure where he could find her.

He felt a bit sorry for the woman since Kwan was capable of just about anything. When Kwan got mad or things didn't go his way, he hurt people. There was not much Hutch could do about that. He needed to look out for himself—not some woman who was stupid enough to get mixed up in the illegal activities of Vince James.

He felt no remorse that Vince was dead and was more concerned about what he would do with the body. At least the guy had died of natural causes, so to speak. They couldn't charge him with murder. Flo had accused him and his sons of kidnapping, but it was her word against theirs on that score. That is if Flo lived to tell the State Troopers about being kidnapped. It would be easy enough to just throw her overboard, although it would be suspicious if her body washed up on the shore somewhere along Chatham Strait. Then again, someone in town could have seen her leave on this boat. Then he would be an accessory to murder, depending on what Kwan or Hendricks decided to do with her.

Then there was Mona's plea to Flo. Mona confessed that she was freaked out because Will had been bitten by Vince, and he needed immediate treatment for rabies. She said Flo had promised to see that Will gets treatment. Except he was pretty sure they had grabbed Flo before she had time to do anything about him. He needed to ask Flo if she had talked with Doc Perkins about Will. He had been so intent on following through on Kwan's demands that he had forgotten about Will. He hoped the boy was smart enough to deal with his injury himself, but he wasn't sure. The boy was not all that smart.

Through the window, Hutch watched Flo accept a cup of coffee and then throw it in the face of her captor and scream at him. She had some fight in her after all, and she looked angry enough to kill somebody. Hutch smiled as he watched, hoping he wouldn't have to intervene. The guy didn't react as he should have. He seemed to be accepting both her verbal and physical abuse like a kid in front of his mother and has been caught doing something bad. He was allowing her to rant and carry on. Hutch shook his head and stayed out of it, electing to remain on deck in a brisk breeze and watching the darkening shoreline.

This whole business with Kwan may have been a bad idea and wasn't improving. What's more, he hadn't heard from AJ or Will since they'd gone into town. He had seen their truck parked in front of the Frontier Pub.

Inside the cabin, the tone of things changed. Something Hendricks said caused Flo's head to snap back. She stared at him for a moment then began talking more calmly. Then she started crying and buried her head in her arms. Hutch suspected the man issued a threat—maybe with the daughter.

He got a thumbs-up signal from her interrogator, who quickly turned and headed for the pilothouse. Flo must have told him where to find the pelts.

Hutch's cell phone rang. He flicked his cigarette butt over the side and pulled the phone out of his shirt pocket. It was Mona.

"Wherever you are, you better watch yourself, Hutch. Two Troopers were just here looking for you. They arrested AJ and Will and are taking them to Hoonah."

Chapter 34

Cal took Brooklyn and Tony out to the boat in his skiff while Bingo, rowing the inflatable, took Wally. The strong winds from the night before had not returned. The bay's surface was calm, and the sky had cleared except for isolated clouds clinging to the higher mountains on the far side of the strait.

Wally got Brooklyn and Tony settled in the cabin then tried to call Trooper Williams to report encountering a rabid animal and killing it. After several attempts, he gave up.

"I can't get through to him." He checked his phone. "Looks like poor cell coverage here."

"I suggest you use the radio and call the Coast Guard," said Cal pointing to the UHF marine radio at the helm. "They can relay a message to him or the State Troopers over in Hoonah who can probably reach Williams."

With the needs of the two young ones taken care of, and Cal and Wally trying to report what occurred at the camp, Bingo took the opportunity to check out the condition of the Jackson boat. Stepping out onto the deck, the bay where they were anchored was no longer feeling like a lonely place. With Cal and Wally now present, he relaxed. He closed his eyes and breathed deep, letting the tension of the last 24 hours ease off. A familiar sound carried over the water, and he opened his eyes to scan the entrance to the bay. Just out of sight beyond the bay's north point, several humpback whales were feeding. He was sure of it. Bingo smiled to himself when he heard their blows get louder, and they finally came into view. A large male surfaced, blew again, and then dove deep—its tail slowly slipping under the water surface as if it was waving to him.

Bingo had climbed onto the Jackson family boat when Cal emerged from the cabin with Brooklyn right behind him. Tony remained sitting at the small galley table eating a sandwich Wally had prepared.

"How is Tony's boat?" Brooklyn asked.

"Appears to be sound. Not much water in the bilge." Bingo answered. He lifted the cover to the battery compartment and beckoned to Cal. "Can you give me a hand checking the electrical system? We need to get some power to run the bilge pump, the radio and see if these outboard motors will start."

While Brooklyn was on deck watching Cal and Bingo work on the cruiser and Tony was busy eating, Wally used the marine radio. The Coast Guard in Juneau answered immediately. He reported finding the Jackson boat and that everyone was safe.

The radio operator, learning he was a Chatham resident, informed him of a developing situation that jolted his senses. He turned down the volume and asked the person to repeat the message. Wally shook his head as he stared at Brooklyn through a window as he listened.

"Our office has issued a broadcast message to all mariners for anyone seeing a black vessel called the *Blackwater* to contact the Coast Guard immediately. The vessel is believed to be involved in the kidnapping of a woman from Chatham. The State Troopers received a missing person report for a Caucasian female approximately 35 years of age, dark blonde hair, five foot six in height, with the name of Florence Whiting. Anyone seeing this vessel is asked to notify the Coast Guard."

Wally wasn't sure what to do. He glanced at Tony, who was flipping through a boating magazine and apparently hadn't been listening. Brooklyn was another matter. He would have to decide what is the right time to inform her.

He lit a small kerosene stove to heat some water, then he dug out some packets of instant coffee and hot chocolate and a couple more mugs from one of the storage compartments. While the water heated, he stepped out of the cabin to see how it was going with the other boat. He saw Bingo had just finished pumping water from the bilge by hand.

"Batteries are dead. Contacts got wet and shorted the system," Bingo said as he disconnected the battery cables, picked one of the batteries up, and handed it to Cal. "Can you hook up this battery to your system to recharge it? The outboard motors seem okay. If I can get one of them started, we can get the other battery charged pretty quickly."

"Let me see," Cal said. "Last time I checked there was a set of cables on board this old tub." Cal took the battery and flipped open a small hatch cover to expose the old fishing boat's engine and batteries. There was a set of jumper cables tucked alongside them. As he connected them to the dead battery, Wally announced parts of what he had just learned from his radio conversation.

"The Coast Guard has called off the search for you folks. There's a search going on for Flo but unless they get more information, they're not sure where to look." He watched Brooklyn's face for a reaction but she seemed calm.

"She will show up right here," said Brooklyn. "I know she will."

Cal looked up at her. "Wouldn't Flo want to be taken to Chatham? She'll figure you're at home and be worried about you."

"I agree, Brooklyn," added Wally. "You and Tony staying here would complicate things. What Cal's saying, is that killing an otter kind of crosses the bats off the list of suspected hosts and confirms my suspicions that the otters are the rabies source and may have already infected other animals. We're gonna have to trap some of them to see if the rabies is spreading to a bigger population. That means hanging around here awhile and we don't have enough food for everybody."

"I'll get them home safely," Bingo said. "You can count on that. And, if you are going to be here a few days and have the time, you might want to check out the mine shaft. I never got the chance to take a thorough loo but there are interesting things stored way inside the mine, including some old mining tools. But be careful. Did you see the grave?"

"We saw the grave," said Wally. "I already knew about it. It's for someone who died from rabies."

"That's not good," Cal said. "I have a strange feeling about this place. Death kind of hangs over it like a raincloud." He closed the battery compartment, stood up, and looked towards the shore. "You know, I've always had an interest in mines like the one at that

272

camp. I've been looking for gold for more than forty years. There are a lot of old gold and silver claims like that one around here. Most of them are played out. I've even got a little dig of my own. But you know, I just might take a look inside that mine before we leave."

Bingo smiled. "You're a hard rock miner? Me, I wouldn't want to spend another minute inside that mountain. I like it just fine out here in the fresh air."

Cal laughed. "So why are you called Bingo, or is it Bob? I think I've seen you around Chatham once or twice. I only stop by occasionally to see my sister Gladys."

"Gladys is your sister? She's a fine lady. She and I like gardening and the challenge of growing flowers in one tough environment. And Bingo will do just fine as I haven't been called Bob, or Robert, in quite a few years. Please don't take that the wrong way. When I arrived in Alaska, I wanted to start a new life. Forget the past. So a different name helped. I hope you know what I mean."

"Oh, I sure do. I've met a hundred guys who felt the same way. So you offered to help Brooklyn locate her mother?"

"More like the opposite." He looked at Brooklyn. "Brooklyn asked for my help. She and Tony needed an adult to come along on this little boat ride. I'm not really sure why I agreed. I just felt like I had to, you know?"

Wally looked at Brooklyn who had been listening to the three of them. "I found some of Gladys' homemade oatmeal cookies when I was getting out some packages of hot chocolate. The water should be hot and you might want to grab a cookie before Tony finishes them off."

Cal chuckled as Brooklyn nodded in agreement and joined Tony in the cabin.

"She's mighty convincing," said Cal after she was gone. "Got to know her a little myself when she hitched a ride with me from Hoonah where she'd gone by herself to look for her mom. She's smart and a real caring young girl."

"Yeah, I think it's been hard on her having her mother missing," Bingo said. "I'm concerned about that too. Flo is mixed up in something that doesn't seem right, especially if it involves this camp. I've seen some pretty frightening things in my life, but the conditions in that camp back there, made me want to throw up. I can't imagine how Brooklyn felt. Or Tony, for that matter."

Cal nodded. "I've watched whales and seals being butchered up in the Arctic. The scene back in that camp was not very different. But I know how you felt, walking in on it unaware." Cal scratched at his long beard. "How did you find this place? I know Brooklyn was looking for her mother. But nothing is obvious to me as to why she would be at that camp."

"Brooklyn had information that her mother might be at a place called the Grotto," Bingo answered. "She asked a lot of folks in town if they had seen Flo. An old Indian woman said she was in the company of a ghost. That kind of scared her. She met with the Native shaman in Chatham who said he knew where the Grotto was, although he discouraged her from trying to find it. Something about an old Indian legend, it is a bad place—a place of death. That didn't stop Brooklyn. She was determined to find it despite what he said. Anyway, when we arrived, we couldn't anchor and the boat ended up on the beach. We had a pretty wet and miserable night. This morning, we found the camp. You know the rest." Bingo finished checking out the cruiser, wiped his hands on a rag, and then joined Cal and Wally back on the deck of the fishing boat.

The men gazed at the rocky shoreline and the wooded slopes surrounding them. Bingo focused on the spot where the entrance of the Grotto lay hidden. "You know, we didn't have a clue about there being some type of camp in there. I figured we would find an abandoned mine or a trapper's cabin that had been fixed up."

"I think we were all fooled," Cal replied. "We found the entrance and the trail using the marks you left and simply followed them. The people who built the camp to process sea otter pelts didn't want to be found—it's a well-hidden camp. You know, we wouldn't be here either if we hadn't been informed by the State Troopers as to where to look for a reported rabid animal."

"Huh!" Bingo said, rubbing his chin and realizing he had shaved off his beard. "That's interesting. Your directions and our directions were to the same place, but for entirely different reasons."

"Well, at least everyone's safe," said Wally. "Now, if we just knew the whereabouts of Flo and whether she's okay. I couldn't bring myself to tell Brooklyn what else the Coast Guard dispatcher told me. "Flo may have been kidnapped by some pretty bad people. I try not to think too hard about the alternatives."

Before he could say more, Tony popped out of the cabin with a cookie stuffed in his mouth to see what was happening. He seemed a lot more relaxed now that he had eaten some food.

"Ah, we can discuss this later," said Wally. "I think I'll get a cup of coffee. It's instant if anyone else wants some."

"I'll take you up on that," said Bingo. He and Wally ducked back into the cabin.

Tony went to the rail and stared at the cruiser. "Mr. Calhoun, is my dad's boat going to be okay?"

"Looks fine, Tony. There are a few scratches on the bottom. We'll know about the motors shortly when we start it up. How are you and Brooklyn doing?"

"We're okay. I sure was hungry." Tony looked over at the beach and the forest. "Why would someone want to kill sea otters, Mr. Calhoun?"

"Call me Cal, son. Poaching sea otter pelts has been on the rise these last couple of years. There's a global market for sea otter pelts. When the Russians came here in the 1800s, the pelts were called soft gold. The fur was highly prized for its warmth almost as much as mink fur. The sea otters were harvested almost to the point of extinction. They were re-introduced in Southeast Alaska in the 1970s and are protected by law from hunting."

"Yeah, and now they're everywhere, thousands of them," Tony said.

"Yes, more like tens of thousands of them, but it's illegal to take sea otter pelts unless you're an Alaskan Native. But with the popularity of their fur in Asia, there's a black market for them. As a result, we're seeing signs of another gold rush."

They joined the others. Wally was making Brooklyn a mug of hot chocolate and grabbed another mug figuring Tony would want the same.

Cal settled his bulk onto a seat and made a statement to all. "Well, I think it's good news folks. If we can get the batteries recharged, you should be able to head back to Chatham in the morning."

"In the morning?" Brooklyn asked as her shoulders slumped. "But what about Mom? I've got to know if she is okay."

"Easy, girl," Wally said. "Both the Coast Guard and the State Troopers are looking for her. They have started a search. I've asked the Coast Guard to contact us when she is found. Like Cal says, you, Tony, and Bingo can head back at first light if this calmer weather holds. Cal and I have work to do and will be staying here for a couple of days. That is, as long as Tony hasn't eaten all of our food."

Everyone laughed at Tony, who was finishing off the last of the cookies.

"But what about the second otter?" said Brooklyn.

"Yeah!" Tony's voice was muffled from another mouth full of a cookie. "You could be attacked like we were."

Wally looked at them. "What? You have seen more than one rabid animal? That's not so good. It increases the probability of the disease spreading to other animals. Looks like we definitely have our work cut out for us, Cal."

"And I'm staying with you. If my mother isn't home in Chatham in the morning, she could still show up here," Brooklyn declared.

Cal threw up his hands. "She's a very determined young lady and made up her mind. It's your call, Wally."

"Not mine," shaking his head. "I guess she stays."

****

A water and land search for Flo Whiting had been mobilized and had generated a steady stream of radio communications between the Coast Guard operations center in Juneau and the State Trooper detachment in Hoonah. The Coast Guard base commanding officer personally took charge of the search. Initially, they didn't have any leads on the suspects or a good description of the vessel in question. That situation all changed when they received a series of reports from Chatham—one was a strange 911 call from Flo Whiting who said she had been kidnapped and another call from a resident seeing her being forced onto a boat called the *Blackwater*. With a probable identification of the boat involved, the Commanding Officer requested additional support. The Coast Guard cutter *Theodore F Stevens* was on patrol nearby in Fredrick Sound and he ordered the cutter to proceed north in the search for the *Blackwater*.

Later that evening, the *Sherry J.* was found. The boat was moored in the Harris Boat Basin near downtown Juneau, but there was no one on board. About the same time, a naked man was pulled out of the water by a fisherman near the Point Retreat Lighthouse some twenty miles from Juneau. The man was Ronnie Waltrip and he was suffering from severe hypothermia. He had an interesting story to tell the State Troopers.

Chapter 35

Brooklyn rolled over on the narrow bench seat in the old fishing boat and stretched as she woke up. Her nagging concern for her mother had led to a fitful night with disturbing dreams. Somehow, they had been reunited only to be in mortal danger. Her dreams carried images of the dark mine, fluttering bats, and escaping an evil presence she couldn't see, but it struck fear in both her and her mother.

A late September dawn was just starting to paint the interior of the cabin in an amber glow. Sounds of two men snoring reached her from the bunks in the forward cabin where Wally and Cal were sleeping. Bingo and Tony were sleeping on the smaller boat tied to the side of Cal's.

Brooklyn propped herself up on an elbow to see out the cabin window. The eastern sky was a thin band of brilliant orange light and expanding as she stared. The colored sky was a welcoming sight, a sign of a clear day, or at least it would start that way. In Alaska, the weather changed quickly and a clear, sunny day in the morning could become gray and rainy by afternoon.

At her home in Chatham, the morning skyline was hidden by a high forested ridge. Through the cabin window, she could see that the entrance to the bay aligned perfectly with the rising sun. The new dawn reflected across the water like the beam of a gigantic lighthouse until it shone into the boat and on her face. Only there was no accompanying warmth, just the touch of color that convinced her this day was going to be better than the last several.

Somewhere out there, her mother could be experiencing the same rising sun, hopefully, safe and sound. She had to be. She trusted in her mother's strength and ability to take care of herself, something she had done all her life. It was something her mother had instilled in her, too. Today, the two were going to be reunited. She just knew it and the excitement of that feeling grew as the sun began to peek over the horizon and the orange glow faded.

When everyone was up, Cal set about preparing breakfast. He was a master at cooking even in a tiny galley. They all wolfed down sourdough pancakes smothered in Gladys' homemade huckleberry syrup. After Tony's third plateful, Cal finally had to throw up his hands and say he was plumb out of pancake mix. The morning sun shining into the boat and joking with each other over pancakes, bacon, and coffee had chased away the problems of the last few days.

After breakfast, Bingo and Wally got Tony's boat ready for the trip back home. Brooklyn watched them work, but her attention kept going back to her mother.

Now that the weather had changed, the little bay took on a different appearance. The small stream trickled over the beach where they had spent a dismal night. Salmon were jumping and finning near its mouth. The outflow of cold freshwater tempted the gathering salmon to enter but they had to wait for rain and the stream level to rise. She looked over at the entrance to the Grotto. There was a stir of excitement and adventure about accompanying Wally and Cal as they explored the valley above the camp and set their animal traps.

She glanced at her new friend Tony who was straightening up the cabin of his dad's boat. Tony would soon be home and back at school. That thought struck her—back at school. She should be in class as well. Mr. Hendricks was going to be upset with her. She remembered her surprise when coming upon Mr. Hendricks on that boat in Hoonah. He seemed like a different person—not her upper-grade teacher for the past several years.

From the other boat, Wally interrupted her thoughts. "Brooklyn, you sure you want to stay here?" Wally had finished helping Bingo load the inflatable back on top of the cabin and stow the sleeping bags and other gear so that the boat was ready for the trip. The two outboard motors were running smoothly and warming up.

"Last chance," Wally said her name again to get her attention. "Brooklyn?"

"Huh?" Brooklyn slowly turned her head. "Yes, I want to stay, Wally. I have this feeling that Mom is going to show up here. She's going to need me—need to hold me. All this…this craziness has made me realize that."

Cal joined them. "Hold on to that feeling, Brooklyn. I know you are very worried about your mom, but you have to keep thinking she's okay. That's what she would want. I just checked with the Coast Guard and they haven't found her yet. There was a report of her leaving Chatham on a boat yesterday. It will be located."

Bingo added his own words of assurance. "Tony and I will be back in Chatham in a few hours. We'll help from there and keep you informed by radio. If she's back home, we'll get her on the radio so you can talk to her."

"If you both are trying to convince me to go home and wait for her there, forget it. I'm staying." Brooklyn folded her arms across her chest. She did not want to get on the other boat and return to Chatham, at least not yet.

"I'm not going to force you to return home," Wally said. "But this isn't like a stroll up the cliffs and watching for eagles. This place may be beautiful, but it's wilderness, Brooklyn. We're going to venture up this valley and could run into a brown bear, or more likely, another rabid animal. You could also get separated from us or lost. With Bingo going back, your safety becomes my responsibility. The day your mother told me she was going away to help Vince James, I agreed to watch after you. She didn't want to worry about you. Do you understand?"

Brooklyn nodded.

"If I let you stay, do you agree on my terms?"

She nodded again.

****

As the cruiser with Tony and Bingo disappeared around the bay's south point headed back to Chatham, Cal guided his skiff into the Grotto. Brooklyn sat in the bow where she had a great view. Wally sat behind her with two backpacks between his legs stuffed with animal traps. Brooklyn wore her own backpack, which contained a rain slicker, water, and some snacks. Cal had insisted she carry a can of bear spray. He showed her how to use it in case she encountered a bear on her own although that was unlikely since she had promised to stick close to the two men.

While they were eating their breakfast, Wally had explained their plan to set the traps along both of the streams that entered the bay and within a three-mile radius of the abandoned camp which included the lake where the two tourists had encountered a rabid animal. Cal was confident they should be able to find where the otters had their dens as it was likely in one of the stream banks. Finding the dens and setting several of the traps upstream and downstream of their dens would improve the odds of either shooting or catching several otters to check for rabies. Regardless of which plan worked out, it was going to be a long, hard day of trudging through dense brush and thick timber.

Brooklyn had renewed confidence that this would be a crucial day, more than any day since the start of her mother's mysterious absence. She could not accept the fact that any harm could come to Flo, who hadn't done anything to anybody. From what she now knew, Flo was trying to help Vince. If it was Vince's camp, then this was where he and Flo would come.

Their skiff emerged from the dim confines of the Grotto into a patch of sunlight. If the clear sky stayed into the afternoon, it would make their wilderness trek easier. Wally tied the skiff to the old dock and he and Cal quickly unloaded the packs. Brooklyn stared at the trail to the camp. The encounter with the rabid river otter and their retreat into the mine made her queasy all of a sudden.

"Brooklyn, are you sure you want to do this?" Wally said. "You could remain here with the skiff."

Brooklyn turned away from looking at the trail and fidgeted with her backpack straps. "How long do you think we'll be gone? Are we coming back here?"

Cal was shouldering one of the packs and getting it comfortable on his back. "If we find the otter den, we could be back here in a couple of hours. Depends on how difficult it is to follow the stream." He looked up the stream and examined the nearshore bank. "It looks like there's an old trail for us to follow. It might be just an animal trail, but at least it's better than bushwhacking one of our own. We'll try to come back the same way."

"That sounds good to me," Wally said. "Cal, why don't you take the lead? Brooklyn, you follow Cal and I'll keep an eye on the trail behind us. We'll be setting some traps soon. I think you'll be interested in seeing what we are doing. It will take your mind off your mom for a while. Let the Troopers find her. They know how to deal with these situations."

The trio set off following the stream. Like the change in the weather, their luck was also improving as they found a well-used otter den in a high bank along their side of the stream not more than a half-mile above the dock. Wally examined the area around the otter den without getting too close and contaminating it with the smell of humans. There were several, animal trails leading from the den onto the stream bank. They looked freshly used. It was perfect for placing a couple of traps. Cal removed two of his traps and explained how they worked as he prepared them.

"These are called soft-catch traps. See these rubber-covered edges? They're constructed to not seriously injure the animal. There is also a device that injects the animal with a sedative, called Gabapentin, so it won't get excited and try to gnaw its foot off trying to escape. It is a drug often prescribed by veterinarians as a post-surgery medication. Only we don't have any and so we plan to check the traps twice a day."

Brooklyn's interest in what they were doing increased when she learned the traps were relatively safe. She liked the fact that an animal caught in one of the traps wouldn't suffer. She had seen pictures of traps with ugly serrated edges that permanently maimed the animal. "Wouldn't a live trap be better?" Brooklyn asked. "We had a raccoon living under our house once and Mom borrowed one to trap it. Then we took it up to the old logging camp and released it."

"Not necessarily," Wally replied. "If we were trying to catch a raccoon or other type of animal to relocate it, like in your case, then a live trap is preferable. But a rabid animal tends to go berserk when caged and would likely seriously hurt itself. With a live trap, there is also the problem of trying to sedate the animal so we can obtain a specimen to send to the lab."

"But how will we know whether we have caught something in one of the traps?"

"Just like in the old days, Brooklyn," Cal said as he tied a piece of red ribbon on a branch close to where he had just buried the first trap in a trail used by the otters. "Each time we set a trap, we mark their location. When all the traps are placed, it's called a trap line. Wally and I will spend several nights on the boat and will periodically check the trap line. Before we leave, we pick up all the traps. We can't leave them unattended. That would be cruel."

It took them a half-hour to finish setting the two

traps near the den.

Wally was emphatic that they find another spot nearer to Evans Lake, that he had seen on Sid's map at the store. So they followed a game trail parallel to the stream hoping it would get them there. To their dismay what they thought was an easy route turned into bushwhacking after all, as the game trail turned away from the stream. Minutes later, they discovered their way forward blocked by a high waterfall.

Chapter 36

The *Blackwater* passed Tony and Bingo in their small cruiser about an hour after the two had left the bay headed for Chatham. Tony opened a side door and waved. Exchanging a greeting is often done by boats passing one another. Tony waved at whoever was in the pilothouse of the black-hulled boat. He frowned when he didn't get a response. Most boat operators waved back as a courtesy and as a way of saying I saw you and stayed clear of your course.

Tony turned to Bingo who was at the wheel. "Huh, the skipper of that big black boat is about as unfriendly as the boat looks. Didn't bother to answer my wave."

The *Blackwater* was moving fast and putting up a large wake. One could usually guess a boat's destination based upon its direction of travel. But it would only be a guess unless the boat happened to be a ferry or a cruise ship with specific destinations or ports of call. Tony had no idea that the black-hulled vessel was heading for the very spot he had just departed. From the equipment he saw on the back deck, Tony assumed it was a fish processing vessel in a hurry to buy fish from an isolated fleet of smaller fishing vessels. Moments later, their wakes crossed with the little cruiser rolling hard from the huge wake of the larger vessel.

An hour later as they were approaching the

entrance to Peril Strait, Bingo and Tony stared at each other in surprise as they listened to a broadcast message from the Coast Guard on their marine radio. "Mariners are requested to immediately report any sighting of a black, steel hull vessel with the name *Blackwater*."

Without a word to Tony, Bingo picked up the radio mike and called the Coast Guard. The answer he got was also a surprise. He was ordered to hold his position and to wait for the Coast Guard cutter *Theodore F. Stevens*.

Less than an hour later, Bingo stood on the bridge of the cutter briefing its Captain and several other officers about the missing Flo Whiting and a place called the Grotto being a likely connection to her kidnapping. After hearing his story, the Captain got on the radio with Juneau. When he finished his conversation, he ordered a seaman be put on the Jackson boat to accompany Tony back to Chatham. Bingo would remain on board and help him find the Grotto.

Bingo found a comfortable place to sit on the bridge of the cutter and sipped a cup of coffee brought to him from the galley. One of the Coast Guard officers was talking with the dispatcher with the State Troopers in Juneau. When he finished, he approached Bingo and the Captain.

"Sir, I've been informed that Officer Dave Williams with the Alaska State Troopers will meet us at the bay. His office reports that there have been previous run-ins with the operators of the *Blackwater*, but there hasn't been enough evidence to make an arrest stick. The Troopers interviewed someone this morning who had been with Flo Whiting and confessed to killing sea otters to sell to the operator of the *Blackwater*. The boat could be attempting to recover a cache of otter pelts hidden near the Grotto. He said they tried to kill him by throwing him overboard last night and could kill the Whiting woman. The crew of the *Blackwater* should be considered armed and dangerous."

"Captain," said Bingo. "There could be three other innocent people at risk. Ms. Whiting's daughter is there as well as two of her friends. They could be on that boat or at an abandoned mine about a quarter-mile inland."

"Okay," said the Captain. "I'm ordering my crew to be prepared to encounter armed resistance. If the vessel is in the bay, I will block the entrance with this ship and one of our rapid deployable inflatables. A second inflatable will assist the State Trooper's patrol boat in boarding the *Blackwater*." He pointed a finger at Bingo. "If your friends are not on the boat, once we have taken custody of the vessel and the situation is secure, I'll request Trooper Williams to pick you up to help guide a landing party to this mine."

****

Flo was asleep on a bench in the salon of the *Blackwater*—never sensing the passing of the other boat and only rousing an hour later with the rattle of the boat's anchor descending into the bay close to the shore. After the anchor was set, a couple of the crew launched two skiffs with outboard motors.

****

While Archie Hutchinson waited to go ashore, he used a pair of binoculars to check out the old fishing boat already anchored in the bay. He kept a wary eye on the shore and was puzzled that there was no shore boat to be seen anywhere. Also, no one appeared on the other boat's deck to greet them. This was not unusual, because fishermen often anchored in small bays such as this one, to grab some sleep, especially if they had been fishing all night. Still, he was suspicious. He had seen this boat before—moored in the harbor at Chatham. It never went anywhere. So why was it here?

A commotion on the back deck caught his attention. Flo was putting up some resistance as she was forced into one of the skiffs. She was furious and fighting back but to no avail as she was handled by two of the deckhands who hoisted her over the rail into the skiff.

Hutch's uneasiness didn't go away as he retrieved a shotgun from the pilothouse and joined the others in one of the skiffs. Where they were headed once onshore was another thing that was unclear to him. All he knew was they were to find the cache of otter pelts and take them. Other than the old fishing boat, the bay looked deserted. There was no sign of a cabin or camp. If Vince James had used this location for processing otter pelts, the guy had done a good job of hiding his operation. Minutes later they all disappeared single file into the hidden domain of the Grotto. At that point, they went on full alert because another skiff was already tied to a dock on the upstream side.

"What's going on here, Hendricks?" said Hutch when he saw the skiff. "I thought this place was supposed to be deserted. Is someone already here? I recognized that boat out there. It's from Chatham."

"I saw it too. That old boat belongs to a Chatham woman's husband who died years ago. The only time I've ever seen it, it has been tied up in the harbor. What it's doing out here is a mystery to me too."

"Doesn't matter," Hutch replied lowering his voice as the outboard motor shut down. Their boat was the first to reach the dock. "We follow Kwan's orders. Get the otter pelts and deal with anyone that gets in our way."

Flo was in the second boat which was behind them and still motoring through the Grotto. As Hendricks climbed onto the dock, Hutch saw a pistol under the man's coat.

"I'm curious, Hendricks. What do you plan to do with Ms. Whiting? I do a lot of things I don't want to when I have to avoid getting arrested, but I didn't sign on to commit a murder."

Hendricks shook his head and watched the second skiff approach the dock. His response was between a croak and a whisper. "Kwan wasn't…clear on that. He doesn't care about anything except getting the rest of his pelts. He said she's my problem, but it wasn't supposed to be like this." He avoided looking directly at Hutch. "I…I'll think of something."

"Well, you'd better think of something soon. We can't hang around here very long. This situation is really screwed up, and I don't want to be caught in possession of illegal furs by the State Troopers or the Coast Guard. My boys have already been picked up on suspicion of kidnapping, and it's going to be a mess for my lawyer to resolve. If Flo Whiting were to have an accident and not make it back home, it would make my life easier—no witnesses to a kidnapping."

****

Flo didn't hear their conversation. She was hardly aware of where she was, being exhausted. The few hours of sleep on the boat had helped a little, but the ordeal with Vince had taken a toll. She didn't even notice the spectacular beauty around her as they passed through the Grotto. It was only when the others got out of the skiff and attempted to hustle her onto the dock that her adrenalin kicked in again. It hadn't occurred to her until then that they might want to kill her or just leave her here. She was in the middle of nowhere surrounded by wilderness. She couldn't run. There was nowhere to run. She wouldn't survive. It was best to go along with Hendricks. Maybe there would be a chance to reason with the man. He was a teacher, for goodness' sake—he was her daughter's teacher. Even though she had lost all of her respect for the man and now hated him, he had to have some compassion.

Hendricks put out a hand to assist Flo onto the dock, but she refused to take it. Their eyes made contact briefly. There was a fire in her eyes and it was directed at him.

"I know you hate me, Ms. Whiting, but you just don't understand my situation. I have to do this. I don't have a choice. So please get out of the boat and follow Hutch. We're going to get Vince's pelts. That cave over there is going to fill with water in a couple of hours when the tide rises. We have to leave as soon as we can."

Flo still refused his assistance and stepped out on the dock by herself. She had to squeeze past Hendricks on the dock, and as she passed him, she slapped him in the face. "Does 'we' include me? Or am I to remain behind? At least I hope you have the decency to bury my corpse so it isn't torn apart by wild animals." She kept walking.

If she had looked back at the man, she would have

seen his reaction to her contempt. His face was red from her slap. With his shoulders slumped and head hanging down, he followed the rest of the group up the trail to the camp. The last vestiges of his self-respect were being stripped away like tree leaves in a fall breeze.

****

The stream Cal was following flowed out of Evans Lake not more than a quarter of a mile upstream of the waterfall. It was a pretty sight in the mid-day sun with the water spilling into a small pool below the high waterfall and partially undercutting the karst rock formation. But the escarpment with its beautiful waterfall might as well have been the wall of a fortress standing before them. Where it wasn't covered in dense moss and ferns, the rock surface was smooth and slick. It reminded Brooklyn of pictures of a water slide. The problem was climbing up to the top of the slide, twenty feet or so above the spot where they stood.

"We've got to find a way over it," Wally said as he sized up the situation. "Up where the stream leaves the lake is where that tourist woman was bitten by an otter. There could be another den for a different otter family. I'd really like to set several of the traps up there too."

"Then we're gonna have to find a way around," Cal said. "The trail ends here. There might be traces of one in the brush on the other side of the stream, but that's not obvious from this side. Maybe we can go to the right until we find a place to climb up."

Wally turned to Brooklyn. "This is going to affect our timetable to get back to the dock and the boat. I know you were hoping we would be back to learn whether your mother had been found or might even show up here. If Cal says it's okay, I'll permit you to go back down the trail alone. You can either wait at the skiff near the Grotto or take it back to the boat and contact the Coast Guard for an update on the search. Give us two hours then come back and pick us up. I haven't seen any bear sign on the trail so it should be safe. What do you think, Cal?"

"Eh, it's probably safe enough. But you have to stick to the trail, Brooklyn. No wandering off for any reason. And keep that can of bear spray handy. It should work even if you encounter that other otter. Better yet, carry it in your hands."

Brooklyn's spirits leaped. She smiled and nodded agreeably, then gave them both a hug. "Thank you and don't either one of you fall over this waterfall."

Cal did one of his belly laughs. "Don't worry, I've got the doctor here to look after me if I bust a leg or my head."

"Your head is more likely," Wally said. He smiled at Brooklyn. "If we don't show up in two hours, give us another hour before calling the Coast Guard or the State Troopers, okay? And, if it's the Troopers, ask for Dave Williams. He knows how to find this place. Oh, and if there are strangers at the camp, don't go barging in. Wait for us to return."

"I will. Thank you again, Wally." Brooklyn gave him another hug, turned, and trotted back down the trail to the Grotto.

****

Along the stream, the brush next to the trail was thicker and closed over Brooklyn's head. She thought it would be crazy to do anything but stay on the trail just as Cal had warned her. There were a few spots where it looked like an animal pushed through it, possibly to get to the stream, but she stuck to the main trail as she had been directed. She hummed one of her favorite songs as she walked. It was one way to announce her presence to someone or something coming towards her.

Rounding a bend, she noticed a dark, steaming mound in the center of the trail. Brooklyn stopped. Up to this point in her hike back to the dock, she wasn't at all nervous. Now all her senses went on alert. "These droppings weren't here when we came through here not long ago."

She approached the spot on the trail in slow, silent steps listening for any sound, but hearing only the gurgling of the stream off to her right. It was the spoor of quite a large animal and looked very, very fresh. She guessed it was left by a bear because of its size.

An animal trail split off towards the stream at that point. As she peered into the opening, she could swear the bent-over grass the animal had trampled was straightening just like the hairs on the back of her neck. She jumped as a loud splash occurred and a branch cracked close by. Something was crossing the stream.

Remembering that she was carrying the can of bear spray, she raised it like a shield to fend off whatever might emerge from the animal trail. She stumbled back a step not even sure she was holding it correctly or whether she could press the trigger. Her arms were shaking. There was more splashing coupled with several huffing sounds.

"Please, oh please, don't come this way." She murmured.

Brooklyn took a second to look back the way she had come. Should she return to be with Wally and Cal?

She looked the other way. The boat had to be closer. She chose the latter. "Breath and walk, don't run." She told herself. "If you run, a bear will think you are prey trying to escape."

After what seemed a lifetime, Brooklyn began to breathe more easily as she walked, but her fingers were numb from holding the bear spray so tightly. From time to time, she glanced behind her. There was nothing there and no sounds other than the thudding of her own heartbeat.

Chapter 37

It took another twenty minutes for Brooklyn to reach the beginning of the trail where they had left the skiff. A noise up ahead made her pause to listen. It was an entirely different type of sound, and it took her a few seconds to recognize it— the sound of an outboard motor. What made the sound odd was the reverberation of the motor as it passed through the Grotto. She started to run, then stopped as she heard men's voices. She listened for a moment. They were arguing—something about finding the camp. Frowning, she wondered what they were doing here and who they were. Something told her to not go barging out to greet them.

Off to her left, a quick movement by a dark shape caught her attention. Her heart skipped a beat, then she relaxed and smiled. A raven landed on the branch of a cedar tree so close she could have reached up and touched it. Brooklyn and the raven stared at each other for several moments without moving. Then the raven bobbed its head, squawked once, and flew off in the general direction of the camp. The raven reminded her of something Old Frank had said—take a minute to think about what you should do in a situation.

The outboard motor went silent, and the voices faded. The men must have walked up the trail to the camp. She looked at her watch. She had left Wally and Cal about an hour ago. Wally and Cal should be finishing their work and heading back. She decided to stay put.

After what felt like ages, she heard the voices again. They were back. Now, she had to see who it was. Using the thick brush to stay out of sight, she crept forward another ten paces until she could see the dock. The voices belonged to two men, one was on the dock, and the other had climbed into a skiff. They were still arguing with each other. The man on the dock handed the man in the boat several bundles of otter pelts, which were haphazardly dumped in the bottom of the boat. Then the man on the dock started to get in the boat.

"Hey, there's no more room," complained the man in the skiff. "Wait here for the other frigging boat to come back." He started the motor, put it in reverse, and backed away from the dock. Then he spun the boat around and headed for the upstream entrance to the Grotto. As he disappeared inside, the man on the dock turned and walked back up the trail to the camp, grumbling to himself about having to do all the heavy lifting. Brooklyn was about to creep closer when another boat with just one man came through the Grotto and pushed up to the dock. This third stranger looked no friendlier than the other two.

The dock guy came back down the trail carrying another bundle of pelts. He handed them to the man in the boat. "I'm coming with you this trip. We're supposed to tell that idiot in the other boat that this is the last bundle. He can take a thirty-minute break, then come back and wait. The boss and that Hutchinson guy have got some unfinished business back at the camp. Probably has to do with what they're going to do with that woman."

Startled by the mention of a woman, Brooklyn dropped the can of spray she had forgotten she was still holding. It clunked on a rock. She froze and watched for any reaction from either of the men to the noise. Neither did.

"Sounds good to me," the guy in the boat said. "The sooner we get out of here and deliver these bundles to Kwan, the better I'll feel. This place gives me the creeps. Those two better hurry, though. The tide is soon going to be too high to get through that cave."

As soon as the dock guy had jumped into the skiff, the boat handler backed up just like the first boat, turned, and headed back through the Grotto. Within minutes they were out of sight, but Brooklyn could still hear their motor, so she waited until the sound faded. Mr. Hutchinson is here? What woman are they speaking about? Then it hit her. Flo was with these men.

"She's here!" Brooklyn said to herself. "Mom is at the camp."

Brooklyn charged out of her hiding place, and up the trail towards the camp.

****

To find a way around the waterfall, Wally and Cal had pushed off from the meager game trail into an almost impenetrable forest. The ground under the dense canopy of cedar and hemlock was thick with moss and ferns. Fallen trees and rotting logs made their route nearly impossible. Tree roots and twisting vine maple tried to tangle their feet and trip them. Grabbing a branch of Devil's Club was like trying to hold onto a cactus to keep from falling down. The little valley they had entered was worse than any place Wally had ever been, and he began to regret telling Cal they had to reach the lake to set out more traps.

Cal led, searching for a way onto the escarpment. Wally was amazed how the man seemed to slip easily through the fallen timber and underbrush while he fought it almost every step. The stream flowed west to east, and they had been forced to turn north into dense brush. It was bushwhacking every step. After a quarter of a mile, which seemed a lot further to Wally, Cal stopped and looked left and then to his right, then back to his left.

"Well, it's about time we cut across an animal trail," Cal said. "And this one seems to be just what we're looking for. There appears to be a cleft in the escarpment, and this trail leads right into it. It must come from the other creek that empties into our bay."

"Glad the local critters are a lot wiser than me," Wally replied. "I wouldn't have seen it struggling through all this brush. Much more of this, and I would have been plumb lost."

"We may be able to follow the trail right up to the lake, find the Forest Service shelter, and then the outlet from the lake."

"Then maybe follow it back to our boat? That will be a mite easier than going back the way we came."

"Maybe, but Brooklyn and our skiff are at the Grotto, and as I recall, there's no way to get there along the shore of the bay."

Wally looked at his watch. "We left her over thirty minutes ago. By the time we finish at the lake and hike back to the skiff, we'll have been gone almost two hours. That concerns me—so let's not waste any more time talking and get this done."

As they started towards the escarpment on the newly found trail, Cal pointed to some droppings on the ground in front of him. "This is a sign of maybe what was the last user of this trail. It's fresh. A big brown bear has been through here, probably looking for berries. Keep your eyes open behind us, and I'll watch up ahead."

"Smart bear. It grabs a salmon dinner at the creek and has berries for dessert," Wally said with a smile. "Hopefully, it's no longer a hungry one."

****

Hopeless and dejected, Flo sat on a wood crate just outside the entrance to the mine. There was nowhere to go, and she sat there ignored as several men under Hutch's direction removed bundle after bundle of otter pelts from the back of the mine and hauled them down to the skiffs. They dismantled the drying racks, took down the tents, and picked up every remnant of Vince's camp. When they finished, there would be no trace of it. Even the grave was made less obvious by placing some tree limbs and brush over the surface.

Her two captors had gone back into the mine with a box just like the one she was sitting on. Flo thought she knew what they were up to. The box was marked dynamite. If they were going to set it off, all traces of the camp would be erased. The trouble they were going to puzzled her.

Vince is dead. One of his friends is dead, and Ronnie Waltrip took off somewhere. There was no one left who knew about the camp except—

Flo stood up with that thought.

No. No. It can't be. Vince told me everything. They intend to erase me too.

Flo realized that she had only seconds to get away from the calamity that was about to happen. She had to run. Maybe they would find her, and maybe they wouldn't. That she might die from exposure or starvation in the wilderness was a chance she would take. With one last glance at the mine entrance to check on Archie Hutchinson and Graham Hendricks, she bolted for the trail to the dock.

Just short of the trail, Flo stopped as she saw the brush move and a flash of color. Someone was coming. She looked around in desperation, trying to decide where else to run or to hide.

Then she heard a familiar voice.

"Mom!"

"Brooklyn!"

Flo's heart nearly stopped as she stared at the person entering the camp.

"What…what on earth are you doing here?"

Brooklyn rushed forward and embraced Flo, who could feel her daughter's body trembling. With tears in her eyes, She finally spoke, "I've been looking for you, Mom. When I finally learned about this place, I had a feeling you would be here."

Flo broke their embrace and looked back to see if the two men were still in the mine. "You shouldn't be here, Brooklyn. These men, they're dangerous. I'm not sure what they're planning, but they shouldn't see you. How did you get here? Were you on that other boat?"

"Yeah, but it's okay," Brooklyn said trying to calm her mother. "We're fine. Wally and Cal—"

Brooklyn stopped and saw one of the men had come out of the mine entrance walking towards them.

"What about Wally? The man asked. "Would that

be Dr. Perkins?"

Brooklyn ignored the question and frowned as she recognized the man. "Mom, what's Mr. Hendricks doing here?"

"I asked you a question, Brooklyn," Hendricks said. "Is Dr. Perkins with you? Where is he?"

Brooklyn glanced back at the trail to the dock. "He's looking for a rabid animal. He...he went up the stream. I came back. He said for me to wait at the skiff for him. That...he might be gone several hours. But why—"

"It doesn't matter." Hendricks took a pistol out of his pocket and waved it at the mine entrance. "In there—we're ready for you, Flo, and bring Brooklyn. She can keep you company."

Chapter 38

There was nowhere Brooklyn and her mother could run as both Hendricks and Hutch were carrying guns. Their only choice appeared to be to do what Hendricks insisted and simply try to delay whatever he had planned, hoping Cal and Wally would show up.

Flo and Brooklyn held hands as they walked into the semi-darkness of the mine passing Hutch, who was busy fussing with some wires strung along the walls.

"Hurry up with that, Hutch," Hendricks said as they passed him. "And look who showed up."

"Isn't that Flo's kid, Brooklyn? What's she doing here?"

"Yes, and she said Doc Perkins is around here somewhere, so we haven't got much time. I'm taking them back further into the mine and will leave them there. We've got to get this done and get out of here."

"Your job. My job is to get rid of the camp. I'm going to bring that other box of dynamite in here. Might as well use both boxes. I'll leave it to you to find the detonators and finish attaching them. I'm going back to the boat."

Flo stopped when she heard the word "dynamite." Hendricks pushed his pistol into her back. "Keep moving. Both of you." She stumbled, grabbing Brooklyn by the arm, then did as Hendricks said.

"You sure you know what you're doing?" Hutch

said to Hendricks as he passed him.

"Yeah, I…I have to do this. I've run out of options, and Kwan isn't going to offer up another one. He's got me in a corner and is saying deal with it. You know you should get out while you can, Hutch. He'll do the same to you. He has no loyalty to anyone except himself and his superiors."

Hendricks paused for a moment, wishing there was someone else to finish this awful task. He looked back at Hutch. "When you're finished, head back to the boat. One of the guys with a boat can wait for me at the dock. I'll be along in a few minutes."

Away from the light from the entrance, he clicked on a small flashlight and shone it on the backs of the two women. They walked past the spot where Brooklyn had waited with Tony and Bingo for the otter to leave.

"This is far enough," he said.

Hendricks took some pieces of rope out of his pocket and tied their hands, then their feet.

"Now, take a seat against that wall and stay there. I'll be outside. I don't want to see either of you."

He left them in the blackness and walked back to the entrance. In the dim beam of his flashlight and his anxiousness to leave, he neglected to notice the abandoned mining tools scattered on the floor of the mine.

****

Flo and Brooklyn were silent until he was out of sight. They were beyond the abandoned side shaft and near the digging works area.

"Don't worry, Mom," Brooklyn whispered as they started to wiggle around the darkness. "I've been in here before. And Wally and Cal will be here shortly.

They'll get us out of this."

There was a sound of a board being pried. "You hear that, Mom? Sounds like…."

"Shh!" Flo said. She heard the sound too and listened for a moment. A picture of Hutchinson opening the wooden crate near the entrance to the mine flashed in her mind. It confirmed her suspicions, but she didn't say anything about it to Brooklyn.

"How soon will Wally and Cal get back here?" asked Flo.

"They were going to finish setting some animal traps and then join me at the skiff. When they see it and I'm not there, they'll start looking for me. Hopefully, they'll think to come up to the mine, and not double back up the stream looking for me. Oh my gosh, if Hendricks or Hutchinson are still here, they could be caught unawares."

"I think they plan to be gone. Possibly back on their boat. Wally and Cal will be too late to help us."

"Then we've got to take care of ourselves, Mom."

"Yes, but how? Is there another way out?"

"I…I don't think so unless you are a bat."

"Hey, I don't think that is very funny at the moment. However, it does mean that we have to get out the way we came in. I wonder, if I had a knife, I might be able to cut the wires to the dynamite charges."

"I've got a knife in my backpack. Oh, it's outside."

Flo felt her wrists. The bindings were loose. "He didn't tie us up very well. Hendricks led us back here and just said to stay put."

"Maybe he is giving us a chance to escape?" Brooklyn said.

"I think he is showing a little pity. Try to untie my

wrists, and then I'll get you untied."

A few minutes later, they were free. Flo got on her knees and started to feel around in the blackness. "We can't just sit here."

Flo moved faster, trying to put her hands on anything, a rock or a piece of wood. She wondered how long they had. There weren't any more sounds from the mine entrance.

"Ow!" She cried.

"What happened, Mom?"

Flo rubbed a dirty hand on her head. "I hit my head on a post. There must be something in here we can use as a weapon."

"Wait, Mom. There are some things a little further back." Brooklyn crawled along the floor of the mine until she bumped into the lanterns she and Tony had left behind. She grabbed one and tried the switch. Nothing. "Darn. Batteries are dead." She found another one and flicked its switch. A bright beam of light lit up the far end of the mine shaft. Shining it around them, she saw something hanging from one of the supporting timbers over their heads.

Flo saw the object at the same time and could see that it was some type of bag. "Keep the beam of the light pointed right there. Vince told me there was stuff still in here from when the miners abandoned it."

Brooklyn was quiet for a moment. "Mom, you don't think they are going to blow up the mine, do you?"

"I don't know, honey. But that's why we need to get out of here."

"Hurry, Mom. I don't hear any more sounds."

Flo's mind was racing trying to put together what

Hendricks and Hutchinson were planning. She was wondering how long it would take them to place the finalize placing dynamite, maybe ten or fifteen minutes if that's what they were going to do. Then maybe another five to ten minutes to get as far away as possible before the blast. She bit her lip to keep from crying, but there wasn't anything she could do to stop her body from shaking. She hoped Brooklyn would not notice.

Flo pulled the bag off the nail. It fell apart in her hands. A couple of objects clattered to the floor of the mine. In the light of the lantern, they could see rusted food and water containers. There were several long objects—probably bamboo chopsticks, which crumbled into pieces when Flo picked them up. They were useless.

Brooklyn waved the lantern to peer deeper into the shaft. "Tony saw some stuff back there, Mom. He said the miners left their tools." They scrambled further into the mine and saw the old tools. They were too heavy to be useful.

There was another canvas bag lying next to the wall. "There's another one," Brooklyn exclaimed as she set down the lantern and grabbed a second dust-covered bag. She shook the dust off and coughed. "Feels pretty light, but there's something inside." Her fingers touched something long and slender. "I think it's a knife, Mom. Yeah, I found a knife."

The wall of the mine where the bag had been lying glittered in the light from the lantern. Brooklyn rubbed her fingers over the rough stone surface. "Hey, Mom. Is this gold?"

"Yes, it is," Flo replied as she examined the knife.

It was rusty, but the blade was strong and sharp.

"Vince told me about it before he died. It's a long story that I hope to be able to tell you one day. Let's move."

Flo's plan was simple. She would try to defuse the dynamite, confront Hendricks, and try again to convince him to stop this craziness. It was something she should have done in the first place, maybe while she was still on the boat. But her mind had been too confused at the time. The man was taking desperate measures, and Flo didn't know why. Kwan somehow controlled him, but she didn't care. Now that Brooklyn was involved, she would fight Hendricks with her last breath if she had to.

Chapter 39

Kneeling in the dim light from the mine entrance, Graham Hendricks struggled to remove more sticks of dynamite from the second box and attach them to the ones Hutch had already placed. He knew very little about explosives and regretted telling Hutch he could head back to the boat. He studied what Hutch had started trying to figure out what else to do. He looked around for the detonators. The wires lead outside the mine where they were attached to what looked like a case with several large switches and a timer. A smaller, partly open box sat beside the case. Hutch's last instructions were to finish placing the rest of the dynamite and then fasten the detonators to the wires. The only explosions Hendricks had ever witnessed were in films. School teachers didn't normally know how to teach Blasting 101. How many sticks did it take to bring down the side of a mountain, and how far away did one have to be and not get blown up?

Kwan had demanded this one last job—pick up the otter pelts, deliver them to his cousin near Ketchikan, and clean up the mess at Vince's camp. Complete the job, and he would destroy the pictures, pictures that he threatened to share with his wife and the newspapers. When Hutch informed him that he was to clean up the mess at the camp, including getting rid of witnesses, he panicked. Flo Whiting's stinging rebukes further fueled his anxieties, so he wasn't thinking straight. On top of all this, he wasn't sure how well he had tied up Flo and Brooklyn.

He pried open the lid and grabbed more sticks of dynamite from the wooden crate. His hands were shaking so badly, he dropped several sticks. His heart was already thumping like a bass drum, and the dropping of the dynamite made it feel like his heart was going to explode. He cursed silently trying to remember how the dynamite had to be detonated. He took a deep breath to try and calm himself.

He thought he heard noises and glanced over his shoulder into the darkness of the mine shaft. There was no one close by in the dark depths.

He thought about Flo and Brooklyn. Did they know what was going on out here? Were they talking about him? They shouldn't have to die. He'd done some pretty bad things, but he'd never killed anyone. Hendricks choked back a sob and pounded his fists against one of the posts.

He mumbled to himself. "There's enough dynamite already." Getting to his feet, he grabbed the last crate in both arms and stumbled outside the mine still muttering.

There were two screams behind him. Still holding the crate of dynamite, he jerked his body around. The bright daylight blinded him for a moment.

Someone kicked him in a kneecap. It hurt and he yelled. He dropped the box and sticks of dynamite spilled on the ground. He tried to pull the pistol out of his pocket when he was hit hard in the chest and went down on his back.

Brooklyn stomped on his hand and kicked the

pistol away as Hendricks yelled again.

Flo was now on top of him. He saw the knife and grabbed her wrist with his good left hand trying to keep it away from his throat.

"You...you evil man!" Flo screamed. "You were going to kill us. How could you do that? How could you?"

Hendricks hollered. "I didn't want to do this. I—"

"Didn't want to do what?" Someone said. "What's going on here?"

Brooklyn, Flo, and Hendricks all squinted in the bright light and stared at the figures of two men standing in the middle of the camp. One had a very big pistol drawn and pointed at them.

Flo's arms failed her, and she slipped to the ground. She began to sob with relief.

Hendricks lay there—his body racked with emotion. "I'm sorry—I'm so sorry." His words came in short gasps.

"Wally! Cal!" Brooklyn yelled.

Chapter 40

Aboard the *Blackwater,* Hutch watched Kwan's men busy transferring and stowing the last couple of bundles of otter pelts from the skiffs. Like everyone else, his attention was directed at the activity on the deck. No one was watching the entrance to the bay and all were taken by surprise when they heard a roar of engines coming from that direction. Two boats were racing directly towards them at high speed with blue lights flashing. One was a bright orange RIB, a rigid hull inflatable boat, with a 50 caliber machine gun mounted on its bow and the second craft was a State Trooper patrol boat.

Behind the speeding boats was a white ship with a wide orange stripe on its bow. Broadside, the ship nearly blocked the entrance. Men were bustling here and there across its decks and had uncovered a deck gun that now pointed directly at them.

Moments later, a loudspeaker on the orange inflatable blared an intimidating message. "Lay down your weapons and do not move, or we will fire. Standby to be boarded. You are all under arrest." The men around Hutch froze in place and raised their hands high. He threw down his pistol and did the same.

****

From the bridge of the Coast Guard cutter, Bingo Bob watched in awe as the two patrol boats closed on the *Blackwater* and their men boarded it. Along with the officers near him, he held his breath hoping not to hear shooting or see signs of resistance. Then, a message from the leader of the boarding crew came over the cutter's loudspeakers. "All secure, Captain."

A cheer went up from the crew of the cutter.

Moments later, Trooper William's voice came on the radio. "Captain, We searched the vessel. None of the people we're looking for are on board. One of these guys says some of their group is still onshore. The woman is there with her daughter. He says we have to hurry as the place is about to be blown up. You better send their friend over in the other RIB. We gotta move quick."

Bingo was given a life jacket and hustled onto a Coast Guard RIB. When it reached the *Blackwater*, he transferred to a skiff which was already manned with Trooper Williams and two heavily armed Coast Guardsmen. They shoved off immediately with Bingo directing them to the Grotto entrance.

As they exited the Grotto, rifles were raised, and the boat operator, who was waiting for Hendricks, raised his hands and offered no resistance.

Bingo jumped onto the dock and charged up the trail to the camp, throwing caution to the wind. Williams shook his head and hurried after him along with one of the Coast Guardsmen. He waved for the other one to take the man into custody.

"So much for planning and tactics," Williams said as they ran.

The passing of time to reach the camp was maddening to Bingo. He couldn't run fast enough. His thoughts raced through his mind as he ran up the trail.

There was an image from his dreams—a little girl in a blue dress struggling to stay afloat in a pond only the image morphed into a picture of Brooklyn. He knew now that he cared about Brooklyn's safety more than his own.

It was a strange sight as they burst into the clearing of the camp. A man in a plaid shirt was holding a monster of a weapon pointed at a man who was lying on the ground and sobbing uncontrollably. Sticks of dynamite lay scattered around him. Two women were huddled together in front of the mine doing the same. Wally Perkins who stood next to the man with the gun turned to see who was entering the camp.

"Brooklyn!" Bingo hollered. He raced past Wally and Cal, surprising them both, and stopped short of where Brooklyn knelt with her arms around her mom. He bent over and caught his breath, shaking his head, and struggling to smile as he tried to determine if they were unhurt.

Brooklyn looked at him, and with a wide grin, jumped up and rushed to him. They hugged and cried and hugged some more.

Chapter 41

It had been nearly two weeks since everyone
returned to Chatham, and while Leroy insisted Flo
return to her job at the café, the mother and daughter
had been inseparable as they recovered from their
ordeal at the Grotto. Brooklyn went back to school,
which was rather chaotic as Miss Greenblum had to
teach all of the kids in the absence of Mr. Hendricks
who had been arrested. Flo and Brooklyn were also
kept busy dealing with the repairs to their home. They
cleaned, painted, and ordered new furniture, while the
town's volunteer firemen, including Wally, spent every
available hour helping with the major repairs.

They had made a trip to Hoonah for Vince's
funeral. It was a subdued affair with a few of the Tlingit
tribal members attending, along with Jake Thompson,
his wife, and their daughter Molly, Brooklyn's friend.

****

To bring closure for Flo, Gladys Tussock invited
everyone to her home one afternoon. True to her nature,
Gladys always offered tea to visitors, and Brooklyn, her
mom, and the others who gathered in her home couldn't
turn her down. Wally and Peggy Perkins were seated
across from Cal, who sat in his favorite overstuffed
chair. His feet, clad in wool socks, were propped on a
pile of magazines on Gladys' coffee table. Duchess,
Cal's cute little Jack Russell, was curled up in his lap.

A grandfather clock standing against one wall ticked gently, and a fire burned in the wood stove in the corner of the living room. At the end of the couch, where Brooklyn and her mom were sitting, was a large basket of colored balls of yarn and a spinning wheel. It was a comfortable room—a welcome place after their horrendous ordeal.

"Your sister is quite the tea aficionado," Wally said. "Sid Jackson told me one time he has to special order her teas from some company down in Oregon."

"That would be correct, but to be honest with you, I'd rather be sharing a beer with you and Bingo at the Frontier Bar than sitting here waiting for Bingo to serve us one of Gladys's special brews." Cal chuckled to himself. "But this is my sister's home, and I have to respect her rules—no liquor until after 5 pm Alaska time."

Wally laughed, knowing how Alaskans thought anytime was a good time to have a sundowner drink. It was usually five somewhere in the lower 48 and close enough to pop a beer or pour a shot of whisky.

Bingo entered the room carrying steaming cups of tea. "I heard that remark, Cal, and as much as I would love to, I have to confess that as of six days, and nine hours ago, I vowed to avoid booze except for special occasions. Gladys has strict rules about everything in this house and being that I am going to be spending a lot more time here, I'd better shape up."

There was more laughter in the room, including Brooklyn, who giggled and squeezed her mom's hand. "I knew it, Mom. It was the flowers growing on Bingo's boat. I knew they have a thing for each other."

Cal pointed at a copy of the Juneau newspaper

lying on the coffee table. "There's an article in yesterday's paper about Kwan's alleged seafood syndicate. The State Troopers turned Kwan over to the Feds, who have charged him with multiple crimes. They handed over Graham Hendricks, too. Hendricks pleaded guilty and was offered a lesser sentence for testifying about Kwan's activities. Rumors are that he'll still be sentenced to ten years in prison."

"That's going to break him if it hasn't already," replied Wally. "I don't regret him going to prison. He was a child predator, and apparently, Kwan knew that and blackmailed him into working for his illegal seafood business."

"It was a good thing that Williams and that Coast Guard cutter arrived when they did," Bingo said. "You and Wally could have walked right into the middle of things, and it might have turned out differently. Tony and I were quite concerned about Brooklyn and you two when the Coast Guard made their radio call about the *Blackwater*. It seems my friend Kenny was the one smart enough and brave enough, I might add, to report Flo being taken. Tony was worried too and wanted to go back."

Brooklyn smiled. Tony had told her this the next day after the ordeal, but hearing it from Bingo somehow made it more important.

"Have you heard anything about Archie Hutchinson and his two boys?" Flo asked Cal. "I gave a full statement to Trooper Williams."

"They were charged by the State's prosecuting attorney on multiple counts, including attempted murder, kidnapping, as well as producing and selling drugs. I think there is a hearing scheduled in Juneau in a few weeks."

"You know, witnessing Trooper Williams handcuffing him and seeing the man in custody was quite a sight," Wally said. "A lot of people on the island are gonna be glad when Hutchinson and his drug-dealing boys are gone."

Cal nodded in agreement. "Yes, but the best part, hee hee, was while Williams and the Coast Guard were rounding up folks on that black ship, Wally and I got the drop on Hendricks. It was like the final scene in an action movie."

Everyone laughed, except Flo. "Now see here, Luther Calhoun! I seem to recall that I persuaded Hendricks that his actions were foolish and misguided, and for his own good, he should let us go. He might have too. He was about to give up when you and Wally showed up. And what if Trooper Williams and the Coast Guard had arrived sooner? Then maybe Brooklyn and I wouldn't have endured being forced into that awful mine and you and Wally would have just been two exhausted fools tramping all over the wilderness totally ignorant of all the excitement back at the Grotto."

Cal faked a laugh, but everyone could see the redness in his cheeks appear over his white beard. "Darn, I guess I can't claim bragging rights for rescuing two damsels in distress. You're robbing me of a great story to tell in my old age."

"Well, maybe I'll allow you to stretch it a little," replied Flo. "After all, you are a teller of tall tales."

The group laughed again as Cal smiled with satisfaction and then changed his expression, remembering something. He put a hand into one of the deep pockets of his jacket and extracted a stone. He held up a piece of gold ore that glistened in the light from the lamp next to his chair.

"A couple of days ago, when Wally and I picked up our traps, I took a peek in that mine you now own, Flo. I think you've got yourself a real nice claim. This is some of the richest gold ore I've come across in all my days of prospecting. If you're willing, I'd be pleased to spend a few weeks each summer working on your mining claim. I suspect you could pull enough ore out of there to pay for the repairs to your home and set Brooklyn up with a mighty nice college fund."

Flo and Brooklyn were speechless.

Gladys heard them talking as she came into the living room with a plate of warm cookies, "Humph, that's quite a generous offer, Cal. Only it sounds like I'm going to be chained to my stove preparing camp meals and baking cookies for a month while you fools play with rocks."

Everyone burst into laughter except for Brooklyn. She was too stunned by the fact that she might have a chance to go to college. Maybe she and Mom could even take a vacation somewhere.

Wally took a cookie, and when the laughter subsided, he made an announcement of his own. "Good news, folks. This morning I received a message from my friend at the CDC in Atlanta. There is no longer a concern about a rabies epidemic here on the island. Samples from the bat colony in the mine, while positive, were not the furious variety like we found in the otters. Cal and I caught the other rabid river otters, and tests on other small mammals caught in the traps were negative. So it looks like an isolated occurrence.

Rabies is a strange disease. It pops up where and when we least expect it—something it's been doing for hundreds of years and will probably keep on doing."

"Here, here," Bingo responded as he raised his cup of tea.

Brooklyn spoke up. "That's what Old Frank was trying to tell Tony and me. There could be some truth behind the Tlingit legend. Stories about strange acts by Nature's animals can be like warning signs."

"Or you can look at it another way," Wally said. "Rabies could have been brought here by the early Chinese miners. The Tlingit story could have originated to warn people to stay away from the Grotto."

He paused a moment and then got more serious. "So, Brooklyn, if you're considering college, hopefully, you will choose the University of Alaska. You know, biological science or anthropology or even computer science, are all great careers. The university offers degrees in all of these fields."

"Maybe all of the above?" Brooklyn replied, raising laughs from the group. She looked at Bingo as she spoke. "Then again, maybe I'll study engineering."

Bingo reacted with a big smile on his face.

"Well, I think you would make a great environmental scientist," Wally said. "Oh, and I forgot to tell you something. I took a walk up to the top of the cliff yesterday. I think the eaglet is about to leave the nest. You might want to check on him."

Brooklyn had forgotten all about her special friend. She jumped to her feet. "Mom! I've got to go see. Do you mind?"

Chapter 42

Brooklyn was glad to break away from the adults in Gladys' living room. They seemed to have a lot to talk about, mostly about her mom might actually be rich if Cal's assessment of the gold mine was correct. Then again, gold mining was expensive to undertake and dependent upon a fickle market that was affected by so many things. She needed to mull over that one by herself and how it might affect her future though she was thrilled that her mother might not have to work as hard.

They had spent a lot of time together since they got back. While they had become much closer, her mom had changed. Flo had always been open and sensitive to other people's problems. Now she seemed hardened, more defensive, and she still wouldn't say much about the last days with Vince. She seemed to have drawn into herself. Brooklyn knew so little about her mother's past with Vince. Maybe eventually, her mom would tell her about it. She sensed that her mom still loved Vince. After all, she had risked her life to try to save him.

Chatham was the same place as always, but coming home, it felt different, too. So many people had helped her and her mom through all of this—Wally and Peggy, Old Frank, Cal and Gladys, Mr. Jackson, the town's volunteer firemen, and of course, Tony and Bingo Bob.

Bingo was different too, and she was happy for

him. It shouldn't have been a surprise that Bingo and Gladys had eyes for each other. They were both lonely people. They both loved gardening, and they each had a past connection to the sea. Each in their own way craved comfort and a simpler way of life. She smiled to think that a love of flowers and the enjoyment of a game of bingo on Friday night had brought them together.

A moment of sadness came over her as she recalled the shock of seeing Mr. Hendricks holding a gun on them and then outside the mine as a broken man. She still couldn't believe that Hendricks was a criminal. Still, he was trapped into working for Kwan and was a desperate man.

As she hurried along the road, she glanced towards the boat harbor. It wouldn't look the same without Bingo's faded blue and white derelict boat with its flower pots lined up along the cabin roof and around the deck. A week after their return, Bingo had cut the dock lines and towed it out of the marina with his skiff. Taking it out into the straits and sinking it was Bingo's way of breaking ties with his past and starting a new life in Chatham with Gladys. While there were a few other boats moored to the docks, the harbor was quiet with no sign of activity—not even a flock of seagulls roosting near the fish cleaning table waiting for guts or a fish head to be tossed to them.

She passed the dead-end street that led up the hill to Wally and Peggy's home. Shortly after, she came to the opening in the salmonberry bushes that was the start of the trail up to the ocean-side cliff. Brooklyn smiled and sighed. This was just what she needed—to spend some time at her special place with just the forest surrounding her, the ocean below, and the eagle family in their nest in the gnarled cedar tree. She'd missed seeing the little eaglet. It would have grown big, being fed by its parents. Birds grow up so fast. Remembering Wally's words that the eaglet might have gotten big enough to fly away, she felt a pang of desperation and picked up her pace.

"Please, please let him be there," she said as she entered the deep second-growth timber. The trail was wet in places, and she saw a fresh set of tracks in the mud, probably Wally's. At one particularly muddy corner, she caught sight of the deep impression of her own feet where she had run down the trail to the sound of the town's fire siren.

Brooklyn was breathing hard by the time she reached the rock cliff and started around it towards the small grassy ledge she loved so much. Quick views of the sparkling waters in Chatham Strait between the tall spruce and cedars gave way to a familiar panorama she knew so well. The mountains on Admiralty Island stretched across the horizon over the strait and northward as if they went to the ends of the earth.

As she trotted up the trail, she wondered if Bingo's family of whales would still be hanging around or whether they had started their annual fall migration back to the Hawaiian Islands. The thought of Bingo trailing behind them in his small, frail boat and headed for certain death once he encountered the rough seas of the Pacific crossed her mind. But he hadn't followed through, and for that, she was really thankful.

As she got close to the cliffs and the eagle nest tree, Brooklyn caught sight of the female eagle just as it let out a shrill call. She grew hopeful that the eaglet might still be in the nest. She slowed her pace to catch her breath. It wasn't far now—just a few more corners of the trail along the side of the cliff. She was anxious to peer over the edge to check on the little guy. Then she would roll on her back letting the smell of the forest ferns and the salt air that crept up the cliff envelop her as she watched the clouds roll north and listening to the eaglet's anxious calls to its parents.

Then she heard it. She heard the loud cry of the eaglet responding to the shrill call of its mother high in the sky. She heard the adult male calling too. Brooklyn dropped to her knees and laid down to peer over the cliff into the nest. The eaglet was there. It was standing on the side of the nest with his wings outspread, flapping them wildly. Brooklyn put her hand over her mouth and laughed. The little one looked so funny as he tried to imitate his parents' flight. He was beautiful now, with full plumage even though it would be a year or two before he would have the adult's glossy black body and white head.

Brooklyn couldn't resist the urge to speak to the eaglet. "Hi, little guy. Did you miss me? You've grown. Want to soar like your parents, do you? Well, your time will come soon."

The eaglet appeared to calm down a little at the sound of her voice. He chirped and flapped his newly feathered wings as he walked around the perimeter of the nest, hopping in and out of the messy interior. The male swooped down and landed on a branch of the cedar tree almost at eye level with Brooklyn. The two looked at each other for a minute. Then the male cocked his head and called to the eaglet once again. He spread his broad wings and dropped from the limb, soaring downward along the face of the cliff and swooping high into the air in the direction of the female, who was keeping up her shrill calls. The eaglet became agitated once more and jumped back up on the edge of the nest and peered down the cliff. Then to Brooklyn's shock, he jumped into the air and plummeted towards the rocky beach far below.

"No, baby, no!" she shouted, jumping to her feet. "You're not ready to fly." She searched below the cliff for the bird's wings to catch the uplifting air, but in an instant, he was out of her sight. For precious moments she waited to see it rise into the sky.

"Where are you? Please don't die. I want to see you again. I love you, little eaglet."

Brooklyn's heart pounded as she waited, not wanting to think of any of the alternatives to sudden death or injury on the rocky beach at the bottom of the cliff. She hesitated, then turned and ran down the trail. If the young bird had landed on the beach, maybe he was still alive. She could rescue him. Wally could help with its injuries. She would take care of the bird and then return him to the nest.

Brooklyn ran faster than she had ever run before, slipping perilously on the muddy corners of the trail, caring little for her own safety. Precious minutes passed. On she ran, slowing only when she had to clamor over the boards placed over a small stream before the trail merged onto the road to the boat harbor.

On the road, Brooklyn turned sharply to the right to reach another trail that led to the beach below the cliff. On the periphery of her vision, something caught her attention in the boat harbor, and she took a second to glance to her left. What she saw caused her to stop and stare. The male eagle was proudly perched on top of one of the old pilings, and on a nearby piling was the eaglet flapping his wings to keep his balance.

"The eaglet is alive," shouted Brooklyn with utter joy. "The eaglet can fly, and he didn't leave. He's staying here in Chatham—my home."

Without a care as to who might be watching, Brooklyn ran across the parking lot to the edge of the bay, leaping and yelling as loudly as she could.

A word about the author…

Adventure Thriller author Fredrick Cooper was born and raised in the Pacific Northwest and lived in Alaska for many years. Before obtaining a doctorate in civil engineering and pursuing a professional career, he worked as a road surveyor, longshoreman, commercial fisherman, cannery worker, and even as a technician and news announcer for a cable television station in a small community in Alaska. He is of Coastal Salish and Lower Chehalis descent and is enrolled with a Northwest Indian Tribe. In addition to his creative storytelling, he is a master woodcarver, specializing in Native American artifacts such as canoe paddles and ceremonial items. He is a member of the Pacific Northwest Writers Association and The Willamette Writers. Currently, he lives in Portland, Oregon, and is working on his fifth novel.

www.ingramcontent.com/pod-product-compliance
Lightning Source LLC
Chambersburg PA
CBHW050037030726
47506CB00001B/316